What readers a

THE D

MAV.. ....

and

The Val & Kit Mystery Series

FIVE STARS! " . . . well-written mystery . . . first of The Val & Kit Mystery Series. The two amateur sleuths, Val & Kit, are quirky, humorous, and dogged in their pursuit of righting what they felt was a wrongful death of someone they knew from the past. It's full of humorous, cagey, and a few dark personalities that keep you on your toes wondering what or who would turn up next. . . . a fun, fast read that is engaging and will keep your interest . . . A tightly woven mystery with a great twist at the end."

FIVE STARS! "Enjoyed this tale of two friends immensely. Was shocked by the ending and sad to find I had finished the book so quickly. Anxious to read the next one . . . keep them coming!"

FIVE STARS! "I thoroughly enjoyed this book, laughing out loud many times, often until I cried. I love the authors' style and could so relate to the things the characters were going through."

FIVE STARS! "This was a fun read! The story was well put together. Lots of suspense. Authors tied everything together well. Very satisfying."

FIVE STARS! "I highly recommend this novel and I'm looking forward to the next book in this series. I was kept guessing throughout the entire novel. The analogies throughout are priceless and often made me laugh. . . . I found myself on the edge of my seat . . . the ending to this very well-written novel is brilliant!"

FIVE STARS! "I really enjoyed this book: the characters, the story line, everything. It is well written, humorous, engaging . . . give us more."

FIVE STARS! " . . . a good, easy read. There is more humanity and humor than actual mystery and action. . . . a perfect read for anyone who wants to relax with a good story. Val and Kit are believable characters, and their escapades are worth reading (about). You will find yourself cheering them on to the very last page. I am looking forward to reading more in this series."

FIVE STARS! "The perfect combo of sophisticated humor, fun, and intriguing twists and turns!"

FIVE STARS! "Debut in The Val & Kit Mystery Series filled with funny and fascinating real estate sales characters flying through a plot that will keep you entertained until the last dark surprise at the ending. Looking forward to more."

FIVE STARS! "I recommend this book if you like characters such as Kinsey Millhone or Stone Barrington . . . or those types. Excellent story with fun characters. Can't wait to read more of these."

The Disappearance of Mavis Woodstock

A Val & Kit Mystery

Rosalind Burgess
and
Patricia Obermeier Neuman

Cover by

Laura Eshelman Neuman
Amy Spreitzer Windsor
Melissa Neuman Tracy

Blake Oliver Publishing
BlakeOliverPublishing@gmail.com
This is a work of fiction.

Acknowledgments

Thanks to our early readers for their comments, corrections, and compliments (especially the compliments): Kerri Neuman Hunt, Jack Neuman, John Neuman, Laura Eshelman Neuman, Betty Phelps Obermeier, and Melissa Neuman Tracy.

For our parents,
John and Miriam Burgess
and
Clayton and Betty Obermeier

The Disappearance of Mavis Woodstock

A Val & Kit Mystery

The Val & Kit Mystery Series

CHAPTER ONE

There was a message on my phone when I got back to the office after lunch. "Haskins Realty? This is Mavis Woodstock. I'd like to meet as soon as possible, to have you sell my house. Would you call me at 555-2456 as soon as you get this message? Thank you, and have a good day."

I thought maybe I should know this person. The name had a familiar ring. I picked up the receiver and dialed the number. She answered immediately, as if she'd been waiting with her hand on the phone. "Ms. Woodstock?" I said, pen in hand, ready to take down the particulars.

"Yes."

"This is Valerie Pankowski from Haskins Realty. You left a message."

"Yes, thank you for calling back. How long does it usually take to sell a house?"

"Well, in Downers Grove, things are still moving pretty quickly."

"How quickly?"

"I'd have to look up some statistics on your particular neighborhood. But why don't we start with you giving me a few details."

"What details?"

"How about we start with the address."

"Oh, of course." She proceeded to give me an address on Maple Lane (nice area, in an older part of Downers Grove).

"Okay, that's great. Now, how about size? Do you know the square footage?"

"No, sorry."

"No worries."

"I don't have a mortgage. It's all mine. Would that make it sell faster?"

"Maybe." I suppressed the urge to assure her I got it: she wanted a quick sale. "How many bedrooms?"

"Three, one I use as a computer room. How fast, do you think?"

"Why don't we meet tomorrow? What time is good for you?"

"Is eight o'clock too early for you?"

"I'll be there at eight. I look forward to meeting you."

I heard Mavis give a deep sigh. "Thank you so much, Ms. Pankowski."

After I hung up, I checked the location of her home on the office wall map. I was right. It was a nice, older neighborhood.

Satisfied that I was onto something really good, I did a little paperwork and then shut down my computer before heading out early. I planned to do some shopping and get my nails done with the gift certificate my daughter had sent me for my fiftieth birthday. It was as good a way as any to spend my last day being fortysomething.

I thought about Mavis Woodstock off and on the rest of the day. I couldn't remember the last time I had dealt with such an accommodating client.

Well, every client has a story, and I was curious why this Mavis Woodstock wanted such a quick sale.

***

Mavis Woodstock lived on a quiet street lined with tall trees. Maple, of course. Her house looked freshly painted in white, with black window boxes standing empty, as if waiting for the season's first snow to fill them. A winding brick pathway led to the red front door. So far, I was impressed.

I got out of my car and took a few pictures of the front of the structure. Then, at precisely eight o'clock, I put my camera back in my shoulder bag and rang the front doorbell. The paint on the door looked fresh, and the entire house was as immaculate as it was charming. I rang again. Perhaps she was hard of hearing. Mavis *had* sounded older on the phone (older than what? dirt? me?).

After the third ring, with still no answer, I walked over to one of the front windows and peered in, but couldn't see anything. So I went back to the front door and knocked several times. In vain.

Not sure what to do, I walked around and took some more photos. Then I drove down the street to check out the neighborhood. I found a Starbucks (always a good sign) two streets over, so I purchased a tall mocha and drove back to Mavis's house. This time I pounded on her door. Finally convinced she wasn't home, I wedged a business card in the door and left.

When I got back to the office, I called her number, with no response. As soon as I replaced the receiver, the phone rang.

"Hey, Val." It was my best friend.

"Hey, Kit."

"Can I take you to lunch for your birthday?"

"Yeah, sure."

"Are you busy? You sound far away."

"No, I'm here. I was just over at a house. Prospective client. A nice woman called me yesterday, seemed desperate for me to sell her home. Kept saying it had to be done quickly. Only she wasn't there this morning. Seems strange."

"You weren't quick enough."

"Kit, she called me yesterday afternoon. How quick do you want me to be?"

"Maybe you're slowing down, now that you've reached the half-century mark."

"Not funny. Anyway, lunch sounds good. Pick me up at noon, will you?"

***

Kit picked me up in her BMW, and we drove to Pappasito's, not far from my office but also not far from Maple Lane. After chicken fajitas and Diet Cokes, I asked Kit to take a detour past Mavis Woodstock's house before dropping me back at my office. I could see my business card still wedged in the front door.

"This is so irritating," I said. "If she's in such a hurry to sell, why isn't she home?"

"Beats the hell out of me."

"Let me try one more time."

Kit parked at the curb and then pulled her visor down to check her makeup, while I followed the winding pathway to the front door. The whole place had a Hansel and Gretel feel to it, which annoyed me since I knew I could sell it. I rang the bell and banged on the front door, with still no answer.

I settled back in the passenger seat and let out a sigh. "Geez. Some people."

"Maybe she changed her mind. Or maybe something important came up, and she had to leave."

"Well, obviously." I bristled at her nonchalance. Unlike me, Kit doesn't work for a living and had no idea of the potential sale I might be losing my grip on. "It just feels odd.

She seemed so determined on the phone. And really sweet, by the way." I felt my irritation dissipate. "I hope Mavis is okay."

"Mavis?" Kit checked her rearview mirror before pulling out into the street. "Now there's a name you don't hear every day. Talk about a blast from the past. Remember Mavis Woodstock from high school?"

So that's where I'd heard the name. Kit was right. We had gone to school with a Mavis Woodstock. Why hadn't I remembered that? Well, for starters, it was more than thirty years ago. "This woman's last name was Woodstock too," I said. "It's gotta be the same one, right?"

"Oh noooo. I think there are probably hundreds of Mavis Woodstocks in Downers Grove. Of course it's the same one, you dope."

"Why didn't I remember her?"

"Mavis wasn't exactly Queen of the Hop back then, ya know."

"You're right." I pictured the frumpy girl with frizzy, dirty-blond hair and pale skin. Tallish, I remembered, and skinny.

"Buckteeth," Kit said. "Huge buckteeth. Oh, and glasses."

"No, she didn't wear glasses. Did she?"

"Coke bottles, hon."

I had a sudden unsettling feeling. Like a bad memory nagging at my consciousness. "Poor Mavis. What happened to her?"

"She got herself a piece of property; we know that much."

"No, I mean what happened to her? Where is she right now?"

***

Kit dropped me off at the office, and I shivered during my short trek up the sidewalk. Last week had been unseasonably warm, but this second week of November was raw. I should have worn my coat.

I pushed through the glass doors, and Perry Haskins greeted me without looking up. His job consists of many things besides computer solitaire, although I'm not sure what. But since he's the nephew of Tom Haskins, who is the owner and my boss, I don't question it. The only other employee is Billie Ludlow, a pert twenty-one-year-old who secretly runs the company. At least she's the only one who fully understands how the computers work and how to manipulate the cappuccino maker.

"How was lunch?" Perry swiveled around in his chair to face me. He's movie-star handsome. Classic George Clooney with a little bit of Brad Pitt thrown in for good measure. "And how is it, being fifty?"

I smiled but ignored his questions. "Any coffee left?"

"No, and Billie's not here."

"I'll make some."

"Okay, good. So, any big birthday plans tonight?"

"Never can tell." I removed my suit jacket and then quickly put it back on. I still felt stuffed from lunch, and the waistband on my skirt was starting to roll over and needed covering. I retreated to the small kitchen in the back of the office and poured water from the cooler into the coffeepot.

"So, how does it feel to be fifty?" It was Billie. She stood behind me, barely five feet tall with glossy chestnut hair and an angel face. She held a white cake box in her left hand. "Here, let me do that; you've put too much water in the pot."

"Oh, would you?"

"Happy birthday, Valerie." She reached over and kissed me on the cheek. It was such a sweet gesture, I thought I might cry. Instead, I put the coffeepot down and hugged her, squashing the cake box between our chests.

"For you." She indicated a shiny gift bag in her right hand. Bubble bath in a lavender glass bottle with matching soap.

"Oh, Billie, how lovely."

"It's not much, but I thought we could have cake with our afternoon coffee. It's carrot."

Perry joined us, and we each drank a cup of hot coffee and ate a hearty slice of the cake, which, like all good carrot cakes, was moist and tasted nothing like carrots. Except for Mavis Woodstock's standing me up and a renegade hot flash that forced me to remove my jacket, my birthday was going well.

We were at our desks, enjoying our second slice of cake, when the glass doors swung open and Tom Haskins arrived. He glanced at his watch (it was nearly two o'clock) and then eyed the three of us. He didn't have to say a word; we could read his thoughts: *why the hell am I paying you to eat carrot cake and drink coffee in the middle of the afternoon?*

Tom is a big man, the stereotypical athlete, albeit a weekend one. But, never a fan of business casual, he always wears a custom-made suit and designer shirt and tie. As if a pressing matter awaited him and he didn't have time to consort with the employees, he proceeded, as always, to his private office, the only room with its own door.

"It's Valerie's birthday; she's fifty," Billie called after him. And so Tom stopped and glanced back at me.

"Fifty?" I couldn't tell if his tone meant *well done* or *tough luck*.

"So, how does it feel to be fifty?" Perry asked me again.

Again, I ignored him.

The rest of the afternoon progressed normally. My mother called from Wisconsin to tell me she had a splinter in her big toe that hurt like the dickens and, oh, by the way, I can't believe you're fifty. My daughter, Emily, called from California and offered a throaty imitation of Marilyn Monroe singing "Happy Birthday" to John Kennedy. Then she put her husband on the phone, and Luke insisted I didn't look a day over forty. My dentist's office called to remind me my teeth were due for a cleaning, but apparently they didn't care how old I was.

I tried Mavis Woodstock's number three times, each without success. I wasn't sure what worried me more, that Mavis Woodstock might have disappeared or that the listing might have escaped me.

At five o'clock Tom emerged from his office, putting on his jacket. He glanced in my general direction. "So, got any dinner plans?"

I hit the *escape* button on my keyboard to hide the evidence of my online shopping on the company computer. "No."

"Okay then, let's go. I'm buying. You pick the place since it's your birthday. But make it a steak place."

"Now? It's only five o'clock."

"Take it or leave it." Tom was already heading toward the door.

I didn't feel like going home to my new apartment just yet, so I grabbed my purse from underneath my desk. "Steak sounds great." But by then my waistband was screaming *salad, you idiot.*

***

I've known Tom Haskins for more than thirty years. We went to the same high school, although he was a few years ahead of me. I've seen him through two divorces; he's seen me through one (but mine was a much bigger deal).

I've been working for him for about ten years, having shown up at his office back then and telling him I was looking for part-time work. I'd recently gotten my real estate license, and my husband was at his financial peak, so I just needed something to keep me busy, something fun, not a real job. That shows how much I knew at the time about selling real estate, even if I did have a license.

But Emily was a busy teenager; and since I could no longer accompany her everywhere (her idea, not mine), I found myself with too much time on my hands. To my shock, Tom hired me, although the job was never really part-time. And even more shocking to me, I proved to be good at it.

"Fifty, eh?" Tom pulled his Mercedes out of the parking lot.

"Yeah. What about it?"

He chuckled. "How does it feel, Kiddo?"

"Well, let me ask you the same question, if you can remember. After all, you've been in your fifties for . . . what . . . five . . . six years?"

His smile faded, but only momentarily. "Three, thank you very much. I'm fifty-three. Just enough older than you to teach you a thing or two."

"Oh, like what?"

He didn't answer, and we remained silent during the five- or six-minute drive to the restaurant. After he pulled into the parking lot and turned the car off, he spoke again. "I'll tell you what I can teach you: where to get the best damn steak in Chicagoland. Follow me." I smiled; Tom often uses the term *Chicagoland*, making it sound like Peter Pan's magical Neverland.

"Thank you," I said, after he opened the passenger door for me.

He winked. "Just showing a little respect for the elderly." When we reached the restaurant, he opened that door as well and then gently ushered me in ahead of him, his hand on the small of my back.

We gave the waiter our order, and then Tom spent most of our early dinner either on his phone initiating or closing some megadeal or raving about the perfection of his slab of beef. I actually did order a salad (but regretted it when I saw the plate put in front of Tom) and picked at it while making mental to-do lists for turning my new apartment into a home.

Tom had me back at the office in an hour and a half, even though he stopped to greet no fewer than three separate acquaintances on the way out of the restaurant. He stopped the car and shoved it into park. Then he reached into the glove compartment for a long, robin's-egg-blue box with a white bow. Bingo: Tiffany's.

"Here." He handed it to me with one hand and put the car back into drive with the other.

"Tom, you shouldn't have." I pulled the end of the ribbon and tried to hide my shock that he'd known it was my birthday even before Billie's reminder. Inside the box was a heavy silver-link bracelet with a heart charm, my name engraved on one side, *Tiffany and Co.* on the other. "It's beautiful, Tom. Really, it's lovely."

"Glad you like it, Kiddo. I gotta run. Got plans. See you tomorrow."

"Yes; thanks for dinner." I shut the car door, and he pulled away.

Then I heard the Mercedes backing up toward me. I turned around to see Tom's window gliding down. "Happy birthday!" he said. And then he peeled out, as I'd seen the teenage Tom do so many years ago.

***

Back at my new apartment, most of my belongings still awaited unpacking. In my new stark-white bedroom, I slid open the mirrored doors that concealed my closet. I ran my fingers over the garments that hung tightly together, the items I had transported to the new place without removing hangers. At my old house, I had enough room inside my closet for two chests of drawers just for winter clothes and a shoe rack that would have satisfied Paris Hilton. But everything looked squashed and unhappy in its new home. Like the bargain rack at a Lord & Taylor end-of-summer sale. I made a mental note to consider some serious downsizing and then pulled out a comfy pair of jeans and a Bulls sweatshirt.

Out in my brand-new galley kitchen, I poured myself a glass of pinot grigio and leaned on the counter that looked through to my still-unfamiliar living room. On the coffee table, which I'd brought with me from the Big House, sat my divorce papers and my lease agreement. They just about said it all: close one deal, start another.

I surveyed the rest of the scene. Or should I say the mess? I had purchased a new couch, which I loved, but it was hardly visible beneath the boxes and miscellaneous junk still to be unpacked and dealt with. Well, I'd do it later. That night, that weekend, that month. Sometime during the rest of my new life.

But first, I was going to call Mavis Woodstock again.

CHAPTER TWO

Not surprised when there was no answer at Mavis Woodstock's number, I vowed that tomorrow I would figure out another way to look for her. Then I turned my attention back to my own home and problems. I had lived here for seven days, after all. I still felt both excited and scared, but decided it was time to feel *settled*.

I took the last sip of my wine and considered pouring myself another glass. Instead, I opened one of the boxes.

The first thing I came across was a framed photograph of me at a dinner party with David. The former husband. We were both dressed up, he in a tux, I in a black cocktail dress looking slim, if I do say so myself. I stared hard at the picture, surprised at how happy we looked since I remembered we'd had a bitter fight that night. But we put on smiley faces, as easily as applying lipstick, when the photographer came by our table. Why had I even packed this picture?

I went to the kitchen, found a white garbage bag, and threw the photograph in it. That felt good. I was getting somewhere.

After an hour of taking things out of boxes, I heard my phone ring. Happy for the diversion, I picked it up.

It was Tom, calling to talk business. "Did you ever reach the woman from Maple Lane?" I could tell he was driving and chomping on a cigar. On the speakerphone in his car, he sounded not quite there.

"No. And I called her a million times." I cradled the phone under my chin and climbed over the boxes on the living room floor to get to the kitchen for more wine. "She's vanished."

"Think she found another Realtor?"

"That's just it. My business card was still in her door frame."

"Keep after her, Kiddo. Maple Lane's a good location. But how come you're home? I thought you'd be out celebrating."

I didn't know how to take that. Did he not really want to speak to me and hoped to just leave a message on the answering machine? Well, if that was the case, I would have outsmarted him, since I had a new phone system and no idea how to retrieve messages yet. "I had a busy day," I said. "I'm bushed."

"Yeah, *right,* Pankowski. Just bring home a listing tomorrow, Kiddo."

I assured him it was in the bag, and I put down the phone, feeling pretty good. I'm not sure if the after-hours check-in calls from Tom are really to check in with me or just to see what I do in my spare time. Either way, I sort of like them.

In the next hour, I filled the garbage sack with what it was intended for. And broke one of my shiny new nails in the process. I began searching for the last box of cosmetics and miscellaneous toiletries to find something to repair it, but the ringing telephone interrupted me.

"Is that you, Valerie?"

"Yes, Mom, it's me. Who did you think would answer my phone?"

"Who knows what kind of neighborhood you've moved to. Anyone could break in and answer your phone. I'd never know."

"Mother, I'm four miles from the old house. It's a perfectly safe neighborhood. The police drive by every five minutes to be sure I'm safe."

"Hmm. Make sure you lock your door."

"Yes, Mother."

"Bad things happen to girls living alone in the city."

I smiled. Only my mom will always think of me as a girl. Gotta love that.

"I'm fine, Mom, but thanks for calling. Again." I didn't remind her that she'd raised me in that "city," which is actually the *Village* of Downers Grove. And that it is a safe suburb within (sometimes) easy driving distance of downtown Chicago.

"Okay, just checking. Bye-bye, dear."

"Mom, wait. Something I wanted to ask you. Do you remember a girl who went to school with me, named Mavis Woodstock?"

"Hmm, Mavis Woodstock." She rolled the name around on her tongue as if she were sampling a fine wine.

"Yes. We weren't exactly friends or anything, but she was in my class."

"Did she have really thick glasses? Like Mr. Magoo?"

"Well, she might have. I don't remember, but Kit seems to think she did."

"Oh, *Kit*," my mother said, spitting out the wine. She was never fond of Kit. Too fast and too brazen, according to her.

"Mavis is selling her house, and she called me yesterday," I said. "I didn't recognize her name. But I think she's the same girl. She probably didn't realize who I was, with my married name."

"Her family had money, as I recall. Yes, I'm sure the father was well-heeled."

I didn't recall Mavis being particularly well-heeled. My recollection was that she was always dressed in clothes that looked like hand-me-downs. "Did she have brothers and sisters? I can't remember."

"Oh, there were a whole bunch of them. But I think Mavis was the only girl."

"Really? I just don't remember anything personal about her." But again, that unsettling feeling nagged at me.

"If you hadn't spent so much time hanging around with that Kit, you and Mavis might have ended up friends."

I doubted that. But I wished my mom a good night and assured her I would go right to bed.

I love my mom; I really do. Even more so since she moved four hours away, up to Door County, Wisconsin, and I'm in no danger of her dropping by unexpectedly.

I decided to hell with my nail and instead went in search of my high school yearbooks. Five boxes later, I found them packed among my tomes on real estate law and selling techniques.

I looked through the four books that each represented a different year of my high school days, finding all the pictures of Mavis. It didn't take long, as she had precisely one photo per book. And back then, a person's popularity and worth could be measured by how many times she was pictured in the yearbook, as well as how many activities were listed by her senior-year photo. The paucity of Mavis pictures was outdone only by the absence of any activities listed next to her senior photo, which, like those of her freshman, sophomore, and junior years, showed teeth still bucked and eyes still covered by Coke-bottle glasses.

Why would a well-heeled father not pay for braces and contact lenses for his only daughter?

And why had I been so mean to her?

As soon as I saw the first photo of Mavis, I had a clear memory of a gym class where we were lined up for archery.

One of the popular (one can only wonder why) girls made a snide comment about Mavis's thick glasses and how she could never hope to see the target. It was an offhand remark, intended to get a laugh from her peers more than to humiliate Mavis. But of course it humiliated Mavis; it had to. And I was guilty of snickering when I should have been standing up for her.

It had bothered me then, especially as I recalled stories of my own mother being ridiculed in her schooldays because of her poverty and limited wardrobe; I'd grown up on stories of mean girls and the hurt they could inflict. I knew I was no better than they were. But still I remained silent. Worse, I had pretended to find humor in the put-down.

And, even though I hadn't given it another thought since that long-ago morning in gym class, it was bothering me again. Maybe that is why I felt I had to make sure Mavis was okay and not lying dead on her kitchen floor or something. Poor thing. She'd probably lived alone her entire life, with her buckteeth and thick glasses.

***

I called Mavis as soon as I got to the office the next morning. Or rather I tried to. There was no answer, which only increased my growing obsession with her and her whereabouts, maybe even her well-being. After all, it had been almost forty-eight hours since she'd sounded so eager to sell her house.

I called her every hour on the hour all day. No answer. Finally, I got the idea (duh! why had it taken me so long?) to see if I could find a phone listing for her parents or one of those many brothers my mom said she had.

There were three Woodstocks listed for Downers Grove, in addition to Mavis herself. I got the ubiquitous answering machine when I called the first two and hung up without leaving a message. What could I say that wouldn't make me sound like an overzealous Realtor?

The last Woodstock I reached, a Lionel Woodstock, did nothing to quell my uneasiness about the whole disappearance of Mavis Woodstock (as I had begun to think of the situation). "Hello. I'm wondering if you are a relative of Mavis Woodstock," I said to the male voice that answered on the first ring.

There was a long pause and then, "Who are you?"

"Oh, I'm so sorry. I'm Valerie Pankowski, a high school . . . um . . . friend of Mavis's. Are you her brother?"

"Mavis didn't have any friends in high school."

"Well, I was a friend. And a classmate." How could he be so sure Mavis didn't have friends? He sounded like a mean older brother who'd probably taunted Mavis about being friendless, and I found myself wanting to defend her, as I should have all those years ago in gym class.

"Why do you want Mavis?"

"Look, I just want to talk to her. About getting together." Not a lie. Nothing that would cost me my Realtor's license, should Mavis suddenly resurface and be ready to list her house.

"Mavis is in Florida."

"Oh. For how long? When did she go there?"

"She spends all her time there."

Well, that explained her desire to sell her Downers Grove home. But it didn't explain how she could have been in both Downers Grove and Florida just two days ago. "Could you please give me her phone number there?" I asked. But for some reason, I didn't think I could believe anything this man said, even a phone number. Something about his tone of voice made him sound both belligerent and wary. But why should he be either?

"Look," he said, "Mavis and I . . . I don't have her phone number." His tone told me he wouldn't give it to me even if he had it. I heard a click and realized he'd hung up.

I didn't have time to decide my next move. I had agreed to meet David to sign some papers. I hadn't listened carefully when he called earlier in the day to rattle off all the loose ends we still needed to tie up, but I knew one of them was the title of our car, the Beemer, which would soon be his, not ours. That was fine by me. I loved my Lexus more than I'd ever loved that blasted BMW.

We agreed to meet at Roland's, an upscale bar/restaurant close to Downers Grove where I often took customers after a successful sale. David had met me there once or twice, but I didn't like his suggesting a restaurant that was clearly mine, not his. Still, papers had to be signed and property handed over to its rightful owner. I just wanted to get it done with.

I grabbed my purse and checked my wallet to make sure I had money and a credit card, noticing my new driver's license in the process. I dug my glasses out of their case to inspect my photo one more time. It was the best license picture I had ever taken, which was surprising since I had been sad that morning. But I'd gone to Mario Tracocci's salon the day before, and my chin-length highlighted blond hair made my eyes look bigger and bluer. With the red lipstick I'd applied at the last minute, I looked almost glamorous.

Pleased, I carefully put my license back in its correct place in my wallet, at the front. I was getting downright meticulous in my old age, especially for someone who used to be more carefree than careful. I knew I better watch it, or I would turn into my mother—one of those anal-retentives who alphabetizes her canned goods (which, come to think of it, doesn't sound like such a bad idea anymore).

***

David was already seated at a table when I arrived, a good fifteen minutes before our scheduled meeting time. How like the new me to be early, and how unlike the old him to be even earlier. He was wearing a business suit and tie, but I could tell he'd put on weight. It had been only a few weeks since I'd last seen him, but his appearance seemed to have changed dramatically. Or had I just never paid attention?

He stood as I approached the table and leaned in to kiss me, but then straightened back up before the kiss could be planted. Instead, he held out his hand to shake mine. For some reason, this made me laugh: shaking hands with the guy I had lived with for thirty years. I used to wash his underwear, for Pete's sake, and trim the hairs in his ears.

"Here are the papers, Valerie." He slid a manila folder in my direction.

I took my reading glasses from my purse and then opened the folder. A sudden sadness engulfed me. Oh, I wanted the divorce more than David did; in fact, I had pushed hard for it. If it had been up to him, we would have remained married, with me tending our home and him dating like a college freshman. The thought of all that wasted time transformed my sadness to anger, and I practically broke the pen as I signed my name, pressing down hard, in David's designated spots.

"So, you wanna drink?" David put the folder of papers, the title to the Beemer and whatever else I had signed, into his briefcase.

"No, I'm meeting Kit. We're going out for dinner." Why was I lying? Maybe I just wanted to rub in the fact that Kit is mine. She'd been a friend of both of ours, but she's my *best* friend, so I got custody of her in the divorce. And she's far better than a dozen BMWs any day.

"Really? You're sure?" He looked ready to bolt, and he downed the apple martini in front of him.

"Really. You go on."

"I hate to run, but I do have a few things to take care of." He signaled the waitress for the check.

"Could I ask you something?" It was me talking, and I'd taken myself completely by surprise. It was the Mavis Woodstock thing again. I suddenly wanted to bounce it off someone, see if I was way off base to think something could be wrong. Really, really wrong.

"Sure."

While he fished his American Express card out of his wallet, I began to tell him about the prospective client who sounded so urgent and then seemed to disappear. "Do you think I should be doing something?"

He scribbled his name and put his copy of the charges in his wallet before answering me. "Yeah, I think you should be doing something. You should be forgetting all about her. Valerie, you've always had that way about you." The disgust I heard should have been my signal to leave it at that.

But no. I had to ask. "What way?"

"Making a big deal of things. If Emily had a slight fever, you were sure it was pneumonia. If she cut her finger, you were sure she had tetanus. If I came home five minutes late . . ."

I was sure you were screwing your secretary, I wanted to scream, but I didn't have the energy.

"So," David was saying, "if you're sure you don't want a drink, I'll be going."

"I'm sure. Go."

He stood up. "Okay then. So call if you need anything. No reason we can't be friends."

"Right." I noticed his pants had wrinkled, and it irritated me. And his belt buckle could have been let out a notch. I took the menu and studied it hard.

He leaned down and kissed my cheek. Yuck. When he was gone, I rubbed the spot with my hand.

And then I turned my thoughts back to Mavis.

CHAPTER THREE

With David off the premises, I decided to order dinner. I had never, ever eaten dinner in a restaurant by myself. But since I'd avoided the hardest part, being seated at a table for one, I thought I'd stay. I was starving, the food there was good, and the place was reasonably dark.

I ordered fish and wild rice and a glass of pinot grigio and then reached into my purse for my Franklin Planner and pretended to be studying it. I didn't want to look like one of those sad people who have no choice but to eat alone. At least I'd look like one of those sad people with something to read.

I could see the bar from where I sat. Two women waved at me. They were both Realtors from a competing firm. I waved back and then returned to my planner as if it contained the true meaning of life. Or the whereabouts of Mavis Woodstock. I didn't want the women to come over, and apparently neither did they, since they turned their backs on me and continued their conversation.

It wasn't so bad. No one stared at me or pointed in horror at the woman dining alone. When I could no longer stand looking at calendar pages and addresses, I took out my checkbook. I carefully perused it as I ate the delicate fish, and made up my mind that the next day I would return to Mavis's house and look harder for a clue there. I could at least peer in more of the windows; I wouldn't be the first Realtor or prospective buyer to do that. I flipped to the back of my checkbook and began to scribble a to-do list on an empty deposit slip. The first item: google Mavis Woodstock.

"How much of *my* money have you got in there?"

I looked up to see Tom Haskins. "What are you doing here?" I set the checkbook facedown beside me.

"Just having a drink with those two." He indicated our two rivals seated at the bar.

"Really? I didn't notice you."

"Just got here." He sat down across from me.

"Oh. Well, I was just having dinner." I couldn't help but notice how much better he looked sitting there than David had. Of course I would have thought the same thing had it been that hideous blob Jabba the Hutt sitting across from me.

"Good for you, Kiddo. So how's it going?"

"What? The dinner?"

"Yeah, the friggin' dinner. The new apartment, Valerie, the new apartment. How do you like it?"

"It's okay. It's nice, really. You should come see it; I could cook you dinner."

"Please, I've had your cooking." He waved his Heineken bottle at me. "Did you get that new listing?"

"Not yet." I paused, realizing he might know one of Mavis's brothers. I told him about my phone conversation with Lionel.

"Yeah, I know Lionel Woodstock. A real jerk. But that doesn't mean he is responsible for your letting a listing slip away. Keep calling her. You'll connect. And you'll get the listing, Kiddo. You haven't let me down yet." He waved his bottle toward the bar. "Gotta go see the bimbos. They always spill their guts. They'll tell me something helpful before an hour's up. Maybe they'll even know where Mavis is." He chortled. "You think I'm drinking with them 'cuz they're so bootiful?"

His gangster imitation made me smile. "Look out, Tony Soprano." I scooped some rice onto my fork.

"Screw Tony Soprano. You gotta get out and discover what the competition is doing. It's all about schmoozing, Val. Haven't I told you that a thousand times?"

"Ten thousand."

"Okay, so listen to your Uncle Tom. Get out there some; keep your nose to the ground." He actually touched the side of his nose as he said it, making me think of a hound dog. "And at this point in your life, I'm guessing it wouldn't hurt none to meet some new people." He leaned back in the chair and downed the remainder of his beer.

"Why do you say that? I know more than enough people."

"Seen anything of Davey Boy?"

"Actually, I just saw him about half an hour ago. Had to sign the title to the BMW over to him."

"Piece of shit."

"The BMW or David?"

"Both. You were way too good for that asshole."

I stopped eating. Dear Tom; that was his way of paying me the highest of compliments. "Thank you, dear," I said softly.

***

I had set up my only television in the bedroom, and it was a luxury at the end of the day to huddle beneath the downy softness of my new duvet. My fleecy pajamas felt as soothing as the bedcovers, and my bowl of Ben & Jerry's

Chunky Monkey awaited as I settled in to watch a rerun of *Law & Order: Special Victims Unit*. My favorite show.

I promised myself this would be the last ice cream I'd eat for a while since a diet was definitely in my future. But not tonight. It was the first time I had afforded myself the guilty pleasure of either ice cream or television since moving in. All the other nights, I'd been too exhausted from unpacking and organizing cupboards—after working all day—to keep my eyes open for more than five minutes after plopping into bed.

And as eager as I was to google Mavis Woodstock, I was glad I hadn't gotten around to unpacking and setting up my computer. It had been so easy to just rely on my office computer, and I would do that again the next day, to google Mavis.

I heard the familiar ping ping of *Law & Order's* opening credits and decided I could get used to living alone. It wasn't so bad. There were no shaving remnants left on the side of the sink every morning. The toilet seat was always down. And no argument with David about watching TV, let alone eating, in bed.

Two minutes into the show, just long enough for a hooker's mangled body to be discovered in a New York alley, the phone rang. (I'd seen the episode before, as I had seen most of them, but one advantage of reaching fifty was I couldn't remember who did it.) I grabbed my reading glasses from the bedside table to read the caller ID, but still couldn't decipher the numbers. I picked up the remote to mute the TV sounds, but couldn't find the *mute* button, either. I answered the phone anyway and was rewarded with a serenade by my best friend.

"My baby does the hokey cokey."

"Kitty Kat," I said. "It's hanky panky, you nitwit. Say, I was going to call you first thing tomorrow morning, but since—"

"Valerie, my darling Valerie, whatcha doin'?" She was drunk, or at least tipsy.

"Trying to sleep, watching TV, nothing important." The thing I needed to discuss with her would have to wait until the next morning, after all. When she was sober.

"Get the hell outta my lane!"

"Kit, are you driving?"

"I am, but this moron isn't."

"Where are you? You pull over right now, and I'll come get you."

"I'm pulling onto Elderberry right now—home free."

"Kit, whatever possessed you to drive drunk?" What a question; if she'd been sober, she would have known better than to drive drunk. But Kit isn't a big drinker, and I'd certainly never known her to drive under the influence. "Where've you been?"

"Some bar, some other bar, and then a restaurant-type bar place. I dunno. Started out as a wedding shower for Lucy Weber, remember her? Anyhoo, I called your office, but you had left already."

"Yes, I met David. We had some things to go over."

"Asshole," she said. "This guy is gonna kill someone."

"Kit! You said you were home."

"They say most accidents happen close to home, ya know. But no worries. I'm here now. Safe in my driveway. See?"

I heard a car door open and close and breathed a sigh of relief.

"So how is David?" she asked. "No, don't tell me; I don't even care. How are *you*?" I pictured her stumbling up her walk.

"I'm okay. Meet me for lunch tomorrow. I need to talk about something."

"Not David; I refuse to talk about David. We've wasted far too much of our lives discussing him."

"Not David. Mavis Woodstock."

"Mavish Woodshtock—"

"Kit, we can't talk about this when you are drunk. Call me in the morning."

"Yes, doctor, that's what I'll do. Bye, love."

I put down the phone and smiled. Dear Kit. I'm really lucky to have her. But I had lost the thread of who killed the hooker, and it appeared that another body had been found. It suddenly occurred to me maybe David was right about me making a big deal out of nothing. After all, I do watch a lot of *Law & Order*.

Well, at least I knew that detectives Benson and Stabler would straighten out *their* mess. But only after I had fallen asleep.

***

Emily called the next morning as I was rushing to leave for work.

"Don't you people in California ever sleep?" I wedged the phone between my chin and shoulder and poured the remains of my third cup of coffee into the sink.

"Just checking on you," she said. "How's it going?"

"It's going great, but I'm just heading out the door. Can we talk later?"

"Sure."

"Okay, honey, I'll call you this afternoon."

Emily had lived in Los Angeles for two years. One winter morning, she and Luke packed all their belongings in their Explorer and left Chicago, heading west.

Luke got a job out there, something to do with computers, which has been explained to me countless times; but I'm still not sure what it is he actually does. Emily wanted to become an actress. In two years, she had joined the actor's union and acquired several waitressing jobs. The closest she'd come to acting, however, was her role as Santa's Helper at Macy's.

I felt proud, and a little envious, of her life, but I still missed my baby desperately.

"Mom," she said, just as I was about to hang up. "You need to get out of that tiny apartment—"

"It's not tiny." I laughed. "Besides, you haven't even seen it."

"Go meet someone, Mom. Find yourself a boyfriend."

Was it every adult child's wish to have her single parent find a mate? Lately it had become my daughter's mission. "Emily, the last thing I want is a man. I'm quite happy as I am, and my apartment is plenty big enough. Now let me go to work, so I can pay for this shoebox."

***

The strange thing was, within two hours of Emily's call I did meet a man who piqued my interest.

I had agreed to cover the phones because Perry was getting highlights put in his hair. Billie sat at her desk doing something important with accounting. Tom was in his office with the door closed, doing whatever it is he does back there.

So I was at my desk when the glass doors swung open, and a second later a tall, handsome man stood in front of me. He wore an expensive-looking suit and a crisp, white shirt (that I figured a dry cleaner, not a wife, had crispened and whitened).

I sat up straight to improve my posture. "Can I help you?"

He smiled, revealing teeth that matched his shirt: white and perfect. "Is Tom Haskins around?"

"Yes, let me tell him you're here. Can I give him your name?"

"Just tell him Fletch is here."

"Okay." I rose and smoothed down my skirt. Geez, if I'd known Pierce Brosnan was going to stop by, I would have dropped ten pounds before breakfast.

"Thank you." He turned sideways to study the homes-for-sale photo gallery on the wall. He was good, showing me his profile like that, although it seemed as if he didn't have a bad side.

I walked backward to Tom's office door, since I couldn't remember what was going on with my rear view today.

"Tom!" I said, in what I intended to be a whisper but which I'm sure was loud enough for everyone at Soldier Field to hear. "There's a guy here asking for you." I took one last look to be sure he hadn't been a figment of my imagination and then closed the door behind me. "Fletch. You know him?" I automatically began tidying up a pile of papers on his desk.

Tom was on the phone, which I hadn't noticed at first, but he pushed his glasses up to his forehead and put his hand over the receiver. "Who?"

"Fletch."

"Who?"

I collected four stray pens and put them in the pen holder I had given him one Christmas. "Fletch. Sounds as if he knows you."

Tom pulled his glasses back down to his nose and said a curt good-bye to the poor soul on the other end of the line. "Why didn't you say so?"

He stood up, threw his glasses onto the desk, and headed past me to the door.

"Fletch, you ol' son of a bitch," I heard Tom roar. "What the hell are you doing here?"

By the time I got back to my desk (two seconds, tops), they were pumping hands and gripping each other by the elbows, in that masculine gesture that stops just short of a full hug. I sat down at my desk and gave a polite cough, just so they'd remember I was there.

"Come in, come in." Tom steered Fletch toward his office.

I spoke up as they passed by me. "Anything I can get you?"

Tom stopped and looked down at me. "Like what?"

"I dunno. Coffee, maybe?"

"Good idea," Tom said. "Billie, bring us some coffee."

Even though she was knee-deep in accounting work, Billie waved a hand in the air, which meant delicious coffee would soon be on Tom's desk.

Dammit. I needed to learn to work that machine.

***

A couple of hours later, after much manly bellowing from behind Tom's closed door, he and Fletch emerged and passed by my desk, presumably on their way to lunch. Fletch waved good-bye and said it was nice to meet me, even though we hadn't been formally introduced. Okay, so he wasn't big on facts, but he was getting better-looking all the time.

Turned out Fletch and Tom had been in the army together, way back when. Ryan Fletcher, who was single (how could that possibly *be*?), was an attorney, the corporate kind, who lived in Florida but was working on a case in Chicago for the next several months. All this information came from Billie, after they had left. Although she never takes time to have much in the way of personal conversations with anyone, she seems to know everything.

***

I spotted Kit as soon as I walked into the restaurant, even though she was sitting at the table farthest away from the door and was almost hidden by a fake palm tree. It must have been the oversize dark glasses she was wearing and the menu she was holding up to her face.

I threw my purse onto an empty chair. "So. How are we feeling today?"

Kit lowered the menu and then raised her glasses. I had to admit, even though she had to be nursing one hell of a hangover, she looked her immaculate self, every dark-auburn hair in place. I guess that's what you get when you pay a hundred bucks for a good cut.

"Don't yell, please." She touched the bridge of her glasses with her index finger before taking a long sip of her iced tea. "Ugh." She almost spit it out. "How do the British drink this stuff?"

"Well, I don't think they drink it cold with forty pounds of ice." I took the menu from her manicured hand. "And why are you having iced tea in November, anyway? Did you order food yet?"

"No food. And again, please don't yell."

I was still chuckling when the waitress appeared at our table. I gave her my order for a chicken-salad sandwich and then closed the menu. "Okay, Kitty Kat. Listen up." I took my checkbook from my purse and turned to the deposit slip that held the notes I'd made. "I got some info for you."

"What kind of info—"

"About Mavis." I put on my reading glasses.

"Wait." Kit raised a hand to stop me, but the effort seemed too much, and she laid her hand down flat on the table. "Now, Valerie. I don't want you to go getting all tied up in a knot about this. There's a perfectly good reason why—"

But my own hand came up to stop her. "Hear me out. Okay, I spoke to her brother, and he said she spends all her time in Florida. But we know she doesn't spend *all* her time in Florida—"

"Lionel Woodstock."

"Yeah, Lionel; that's who I talked to. How did you know?"

"I know Lionel is one of her brothers."

"Tom said he knows a Lionel too. How many brothers are there?"

"Three, I think; at least three that I know of. Lionel, the oldest, and then Marcus, and one other one, her twin. I don't remember his name."

"She has a twin? Geez, how could I not remember that?"

"They aren't identical."

"Duh. But you'd think I'd remember. Did you know any of the brothers in school?"

"Not really." She shrugged and took another sip of her hated iced tea. "I remember Lionel best, really tall and geeky-looking. Larry might remember them. I think at least one of them is his age."

At the mention of Kit's husband, I wrote his name on a fresh deposit slip and decided I should buy a notebook. "Oh, that's good. We'll ask Larry."

"Now hold on there, Nancy Drew. Just what do you have planned here?"

"I'm just thinking, that's all. The whole business is strange."

She sat up straighter, took off her glasses, and then quickly put them back on again. "Are you feeling guilty?"

"Guilty? Why should I feel guilty?"

"Because we were all so mean to her," Kit said.

"We weren't mean. Some of the other girls were, but not us. Okay, we could have stuck up for her a bit more, but what did we know back then?"

"Yeah, we were pretty stupid, all right."

"I'm just curious, that's all. I stopped by her house on the way over here, and still no sign of life. Where can she be? If she was in Florida when she called, why wouldn't she mention that?" My sandwich was placed before me, and I took a bite. "All I'm saying is that I'd just like to know what happened to her. Is that so bad?"

"Not so bad." Kit took a potato chip off my plate and then another and managed to eat, as she always does, without disturbing her perfectly lined lips.

After I finished my sandwich and the check arrived, Kit took off her glasses once more and placed them in their Prada case. I put some money on the table, and she stood up. "Okay, Nancy, let's go," she said.

"Go? Where?"

"Back to the scene of the crime." A grin spread across her face. "Let's go check out her house again."

"Oh good, but I told you, I was already there this morning. There probably won't be anything—"

"We'll see." She took my arm. "And you drive."

CHAPTER FOUR

S o our Mavis moved to Florida. Yikes." Kit gazed out the window as we drove to Mavis's neighborhood.

"What's wrong with Florida?" I asked.

"Too hot. Too many hurricanes. Too many old people. And no one speaks English. I don't know why anyone would want to live there."

"Oh, that reminds me. Did I mention that a really good-looking guy came into the office this morning? He's an old friend of Tom's, and they went out to lunch together. *He* lives in Florida, and he's not so old, and he speaks English. But you are right about one thing: he was definitely hot."

"What? You wait until now to tell me this?" Kit applied a deep-copper shade of M.A.C. lipstick; and with her auburn hair, it looked stunning.

I turned the corner onto Mavis's street. "No big deal. We often have attractive men in our office."

"Right, it's like *GQ* headquarters over there." She put her lipstick back in her purse. "Single?"

"Apparently so."

"Money?"

"Well, I didn't see his bank statement. But he has all his own teeth, and he was wearing shoes."

"You should doll yourself up, ya know, make a move."

"I'm dolled up enough, thank you." But I found myself wishing I had worn more makeup that morning. I made a mental note to wear my red lipstick all the time.

I pulled up in front of Mavis's house and killed the engine. I was getting so familiar with the place, it was almost like coming home—if you lived on the outside instead of the inside, that is.

Kit bolted out of the car and scurried up the path to the red front door. By the time I reached her, she was ringing the bell with one hand and tapping on the door with the other.

"Let's go around to the back," she said.

"Well, okay, but let's try not to get arrested for trespassing."

She gave me a look that said *no problem*, and suddenly we were kids again, doing stuff we shouldn't have been doing. And as always, Kit was in the lead, and I followed behind in nervous awe.

The backyard was neat and orderly, much like the front. Even the leaves from the huge old maple trees had apparently been raked and hauled away. Only a slight scattering remained to blow about in the cool breeze. If Mavis was indeed living in Florida, she'd made arrangements to have someone tend her yard.

"Looks like someone's cleaned this out," Kit said. She pointed to a perennial garden where only the autumn joy remained to provide its lasting burgundy color. All other foliage had been clipped and removed.

As always, Kit seemed to have read my mind. "Maybe a neighbor takes care of it," I said.

"Yeah, or maybe Hannibal Lecter came for a salad to go with lunch."

A chill went through me, and I shivered. "Stop that," I said. Then I followed her onto a deck that stretched the full width of the house, with access from a back door positioned between two large windows. We each chose a window and peered in.

"See anything?" I asked.

"Er, I think I can see—wait, yes, I think I see some shoes. And they have feet in them! And yes, yes, I see legs . . ."

I rushed to her side and looked over her shoulder. With relief, I slapped her on the back. She could see nothing. But she turned and gave me her devilish grin. She was having a little too much fun to suit me.

She straightened up. "So, you wanna break in?"

"Of course not. Don't be ridiculous. We can't do that."

Kit shrugged and moved to the back door.

"We can't," I said. "Can we?"

A sudden flashback hit me, like handcuffs being slapped on my wrists. We were thirteen and headed for a life of crime. Shoplifting in Kmart. Okay, so it was the only time we ever did it, and it was definitely an activity all the cool girls in our school were trying out; but I was sick with anxiety for about a month afterward.

The items we stole were unimportant (me: a powder compact I never used; Kit: a bottle of awful-smelling lilac cologne). The idea, as Kit explained to the thirteen-year-old me, was the thrill of not getting caught. But as I stood on Mavis's deck, I could feel my stomach lurch at the seriousness of our crime.

Kit tested the doorknob, and her grin spread into a full smile. "Looks like we don't have to break in. Seems like we've been invited." I watched in amazement as the door opened.

We entered Mavis's kitchen, and my Realtor eyes took it all in: the shiny tiled floor, up-to-date appliances, taupe walls, and clean white cabinets and countertops. Only an empty chardonnay bottle and a lone wineglass, which looked as if it had been rinsed if not washed, stood in the spotless stainless-steel sink.

If Mavis were here, I could have told her it would be an easy sell.

Kit had already proceeded into the living room, and I followed. Nice wood floors, also spotlessly clean. A couch with a throw blanket over the back, two black Labradors woven in. A large comfy armchair. On an end table sat a wooden duck, and on the coffee table lay an issue of *Real Simple* magazine. Once again, I appraised the room with my Realtor's vision. It was nice. Cozy and well cared for. Much the way I would stage a house before bringing in prospective clients.

Kit was already in the bedroom, and I heard her call. "Come look at this."

"What did you find?" I tiptoed across the wood floor, my mind trying to form a good—a legal—excuse for our being here, in case Mavis suddenly appeared.

On the off-white dresser stood a silver frame that held a photograph of a woman and a young boy. The woman looked tall and slim and had silvery-blond hair cut just below her chin in a timeless style. She wore a fitted suit and had her arm around the boy's shoulders. He looked about twelve. They both smiled at the camera, although the woman had a hurry-up-and-take-the-picture look.

"This can't be our Mavis," Kit said.

"The woman looks about forty, so she's too young. Unless the picture is old. I wonder who the child is."

"Mavis's love child?"

"No, it can't be Mavis. She looked nothing like this."

"She could have gone under the knife, ya know. Or not even that drastic. She could have just gone to a good optician and dentist." Kit started to open a drawer.

"Don't. That's going too far. We should leave."

"Don't you want to dust for fingerprints?"

"Very funny. Let's get out of here. It's getting creepy."

On my way back to the kitchen, I glanced in the remaining rooms: two other bedrooms, one that might have been the computer room Mavis mentioned on the phone—though I saw no computer—and a bathroom and small dining nook.

Kit was already in the kitchen by the time I got there. "I didn't find anything," I said. "You?"

"No dead bodies, if that's what you mean."

"Well, it's all very neat and tidy, nothing out of place, don't you think?"

"Except for the bed, of course."

"What?" I returned to the bedroom and stared at Mavis's queen-size bed. Kit was right. It was unmade. The pillows and the duvet were tossed around as if a tornado had ripped through the room. I couldn't believe it hadn't struck me earlier. Guess my Realtor's vision wasn't 20/20. Besides, I'd been so focused on the photograph.

I rejoined Kit in the kitchen. "You're right. It's strange, isn't it?"

"Do you always make your bed?"

I conjured up a vision of my own bedroom, with its clutter of boxes and piles of clothes waiting for a permanent home. "Well, I can hardly find my bed nowadays, much less make it. But the rest of Mavis's home seems so tidy. This could be something."

"Something? What do you mean?"

"I don't know what I mean, but this is freaking me out. Let's go."

"Don't you think we should look a little more? As long as we're here?"

"No, I don't. Let's go."

I headed toward the back door and then realized there was another way out of the kitchen. Once again I thought how *un*Realtor-like of me to have missed something as obvious as a door. I *was* nervous about our break-in. But I knew Kit was right again: as long as we were here . . .

My voice cracked as I spoke. "This must lead to the garage or basement, do you think?"

Kit was already there. She opened the door and then turned back to face me. "It's the garage. And this is weird."

"What?" I wasn't sure I wanted to know, but I approached the garage door and Kit. "You mean that smell?"

"What smell?" Kit crinkled her perfectly made-up nose. "That's just the garbage." She nodded her head toward an overflowing can in the corner that I could barely see in the dark garage. "No, I mean that." She swung the door open fully. "Mavis's car. How do you like them apples? Wherever Mavis went, she didn't drive herself."

I grabbed her arm before she had a chance to explore further and take Mavis's car out for a spin. "That's enough. We're going."

***

"Hey, Kiddo. Anything going on?" It was no doubt just one of Tom's regular evening check-in calls, but I wondered if he knew Kit and I had been at Mavis Woodstock's house earlier that day.

"No. Nothing, really." I wasn't ready to tell him I'd become accomplished in the art of breaking and entering (okay, no breaking, but definitely entering).

"What happened with Mavis Woodstock? Did you get her straightened out?"

"What?"

"Did you reach her? By the way, Fletch was asking about her. I guess he knows her from Florida. I suppose he gave her our name to sell her place. I told him she called you."

That was a surprise, but probably a good one. If Fletch knew our Mavis, he might have some information that could lead me to her. "No, I didn't reach her. And she never called again."

"Keep after her, Kiddo. Hey, did Perry get that contract out?"

"Yes."

Actually, *I* had taken care of the contract that was supposed to have been Perry's responsibility. When I'd returned to the office, I learned his hair appointment had run over, and he would have missed the deadline.

"So how was your lunch?" I asked Tom. "Good to see your old pal, I bet?"

"Yeah, Fletch is one in a million. Did I ever tell you he saved my life?"

"Yes," I lied. I'm sure it was a great story, but Tom never stays on the phone too long, and I was more interested in the details of Fletch's present life than his military career. "So what's he doing here? How long is he here for? How old is he?"

"Why do you wanna know?"

"Well, Billie says he's single, and he seems very nice."

"He ain't that nice."

"You just said he was one in a million."

"Not in Downers Grove."

"Well, he seems nice."

"Valerie." When he says my name that way, I know a lecture is on its way, so I braced myself. "To begin with, you can't count on the guy—"

"You just said he saved your life." The lecture had to be squelched. Besides, I didn't want to hear anything bad about good ol' Fletch.

"Will you listen to me? That was a long time ago. Things were different in the army—"

Wow, I really had to cut him short. Tom's army stories were the worst, not to mention the longest. "Okay, forget Fletch," I said. "Are you going to be in the office tomorrow?"

"Don't know yet; I'll see you when I see you. You okay?"

"Yes, I'm fine."

"Okay then, go to sleep, Kiddo."

"It's seven thirty!"

"Good; you look like you could do with more rest. See ya."

***

The next morning, while I was reassuring Perry for the umpteenth time that his highlights were perfect, who should show up but Fletch (speaking of perfect). He was wearing another suit that looked custom-made, this one with a pale-blue pin-striped shirt.

"Is Tom around, Valerie?" Tom must have given him my name. Maybe he'd *asked* Tom about me.

"No, I haven't seen him yet, or heard from him. Should I call him? Were you expecting to meet him here? I could call him, at home or on his cell." Babble, babble, babble, while Fletch sat down on the other side of my desk, in the chair reserved for prospective customers.

"No need," he said. "Are you free for lunch?"

I looked around the office. Perry had disappeared into the bathroom to study his hair in a better light, and Billie was on the phone, engrossed in a conversation with a mortgage company. Still, I had to ask. "Me?"

"Yes, you, if you're free. I need to see about renting an apartment or something while I'm here. The corporate place I'm in is pretty dismal. I need something with access to a gym, and close to a park would be good. I like to run every day."

"Who doesn't?" (Even *I* didn't believe that lie.) I pushed my feet back into my shoes under the desk. "We don't really get into leasing, but let me call a few people." Of course I had no idea who to call, but surely knowing "a few people" sounded good.

"And lunch?"

"Lunch would be great. I'm free, as long as we go early."

We agreed to meet at Italiano's, a quaint eatery in downtown Downers Grove, at eleven thirty. After Fletch left the office, I called and pushed back my already-existing lunch date with the Coopers. Okay, so the Coopers were on the verge of signing a purchase agreement, but they were in their twenties. A late lunch probably wouldn't mess with their metabolism. As for me, I could always eat twice.

I didn't get a chance to google Mavis Woodstock before I had to leave to meet Fletch on time. I promised myself I'd do that before leaving the office at the end of the day. No matter what. In the meantime, I felt certain I could learn something from Fletch about Mavis, since he knew her.

***

I ordered pasta fasul, convincing myself that the savory broth was, after all, only soup. Fletch ordered an Italian salad and manicotti. We finished with two espressos, and when Fletch took out his American Express card to pay the bill, he complimented our waiter on the delicious food.

After we took our final sips of the strong coffee, Fletch asked me to show him around the downtown area—on foot.

I glanced at my watch. "Let me see if I can push back my afternoon lu . . . er, appointment." I fumbled in my purse for my phone and called Billie to ask her to wrangle an extra hour for me. Within minutes—bless that Billie—my cell phone sang its tune.

After Billie assured me the Coopers were fine with the further delay, I plopped my phone back in my purse. "You're in luck. Looks like a grand tour of Downers Grove is on your afternoon agenda."

"Perfect," Fletch said. And heaven help me, I thought for the second time that day, he was.

The sun was shining as we left Italiano's, but it still felt brisk enough for me to tighten the belt of my camel-hair coat around my waist.

I couldn't remember ever having such rapt attention from anyone. Oh, maybe Emily—but not since she was young enough to sit on my lap for a story. As we walked down the street, past the cutesy shops, Fletch wanted to know all about me.

I tried to stick to facts about my work with his friend Tom, how I'd gotten my real estate license after spending so many years as a stay-at-home mom, and how I really enjoyed both selling houses and helping people buy just the right homes for them. I sounded like Mother Teresa describing her work with the down-and-outs in Calcutta.

But before I could nominate myself for the Realtor equivalent of a Nobel Prize, Fletch steered me onto my personal life, which he seemed more interested in. Soon I was telling him about my recent divorce and the marriage that preceded it. In fact, I was so busy talking about myself, I almost forgot about poor Mavis. (And wasn't that the problem back in school? We all forgot about her, unless we were making fun of her.)

All too soon, I led us back to my car and groped in my purse for the keys.

"When can I see you again, Valerie?"

My name on his tongue sounded lyrical, and somehow I didn't think he wanted to see me again just because we still hadn't discussed his living accommodations. I felt goose bumps form on my arms. They spread throughout my whole body, inside and out, as I looked up at him and he leaned in close to my face. I was glad I'd avoided onions at lunch.

I remained speechless while his face hovered around mine, around my lips, ready, I felt sure, to seal our plans with a kiss.

"I'll be done with my meetings by six," he said. "Can we have dinner tonight?"

"Yes. No. Uh . . . call me, okay?" *What was wrong with me?*

He stood up straight, leaving my face feeling exposed and unprotected. Disappointment coursed through my body, even as I knew *I'd* disappointed *him*. And I felt sure he wasn't used to being disappointed.

"I have to leave Monday," he said, "after my last meeting, and I won't be back for a few days. See what you can work out." Suddenly he sounded more like his friend Tom than the Fletch I was getting to know.

"Yeah, I will." I climbed into my car and put my key in the ignition. Then I powered down the window. "Oh, Fletch, one thing I wanted to ask you. Mavis Woodstock. Tom says you know her?"

He put his hands in his pockets and gazed up at the sky, as if trying to decide how best to respond. After what seemed a ridiculously long time to answer a simple question, he spoke. "I know Mavis." Then he pulled a hand out of his pocket and his eyes focused on his watch. "I gotta go. I'll call you, Val."

"But about Mavis . . ."

He smiled. "I'll tell you at dinner." And then he walked off to his own car.

CHAPTER FIVE

When I was finally back at the office, I fixed myself fresh coffee in an attempt to counter the stupefying effects of my two lunches. Then I sat down at my computer and took a sip before opening my browser.

When I saw I had seventeen new messages in my in-box, I cursed myself for not checking my e-mail sooner. Ever since my move, I'd let everything slip. Well, it wasn't the e-mail account I used for work, so I didn't think any of the messages could be too important. I focused instead on the blank space next to the magic words *Powered by Google*.

I typed in *Mavis Woodstock*, hit Enter, and waited for the list of sites I knew was forthcoming in a matter of seconds (a list of four thousand two hundred thirty sites, to be precise, presented to me in exactly a tenth of a second).

But not one of the four thousand two hundred thirty revealed anything. That, of course, I found out only after I'd wasted the rest of my day clicking on site after useless site that offered information on everything from the great rock fest of 1969 to brand-name tires at discount prices—everything but my Mavis Woodstock, that is. I felt like the fool who buys a lottery ticket and, against all reason, feels certain it's a winner.

I heaved a sigh and clicked on to my Gmail. For a second I thought the Mavis Woodstock listed in my in-box was somehow part of my Google search, and I began to page down past it. Then I did a computer double take and paged back up.

With my heart pounding, I noted the message was dated five days ago, which meant Mavis wrote it shortly after our one and only phone conversation. My excitement ebbed when I realized the message didn't say much. Just one sentence spelled out the end of our almost nonexistent relationship: *Sorry to have bothered you, Valerie, but I won't be selling my home, after all.*

I hit *reply* and typed my own brief message to Mavis. (Even if she *was* dismissing me, I was glad she'd put us on a first-name basis.) *May I ask you why, Mavis? Just to help with my record keeping and such. Say, do you remember me from high school? I always wanted to get to know you better. Maybe we could get together sometime. I have something important to tell you. Valerie*

I pushed *send* before I could come to my senses and discard my message.

***

That evening I found myself regretting I hadn't agreed immediately to have dinner with Fletch. Still, I felt like a schoolgirl—a smoking-hot schoolgirl—as I replayed my lunch with him. And like a schoolgirl with a crush, I hoped he would call that night and still want to see me. I'd get ready just in case.

I entered the living room after my shower, to escape the heat and steam that spilled from the bathroom into the bedroom, so close were my new living quarters. With wet and uncombed hair and a towel wrapped around me twice, the end tucked over my left breast, I held my hairbrush up to my head. But just then Tina Turner began demanding *you better be good to me* through the speakers of my tiny Bose radio, so I jumped into the largest space I could find in the living room and began belting along with her into the hairbrush. My fluffy bunny-rabbit slippers stood in for Tina's Manolo Blahniks, and my white Sears bath towel substituted for her black leather miniskirt.

When we were both done, and Tina was replaced by a commercial for an antacid, the phone rang. Could it be? I hobbled to the counter and picked up the receiver. How did Tina do it in four-inch heels?

"Hello," I said breathlessly. I still felt a tad like Tina.

It *was* Fletch. And by the time we hung up a few minutes later, I'd agreed to a dinner date with him. *That night.*

I dropped the phone on the couch beside me. I could hear Faith Hill warbling from the radio, but I had no interest in singing along with her. For the second time that day, I felt unsettled. Like there was something I should be doing, something I should be worrying about, but I didn't know what it was.

Before I could figure it out, Tom called. "What's wrong? You sound funny."

"Tom, I just said *hello*. How funny can that sound? And nothing's wrong. In fact, I just got a call from Fletch. We're having dinner tonight."

"What? You're kidding, right? He didn't say anything to me about dinner."

"Well, I don't think he actually intends for the *three* of us to dine together. Just he and I."

"What?"

I sighed. "Fletch asked me out—"

"That guy is all wrong for you." I could hear Tom sucking on his cigar, and I knew he was having his usual trouble lighting it and keeping it lit.

"Really? Well, so far I find him charming and—"

"Don't interrupt. I haven't finished yet." I could almost see the enormous waft of smoke as I heard him blowing out. "Now listen, Fletch is not who you think he is—"

"Is that so? And how do you know who I think he is?"

"Because he's probably given you a big line of bullshit. Trust me on this one, Kiddo; he's not the guy for you. Now, I know you're probably lonely, and let's face it, you're not getting any younger. So when a guy like Fletch breezes in and asks you out, naturally you fall for it."

Tom's two wives popped into my head. The first one, around his age, had almost ruined him financially after their divorce. Her drinking and gambling problems left him shattered and broke. But being the real estate mastermind that he is, he rebounded quickly enough to amass another small fortune before marrying wife number two, who was twenty years his junior. He was smart enough to have her sign a prenup, but the discovery of her numerous lovers also left him shattered when divorce became inevitable. At least number two didn't leave him broke.

He was babbling on, no doubt waving the cigar around for emphasis, but I had stopped listening. Perhaps *he* was lonely. And *he* certainly wasn't getting any younger, either (although he has the unfair advantage that age on a man is not cause for despair, the way it can be for a woman).

"Look," I said, "I don't want to hear any of *your* bullshit. I'm going to dinner with Fletch, and that's that."

"Fine; go ahead, but don't go falling for this guy. He'll break your heart."

"It's dinner, Tom; we're not running off to Vegas to get married."

"Do whatever; you'll find out."

"Find out what?"

"Nothing."

"Come on, what will I find out?"

"That he's nowhere near good enough for you."

It was such a sweet thing for him to say—for *anyone* to say, let alone big, tough Tom—that I think I felt a need to reciprocate, or reward him. So even though I needed to hurry and get ready for my date with Fletch, I decided to confide in Tom about the latest Mavis discovery. "Tom," I said softly, and then I told him about entering the house with Kit and seeing Mavis's car in the garage.

"*What?* What the hell were you doing *in* her house at all, let alone with that nut-job Kit?"

I couldn't tell what made him angrier, that I had gone into the house, or that I had taken Kit with me. It didn't help when I insisted I wanted to get the listing for the good of *his* company, and Kit just happened to be with me at the time.

"Valerie, I forbid you to go anywhere near that property again; do you hear me? You or any of your friends. It could cost me my company's good name, and it will, I promise, cost *you* your job if you go anywhere near anything to do with Mavis Woodstock again."

***

Getting ready for my date with Fletch took some doing, and not just because Tom's tirade had left me feeling more unsettled than ever. Actually, it was pretty easy to brush off Tom's outburst as, well, Tom just being Tom. I've seen him have a major meltdown when we've run out of cream for his coffee (only on days when Billie isn't in the office, of course).

The chilly weather should have made it easier to find something suitable to wear without breaking my two rules: no bare arms and absolutely, under no circumstances, was there to be any cleavage. Fifty-year-old breasts need to be covered.

But still I tried on six dresses. The first three were all too tight. Number four displayed a small amount of cleavage (although it hadn't when I bought it and weighed ten fewer pounds). Number five had a rip in the seam under the arm that I didn't have time to fix. And the last one was too short.

Okay. No dresses. I went to the suit section of my closet and pulled out a brown wool skirt and matching jacket. Maybe I wouldn't be too warm. But just in case, I chose a white silk blouse that would look okay if I had to take off my jacket.

Fifteen minutes before Fletch was due to arrive, I was dressed, made-up, and ready for him. Fourteen minutes before he was due, I was so hot I ripped off my suit jacket. A minute after that, the silk blouse came off. And then I spent the rest of the time before Fletch arrived searching my closet for something cooler yet fallish—and above all, stunningly stylish. If my mother had been there, she would have said *you can't get blood out of a turnip, Valerie; so don't even try.*

Well, I thought, in answer to my mother's imagined remarks, *maybe I won't get blood out of a turnip, but I* will *get some information about Mavis tonight.*

***

Fletch greased the maître d' with a twenty-dollar bill, and we were seated immediately. The only other person I had seen do that, in real life, was Tom. My ex-husband had tried it once at a snooty French restaurant, and the maître d' had glanced at the bill as if David had placed a dead haddock in his palm. We'd spent the next forty minutes waiting for our table and arguing over the pretentiousness of the French versus the sucking up of Americans.

Our table for two was at the back of the room, set against French windows, through which I noticed a light dusting of snow outside. The waiter held out my chair and then produced a lighter from his pocket and lit the red candle tucked into the table's floral centerpiece. The soft glow provided just enough light so I could study Fletch as he studied the leather-bound wine list. I became aware of some soft jazz playing somewhere in the background, and I smiled back at Fletch when he gave me a little wink. If I hadn't had

Mavis at the top of my mind, I might have found the whole scene romantic.

In fact, it flashed through my mind that it would have been a more romantic date for a proposal than the one I'd actually had. David and I had gone to a Bears game at Soldier Field, and during halftime, he proposed marriage and produced a tiny diamond ring. In the retelling of that date, David always seemed more impressed with the score of the game than the fact that I had agreed to become his wife.

I pushed the feelings of regret out of my mind and concentrated instead on my current dinner date.

I decided Fletch was as nice as he was handsome when I listened to him give the waiter our wine order and watched as he flashed his warm smile. I was, however, determined not to be sidetracked by the ambience and to get Mavis Woodstock out on the table, so to speak, even though the Mavis I remembered would have been more suited to washing dishes in the kitchen than sprawling out on one of the tables.

After the waiter returned and poured our wine, Fletch raised a glass in toast.

And then I said, "So. About Mavis Woodstock. Tell me about her."

"Ah, you remembered."

"She was the carrot you dangled in front of me. Do *you* remember?"

"I hope she's not the only reason you agreed to dinner."

"Of course not. But I would like to hear what you know about her."

"And just why is that?"

For some reason, I wasn't sure I wanted to share everything I knew—which was basically nothing. But his seeming reluctance added to my sense of unease about Mavis.

"Well, if you must know, she's an old friend of mine," I said at last. "I'm just curious how you know her. You must admit it's a small world, your coming all this way from Florida and knowing my old pal."

Well, it wasn't a total lie.

He sipped his wine. "When did you last see her?"

"Not for a while. But we e-mail. You know how it is, a great way to keep in touch." At least that was true. Partly.

"Are you selling her house?"

"Well, it certainly won't be difficult. It's a great place."

"Oh." He raised an eyebrow. The light from the candle between us gave him a suddenly sinister air. All he lacked was a black mustache to twirl with his fingers. "Where exactly is this house?"

"In Downers Grove."

He smiled. "That much I figured, but where, exactly?"

I realized it wouldn't be difficult for him to get the address, as simple as looking in the phone book. But I thought he should work for it. "You haven't answered my question," I said. "How do you know her?"

He was slow to respond, the way he had been at his car when we last said good-bye. He took another sip of wine and then dabbed at his mouth with his linen napkin. "We were acquaintances in Boca Raton. I helped her out with a few legal problems she had, nothing too major."

I noticed immediately that he said they *were* acquaintances, past tense. And when he didn't continue, I pressed on. "What was she doing in Boca Raton?"

"I thought you said you were friends."

Uh-oh. "Well, you know Mavis. She's hard to figure out. Did she seem happy there to you? I got the impression she might have wanted to move back to the Midwest."

"Who isn't happy in Boca? It's paradise."

"No kidding." I was glad to see the waiter, who handed us menus that were longer than the lease on my new apartment.

After we ordered—steamed mussels in white wine for him, and steak Diane in shallot sauce for me—Fletch toasted again.

I set my wineglass back on the table. "So what kind of lawyer are you? Criminal?"

He laughed. "Nothing so exciting, I'm afraid. Mainly estate planning, that kind of thing; very dull. Some corporate work; even duller."

"Oh."

"You sound disappointed."

"No, not a bit. I'm sure you have to be brilliant to be a corporate lawyer."

"Not at all. You have to be methodical. More wine?" He took the bottle from the silver wine cooler at the side of our table.

"Thank you. Do you know why Mavis wants to sell?"

"Really, Valerie, I'm beginning to think you don't know Mavis at all. Didn't she tell you? You are her Realtor, right? Not to mention her old friend." The glow from the candle illuminated the twinkle in his eyes.

Damn. Clearly, I could never be any kind of secret agent. Not only would I crack under the slightest interrogation, but I'd also blow my cover in two minutes. "Yes, of course, but you know Mavis, she's hard to—"

"Figure out? You already said that."

"But it's so true." I gave a canned laugh and shook my head as if I were reminiscing about all the hours I'd spent trying to figure out my old friend Mavis.

"You were in school together?"

I silenced my fake laugh. "How did you know that?"

"Tom mentioned it."

"Oh, Tom."

"Yes. He knows her too. Although not nearly as well as you seem to."

We stared at each other across the table, and I could tell that behind his smug look, he was laughing this time. And *his* laugh was real.

"Yes, Mavis and I go back a long way," I said.

Luckily, before I launched into an account of all the happy times Mavis and I had spent together, I was saved by the arrival of my French onion soup and Fletch's spinach salad vinaigrette.

The food looked delicious, I was with a gorgeous man, and I was done with Mavis for the night.

CHAPTER SIX

Fletch and I arrived back at my apartment in high spirits. I unlocked the door. "Come in; let me get you a drink."

"I don't think I need any more." He glanced around my living room. "This is nice, Valerie."

"You don't think it's too small?" I dropped my keys and purse on the counter that separated the kitchen from the living room.

"I like small; it's cozy."

"Sure you don't want a drink?"

"No. Really. In fact, I should be going. I have a breakfast meeting tomorrow."

I wasn't sure if I was insulted or relieved. I glanced at my kitchen wall clock, which showed it wasn't even ten thirty yet. "It's still early," I said.

"I know, but I have to prepare for my meeting."

"You work on a Sunday, and you're not even in real estate?"

"Is tomorrow Sunday? Seems like I work every day. But how about we both play hooky one day this week and you show me the Midwest? Looks like it could be a true winter wonderland you could show me." He motioned out the window at the falling snow. Then he wrapped his arms around my waist, and I could feel his sweet cabernet breath on my cheek.

"It's a big area, the Midwest," I said.

"Hmm, how about we stay east of the Mississippi?" His lips found mine.

I waited until he removed his tongue from my mouth, and with it, the last vestige of any unease I'd felt about him. "We'll just stay within the tristate area."

His tongue was back in my mouth, and I could feel its magic all the way down to my toes. Then he pulled away. "Okay, lady, you're on. I'll call you tomorrow."

I didn't want to let him go. I could smell his sexy aftershave. The collar of his shirt was crisp, and I resisted the urge to pull at the knot of his silk tie. Instead, with my hands flat on the lapels of his jacket, I gently pushed him away. Fletch was the first man I'd been this close to since David, and that seemed like centuries ago.

We held hands during the walk to the front door (four steps, at most).

He kissed my forehead. "Thank you for a perfect evening. It was lovely, and so are you."

Then he left. And when my feet touched the carpet again, I twirled around and let out a huge *whoopee*. He was coming back.

I poured myself a glass of pinot, kicked off my shoes, and plopped onto my sofa. Then I called Kit. "Whatcha doing?" I felt like that schoolgirl again, just home from my first date.

"Playing Texas Hold'em with the Whittackers. What are you doing?"

"Just sitting here thinking about Fletch."

"Oh yeah, and how is that going?"

"First date. Pretty damn near perfect."

"Good for you," Kit yelled, and I wasn't sure if she was yelling at me or one of the Whittackers.

"Me?"

"Yes, you. Way to go. But I'm assuming since it's not even eleven yet, and you are calling *me*, that he's not there and you didn't have sex."

"Yes, he's not here, and no, we didn't have sex." Then I switched to a singsong voice. "But it might come up in the future."

She laughed. "Good for you." Again I wasn't sure if it was good for the Whittackers or me.

"Okay then, I'll let you get back to your game. Just wanted to check in."

"Hey, Valley Girl." She was whispering. "Really, good for you. I'm glad you like this guy. But what did you find out about Mavis?" I had relayed the connection between Mavis and Fletch to Kit earlier in the day, during one of our many phone conversations, and I was pleased her curiosity had been piqued.

"Well, that's the odd part. He was definitely reluctant to say what he knew about her. Yet I had the distinct impression he wanted to know what *I* knew."

"Val, you didn't go all goofy, did you, with your murder theories and bodies hidden in the attic?"

"Give me some credit. I was very discreet."

I hoped her howl of laughter was aimed at the Whittackers and not me. But then, no longer bothering to whisper, she said, "Discreet? You? That's a good one."

"Well, I'm glad you are so amused. I'm going to bed, and I hope the Whittackers take all your money."

She burst into laughter again. "Yeah, right; that's about as likely as you being discreet."

"Call me tomorrow."

"I will. Love you." She was still laughing as she hung up, and I only hoped the Whittackers knew how to bluff (unlike me, apparently).

***

"So how did you do with the Whittackers?"

"We kicked their asses."

It was Sunday morning, and I was in Kit's immaculate kitchen, sipping fresh, hot coffee. The *Chicago Tribune* was spread out before me, and I was checking out the real estate section.

Kit was deep into the entertainment news, and Larry was at the stove fixing us omelets. I was hoping we were starting a Sunday tradition, now that I had established a much smaller, but cozier, home of my own.

Larry is a good guy. I'm not surprised he turned out that way because all through school, he had the makings of a good guy. I never knew him and Kit to date anyone else; and even though on the surface it appears that Kit is way too flamboyant for the regimented CPA, they make a perfect match.

In school, Larry had been one of the cool guys (but always a good one), even though—or maybe because—he was shy. And in middle age he has gained only enough weight to make him look cuddly, not fat. He has lost a lot of hair, but it isn't an unattractive look. And he adores his wife, their one married son who lives in Texas, and their comfortable lifestyle. These two lifelong friends are family to me. And spending time with them together reminds me that some marriages really do work.

"Kit says you had a date last night, Val." Larry put a perfect egg concoction in front of me. He wore an apron with instructions to *Kiss the Cook*.

"You bet she did," Kit said. She nibbled on a piece of toast. "I'm reading all about it here." She indicated the newspaper. "Valerie Pankowski and her date were chased by paparazzi in Downers Grove."

"Very funny." I dug into the perfect eggs. "And yes, Larry, I did. A real nice guy."

"That's great, Val." Larry returned to the stove. "You deserve a nice man." Didn't I say Larry's a good guy?

"By the way, did Kit tell you about Mavis Woodstock?" I asked.

Larry turned off the stove and came to join us at the counter, a cup of coffee in his hand. "Yeah, I understand you two broke into her house."

"Larry, we didn't break in," Kit said, without looking up from the paper. "I told you, the door was unlocked."

"How convenient."

"Do you remember her brothers?" I asked.

Larry stretched out his long legs, and his feet landed under the stool next to the one he was perched on. "Yep. Let's see. There was Lionel, the oldest, Marcus came next, and then Will, her twin. Marcus and Will were okay guys, but Lionel was . . . not very nice."

"You mean he was an asshole?" Kit turned the pages of the newspaper.

Larry gave his wife an amused look. "You could say that; you could definitely say that. I remember him picking Mavis up a couple of times after school, and I thought he was pretty rough on her."

"Oh no," I said softly. An image of poor Mavis being dragged from school property by a goonish brother made me lose my appetite. "What about her folks? Do you remember them?"

"Her mother probably still lives in the area. At least I never heard anything about her passing away. I think her dad died not long after we were out of college."

"Did Mavis go to college?"

"I don't think so; I never heard about that. Her brothers all graduated from DePaul. The family had money."

"So I hear. Where did that come from?"

Before he could answer, my phone rang in my purse, and I scrambled to get it. It was Tom, who will probably always be part of my Sunday-morning ritual. "It's the boss," I said, and I walked toward the living room to take the call.

"Tell the boss it's Sunday," Larry called after me. "And tell him to bet on the Bears today." For some reason, Tom favors the Packers over his home team, and he and Larry carry on a friendly rivalry that's lasted since we were all in school.

"You ever listen to your messages?"

"I'm having breakfast with Kit and Larry. And good Sunday morning to you too." I fell onto one of two leather couches cradling the fireplace.

"Haven't I told you a thousand times that Sunday is Monday for Realtors?"

"Ten thousand times."

"So while you were with lover-boy last night, we lost the property on Gilmore. I had to call that idiot nephew of mine to get his ass over there, and you won't be surprised to learn it was too late."

"Perry was working on a Saturday night?"

"Val, Saturday night is Thursday night for Realtors."

"Well, I'm sorry we lost the listing, but—"

"We might not have lost it entirely. You can get over there today, sweet-talk the geriatric couple who own the joint into going with us. They probably didn't sign anything yet."

"Well, did they, or didn't they?"

"How the hell do I know? I don't know every little detail. That's your job. And if you concentrated on it a little bit more instead of running all over the state with every Tom, Dick, and Harry, you might be on top of things."

I suppressed a giggle. "Aren't you going to ask me how my date was?"

"Okay. How was it?"

"Actually, it was wonderful."

"Listen to me, Kiddo, don't go getting yourself all hot and bothered over that guy. It won't come to anything good. You're on the rebound. You need to play the field a bit."

"Oh no." I put my hand on my throat in mock horror, even though Tom could not see my dramatics. "And I just had the wedding invitations printed this morning. Do you think I can get a refund?"

Tom laughed. But it wasn't a good laugh. It was a joke's-on-you kind of laugh, and I heard him latch his briefcase shut. "One thing I can assure you, there ain't gonna be a wedding, at least not one with Fletch as the groom. That I can guaran-damn-tee you."

***

I left my pals after finishing my omelet and one more cup of Larry's gourmet coffee. While I drove to the house on Gilmore that Tom was all worked up about, I practiced my role of running interference for Perry. I had done it many times before.

Perry has some good points, but they mainly center on him staying in the office and not meeting any potential clients. His people skills are . . . well, not much better than his uncle's.

In fact, as I drove and thought about it, I decided Perry is the softer, kinder version of Tom—without Tom's sharp wit, intelligence, and amazing intuition.

That got me pondering Tom's warning about Fletch. There had to be more to our mutual acquaintance than Tom was telling me.

I reached Gilmore Street and introduced myself to the Gilmores. (They were quick to assure me the street had not been named after them.) They were in their late seventies, I guessed, and far from snatching their listing away from Perry, they seemed disappointed he wasn't with me. A dear boy, Mrs. Gilmore told me. And smart as a whip. Which, of course, only made me question *her* smarts.

With the listing safely secured for Haskins Realty, I got back in my car to deliver it personally to Tom—but only after a stop at Oakbrook Center. With my role as tour guide coming up, I decided to splurge on some appropriate clothes for driving Fletch around. Something casual but stylish.

As I pulled into the parking lot near Lord & Taylor, my phone rang. It was Kit.

"Hey, can you talk?" she asked.

"Yeah."

"Are you on your own?"

"Yeah; what's going on?"

"Okay, listen to this." I heard a rustle, like the sound of a newspaper. "This was in today's paper. Just a tiny blurb, way at the back. Ready?"

"I'm ready, for Pete's sake. What is it?"

"A neighbor called police late Saturday night to the twenty-three-hundred block of Maple Lane in Downers Grove, where the body of a woman was found in the garage, in her car. The coroner determined the woman died of carbon monoxide poisoning. She was pronounced dead at the scene. Identification of the body remains undisclosed, pending notification of next of kin."

When Kit stopped reading, I spoke. "Mavis?"

"Mavis."

"Mavis? Oh dear God, poor Mavis. But we don't know for sure."

"Honey, think about it. Mavis has gone missing; you've been trying to convince me of that yourself."

"Okay, okay, but the twenty-three-hundred block of Maple Lane is a long block. It might *not* be her."

"Wanna bet?"

"No, no bets. Oh, Kit, it's Mavis, isn't it?"

"I'm afraid so. And ya know what else?"

"What?"

"Think about it. They found her Saturday night. We were there on Friday afternoon, ya know. We even looked in the garage—"

"Oh no; do you think she was there, in the car, when we were there? It *was* dark, and those car windows were dark, and—oh, Kit, how horrible!" I gagged as I recalled the nasty smell we had dismissed as garbage. The thought that it might have been Mavis's body made me almost throw up.

"I know, honey. Look, just come back over here and we'll talk."

I nodded mutely, and although Kit couldn't see, I figured she knew it. She didn't even mention that I was the one who kept us out of Mavis's garage. She has her faults, but Kit isn't an I-told-you-so kind of gal. She would definitely have checked the car if I hadn't been so eager to leave Mavis's house. "I'm on my way. Tell Larry to make some more coffee."

"Coffee, hell. I need a Bloody Mary, at the very least."

CHAPTER SEVEN

On my way back to Kit and Larry's, I did, of course, drive past Mavis's house. No police tape, no activity at all. I said a silent prayer that it wasn't Mavis who had died, although the words in my head felt futile.

Since nothing looked awry, I kept driving.

Then, about a block away, without even realizing what I was going to do, I pulled into a driveway and turned around. Driving back to Mavis's house, my heart began to beat so wildly I thought there might soon be another death on Maple Lane. It got even worse as I pulled into Mavis's driveway, climbed out of the car, and crept up to the garage. I pulled on the handle of the door, trying to lift it up, but it didn't budge.

"Fancy meeting you here," said a familiar deep voice from behind me.

I whirled around and saw Fletch. "What are *you* doing here?"

"You took the words right out of my mouth," he said, and I realized once more that he did more evading than answering.

"Oh. I was just wondering how Mavis was." I managed not to stammer, in spite of my still wildly beating heart.

"And you thought you'd find her in the garage?" By his tone, you would never have suspected that he'd had his tongue in my mouth just the night before. Or that he was planning a driving tour of the Midwest with me. He sounded suspicious of me. But what possible good reason could *he* have for being there?

"Fletch, I'm trying to get a listing. What are *you* doing here?" I asked again. Across the street I could see his rented Buick parked in front of one of Mavis's neighbors.

"I'm afraid you're going to have to forget about that listing. Unless you get it from the deceased's beneficiaries."

"What . . . do you mean that *was* Mavis in the paper?"

"So you did know. What did you expect to find in her garage, then, her ghost?"

Fletch took a couple of steps toward me, and only the fact that I was already pressed against the garage door kept me from backing away from him. I was glad it was broad daylight.

But when he got within touching distance of me, he pulled me to him gently. "You're as white as if you did see a ghost. I know it must be shocking, such an old and dear friend of yours." He leaned forward and kissed me lightly on the cheek.

It was weird, because last night I wanted nothing more than to spend the rest of my life with my lips locked against his, and suddenly all I wanted to do was wipe my cheek with a Handi Wipe. And I didn't know why, exactly. I pulled away from him. "What's going on? And how did *you* know about Mavis's death?"

"I'm the one who discovered her body," he said. "I came by to see her, and when she didn't answer the door, I looked around and found the back door unlocked. So I went in to look around and then . . . Valerie, it wasn't pleasant. I called the police."

I felt shaken. Part of me wondered how I'd ever gotten involved in something so grisly, and other parts felt both regret and relief that Kit and I hadn't gone inside the garage. I could feel my whole body tremble, and my voice quavered as I spoke. "Wait a minute. You came to see her? When exactly was that? You were with *me* last night. And the report in the paper said a neighbor found her."

"They got that part wrong. After I left your place, I drove by here. I wanted to see Mavis. All your concern for your dear old pal made me a little anxious. I thought I'd just swing by her place and have a visit."

I was speechless, but I wasn't sure why. Fletch's tone was accusatory, as if I had done something wrong and he was about to catch me in a lie. I almost expected him to take out a notepad and start jotting down my words.

Then he softened a bit, but there was still an edge to his voice. "Er, that's okay with you, isn't it?"

"Fletch, I'm just shocked, that's all. First, that Mavis is dead, and second, that—"

"What? That I'm here now, today? Returning to the scene of the crime, as they say?"

"You said it, buddy, not I."

"Look, Val." He took my arm. "Last night was the worst fucking night of my life."

"I'm assuming you are not talking about our date."

He gave a short laugh and then grew serious again. "No, of course not; that was wonderful. But this . . ." He looked toward the house. "Ever find a dead body?"

"Yes. I mean no. I haven't found a dead body, of course, but yes, I can see that it must have been upsetting."

"Upsetting?" He ran both hands through his hair. His bare fingers were red from the cold. "Losing my wallet would be upsetting. Finding Ma . . . Mavis . . . was . . . it was devastating." He walked over to my car and slid his back down against one of the front wheels. His feet made a scrunching sound on the snowy driveway. His hands were still lost in his hair somewhere, and when he looked up at me, his eyes were wet with tears.

"Fletch, I'm so sorry. Tell me what happened."

"When I couldn't find her in the house, I checked the garage, and there was her car." He stopped for a moment, as if the memory was too painful to recall. "She was inside. Dead. I'm afraid she'd been there a while too. It was horrible, Val."

I knelt down beside him and put a hand on his shoulder. I didn't know what to say.

He took a big gulp of the cold air and continued. "The police asked a lot of questions. They finally let me go about three o'clock this morning."

"Do they think it was suicide?"

He looked up at me, his wet eyes wide, like a child. "What else would they think? They concluded she got in her car, maybe as long as several days ago—it's harder to tell with this cold weather we've had. She turned on the engine and eventually died from carbon monoxide poisoning. By the time I found her, she was long since dead."

I removed my hand from his shoulder and stood up.

He wiped his wet cheeks with his palms, and a little smile returned to his face. He rose to his feet. "By the way," he said, "in case they have other ideas, they might call you."

"Me?" I backed away as I said it.

"Of course. You've sure shown an undue interest in Mavis ever since I've been here."

"*She* contacted *me*." I sounded calmer than I felt. Fletch's sudden change in tone was disconcerting. Plus I was sickened by the knowledge that poor Mavis had indeed been lying dead in her motorized coffin while Kit and I were sneaking around her home. And I supposed if they knew that, the police probably would consider me a person of interest.

As I watched Fletch rub his hands together to get some circulation going, I dug my own gloved hands deep into the pockets of my coat. "But one thing I still don't understand," I said. "Why are you back here now?"

"I don't understand that, either." He sounded sad, but I couldn't help but doubt his sincerity.

"I've got to go, Fletch. I'm swamped with work stuff."

I thought he looked at me with a smirk, but I couldn't be sure, in my haste to leave. After I pulled out of the driveway and glanced at the digital numbers on my dashboard, I realized I really *did* have work stuff to do: I had to drop the Gilmore papers off at Tom's. In what seemed like a lifetime ago instead of about an hour, I had intended to do that when I finished shopping at Oakbrook.

I grabbed my phone and called Kit. "I've got to drive some papers downtown to Tom. I'll be a couple of hours. And you better fix something a lot stronger than Bloody Marys."

***

Tom Haskins lived in a three-bedroom condo in a swanky building on Lake Shore Drive. It came complete with covered parking, a marble lobby that was good enough for Donald Trump to hold his next wedding, and a doorman in a green uniform with gold-fringed epaulets. From the floor-to-ceiling windows in his nineteenth-floor living room, he had a perfect view of Lake Michigan, including Navy Pier. I loved it. My whole apartment could just about fit into his front closet. Tom had lived there for only a year; he takes advantage of his real estate connections to buy and sell homes for his personal use on a regular basis.

I tried to call him as the Chicago skyline came into view.

"This is Tom Haskins. Leave a message. Beep." Very nice. So inviting.

"Hey, Tom, it's me. I'm on my way; I'll be there in about twenty minutes. I've got the Gilmore contract with me, and I need to talk to you about something."

I set my phone down next to me on the seat, and it rang a couple of seconds later. "What do you need to talk about?" No *hello*, no *thanks for making the trip into the city*.

"Ah, Tom, in a good mood, I see. Look, I'll tell you when I get there." I dreaded what I had to tell him about Mavis and especially the fact that I stopped by her house. But I knew he'd hear of her death and, worse, he'd hear from Fletch that I'd been there. I also wanted his take on Fletch's having found her body, not to mention how completely broken up his tough military friend had seemed over a mere acquaintance.

"Just leave the papers with the doorman," Tom said. "We'll talk tomorrow."

"What? Are you nuts? I've been nearly killed three times driving in here. The least you can do is listen to me for two minutes." Maybe if I put him on the defensive, he wouldn't blow up when I confessed to him that I'd ignored his orders.

"I'm busy."

Suddenly it hit me. Was Tom entertaining a woman? In some circles, Tom is considered attractive, in that rough, Tony Soprano way. Of course he isn't attractive to me, but then I've known him for most of my life.

"Busy doing what?"

"None of your damn business. Just leave the contract with the doorman."

"Tom, they have to be at the bank first thing tomorrow morning."

"Relax. I'll sign them and have a messenger take them over."

"No good. They have to be explained. I made several changes."

"Val, the bank isn't run by monkeys. They've seen a real estate contract before. Just leave them with the doorman, and don't worry about it."

I was about to explain to him how the intricate verbiage I had slipped into the contract was sure to astound even the smartest Chicago banker, not to mention the cleverest Chicago monkey, but he'd hung up on me. I did one of those things you see in the movies: stared at the phone in disbelief. Well, I'd show him. I was a lot closer to his building than he knew. And I wasn't leaving anything with the doorman, who remembered me and cheerfully let me in.

So fifteen minutes later I pounded on Tom's door. I could hear a shuffle coming from the other side, and then more shuffle, and then he opened the door. He wore a burgundy bathrobe and held a cigar in one hand.

"What the hell did I tell you?" His hair, what little he had of it, was wet and combed down flat, as if he'd just taken a shower.

"Tom, you know I don't listen to what you tell me." I hoped that was preparation enough for what I had to share with him about Mavis. I walked past him into the spacious hallway. There was a set of golf clubs leaning against a hall table, and I wondered if he had a trip planned.

"Give me the contract." He did not move from his position at the front door.

"Okay, okay. Keep your hair on." I glanced again at his nearly bald head. "Oh, never mind. Too late."

I walked into the living room, admiring its whiteness and the panoramic view. Sitting on one of his plush sofas, I placed my briefcase on the marble-topped coffee table.

"Hello." Another person appeared.

I looked up to see a woman in her early forties, dressed in a pink suit that looked as if it might be Chanel. She had short, silvery-blond hair; and in addition to her high fashion, she smelled of something delicious. Her shoes were a darker shade of pink than her suit and looked as if elves had made them for her the night before.

"Hello." I rose and extended my hand. "I'm Valerie." For some reason, I couldn't remember my last name.

"Nice to meet you, Valerie; I'm Celeste DuBois." Naturally. She looked the type to have a French name (although her accent was pure Chicago).

"Here, give me the friggin' thing." It was Tom, come to play with us. I handed him the contract, and he sat down on the couch, his cigar sticking out of his mouth. He was wearing suit pants under his bathrobe, I noticed, and he pulled a fountain pen out of the top pocket of his robe. (Who the hell keeps a fountain pen in a bathrobe?)

No one spoke as Tom glanced over the contract. Celeste DuBois remained poised in her standing position, as if ready to sashay down a runway and show us the upcoming spring line. Tom flipped the pages of the contract and then began scrawling his illegible signature in all the right places.

"Er, Tom." I sat down beside him. "Did you notice—"

"Notice what?"

"Here, look, on page six, see, I added this line."

"Yeah, I noticed. You think I'd sign something without reading it?"

"Yes, Tom." I placed a hand on his arm. "We all know you graduated first in your speed-reading class. But what do you think?"

"You're a genius. Now get out." He stood and handed me the signed document. Tom's demeanor was gruffer than usual (I hoped Celeste was taking notes), and I decided it was not the time to tell him about Mavis's death.

I opened my briefcase and put the document inside. "Nice to meet you, Celeste," I called, as Tom ushered me out into the hall. Over my shoulder, I saw Celeste smile and give me a wave, as if she'd just christened an ocean liner and was watching it launch into the water.

"Who's she?" I asked Tom, when we were out of earshot.

"Celeste DuBois." He had one hand on my back, the other reaching to open the door.

"I know her name, but who is she?"

"A friend."

"A friend?"

"Yeah, a friend. I can have friends."

***

Finally back at Larry and Kit's, I found the desire to tell her about Tom almost as compelling as the report on my stopping by Mavis's. In fact, I addressed that issue first.

"He had a woman there."

"Get out," Kit said.

"Seriously. And she was gorgeous, if you think tall, thin, and blond is gorgeous."

Kit smiled and raised her eyebrows, waiting for me to continue.

"But I was so—"

"So what?" Kit put on her reading glasses, as if, like most fiftysomethings, she could think better that way.

"Well, surprised. She didn't look like the type Tom usually goes for."

"How do you know he goes for her? Could be business."

"Surely he would tell me if it was business. He was acting as if I had the swine flu, and he couldn't wait to get me out of there."

"What is the swine flu, anyway?"

"Focus, Kit, focus. We are talking about this woman. Celeste DuBois."

"Oh, like Blanche DuBois from *A Streetcar Named Desire*."

"Okay, let's forget it. We need to talk about Mavis. You aren't going to believe what happened. Where's Larry?"

"I dunno. Probably in the den."

"Well, he's gotta hear this too." I was glad to see my friend head into the hallway to yell for her husband. I felt exhausted.

"Okay, he's coming." Kit sat back down on her stool at the kitchen counter. "By the way, Celeste DuBois . . . it sounds made-up. Who has a name like that in Chicago?"

"Exactly."

***

"I feel like such a fraud," I said.

Kit was driving her BMW way too fast. I nearly told her to slow down, that we weren't late for a funeral. But the truth was, we *were* late, and we *were* going to a funeral. "I don't see why." Kit pushed harder on the accelerator. "It's not as if we didn't know Mavis. She is . . . was . . . an old friend of ours, ya know."

I grabbed the armrest, as if that might slow the vehicle down a little. "Well, that's not exactly true, but I suppose it's close enough. And I suppose we might even see some of the other kids there." I laughed. The *kids*, obviously, would no longer be kids. Since Kit and I had aged normally, it was reasonable to assume all of our classmates had too.

I had easily found the funeral notice in the obituary column of the newspaper, and convincing Kit to go with me had been a breeze. I still, however, felt like an interloper.

We got to the First United Methodist Church at precisely three o'clock, and Kit whipped into one of the many empty parking spaces. "See? Right on time," she said.

"There aren't many cars here. Are we sure the paper said three?"

"They didn't exactly give people much time to clear their calendars, ya know. I mean she died only two days ago. And besides, if Mavis has been living in Florida, she probably lost touch with any friends here, so who's left?"

We were both silent for a moment, neither one of us saying the obvious: poor Mavis never *had* many friends.

Thinking suddenly of my own demise, I wondered how many people would show up for my funeral. "Kit, when I die, make sure I'm cremated. And no funeral."

"Right." She looked in the rearview mirror and fluffed her hair. "I'll put you in a Jewel sack and toss it into Lake Michigan. How's that sound?"

"Sounds good." Then I added, without realizing I was going to, "They *found her body* two days ago. We don't know *when* she died." I reached for my purse with one hand and the door handle with the other. "Let's go."

As we walked up the sidewalk to the church entrance, it suddenly occurred to me that maybe it hadn't really been Mavis who'd called and then e-mailed me. Maybe it was the murderer, trying to make it look as if a dead Mavis were still alive. Then I quickly reminded myself there might not even *be* a murderer.

CHAPTER EIGHT

We passed rows of empty pews as we made the long walk up the center aisle. Only the click of my boots on the stone floor broke the silence of the church. It sounded like an army marching toward battle. I went up on my tiptoes to soften my steps, but I still felt like an intruder.

When we finally got to civilization, there was a small group taking up only the first three rows on either side. We sat in the fourth row and solemnly took in the scene. At the front of the sanctuary the closed casket looked like an empty dining room table waiting for someone to set it. In the first row a tall man sat next to a much older woman. Mavis's brother and mother, perhaps?

At that moment a minister appeared behind the coffin and started to speak. It was clear he knew even less about Mavis than we did. His eulogy was brief and impersonal. It made me sad for poor Mavis all over again.

While he spoke, my eyes roamed over the other people. Of course, since I could see only the backs of their heads, it was difficult to even guess who they were. I had a strong hunch—or maybe a repressed memory come to light—that the tall man next to the old lady was Lionel. There was a guy—Marcus or Will?—at the end of the second row sitting beside a blond woman about our age. And then I knew it must be Marcus because I spotted Will, Mavis's twin, in the row just in front of us, away from his family, sitting alone and looking sad.

A memory of Will flooded my brain. He'd worked as a checkout boy at Dominick's one summer. I remembered how his spotted face had turned a deep crimson when I thanked him once for sacking our groceries. My mother was with me, and she gave him a quarter for loading numerous sacks into our station wagon. He looked at the coin as if it were a gold nugget and shoved it into the pocket of his jeans before scurrying back into the store. I recalled chiding my mother for not giving him a whole dollar and her rebuttal that the Woodstocks could buy and sell us many times over.

Even though I could see only Will's profile, his resemblance to Mavis, as I remembered her, was startling: tall and skinny, with frizzy, dishwater-blond hair. I nudged Kit and then cupped my hand around my mouth, leaving an opening so she could hear my whispering. "Look, it's Will, her twin."

"Didn't this family ever hear of hair conditioner?" She didn't cover her mouth, but at least she whispered.

When the minister finished his vague tribute to Mavis, he led us in a prayer, but I kept my eyes on the bowed heads in front of us. Then, unaware that the service was completed, I was surprised when everyone stood and shuffled down the aisle past Kit and me.

"Let's go." Kit grabbed my arm. "I think we should say something to the family."

We were the only mourners left, and I followed her out of the church. The group headed immediately for their cars, and I scrambled behind Kit as she rushed up to Lionel, who was leading the elderly lady by the elbow to his old Pontiac parked near the entrance of the church.

"Lionel," I heard Kit say, as she touched the back of his shoulder. "Lionel Woodstock?"

He turned, and again the family resemblance struck me. They seemed to have a monopoly on long and lean with bushy, light-colored hair. Clearly, the Woodstock men had no problem with baldness, though baldness would have been a gift in their case. Lionel's mop would have served him better if he'd put it on the end of a long handle. He wore a faded black overcoat and a yellow wool scarf that emphasized his bloodless face.

"Do I know you?" He stared down at Kit, and I saw his Adam's apple protruding above the scarf, bobbing up and down as he spoke.

"You might remember me. I'm Katherine James. Used to be Juckett. This is Valerie Pankowski. Used to be Caldwell. We went to school with Mavis. I'm so sorry for your loss."

He opened the passenger door and attempted to shove the elderly woman inside. "Pankowski?" he said, his back to us. "Didn't you call looking for Mavis the other day?"

"Yes," I said. "I was actually supposed to meet her."

"Mother, please get in the car," Lionel said.

Mrs. Woodstock gave us both a sad smile. Although age had left its mark on her plump face, I could see that she had once been pretty. Mavis must have gotten her looks from her father.

"You knew Mavis?" she asked, her hand on the door frame preventing her son from shoving her in. Her brown leather gloves didn't match her black coat or the navy purse hanging over her arm. It made me feel as though she'd dressed in a hurry, without time to prepare herself for her only daughter's funeral.

"Well, we hadn't spoken for many years," I said, "but yes, we did know her. We were in high school together."

"She was a wonderful daughter." I could see tears form in the corners of her eyes behind her silver-framed glasses.

"Mother," Lionel said, "will you please just get in the car."

"We are having some people to my house," Mrs. Woodstock said. "Please stop by if you have time; I'd love to have some of Mavis's old friends there."

Lionel turned back to face us. A cold smile formed on his thin face. "Really, that won't be necessary." Then he raised his eyebrows and gave a little nod toward his mother, as if to indicate she was slightly daft and nothing she said was to be taken seriously.

"We'd love to," Kit said. "What's the address?"

"I live on Preston Avenue," Mrs. Woodstock said. "Number ninety-three seventy-eight. Can you find it?"

"Mother!" Lionel gave her a final shove so that she landed in the front seat with one leg still sticking out.

"We'll be there, Mrs. Woodstock," Kit said.

Lionel picked up his mother's ankle and practically tossed it into the car, as if it were a piece of luggage. Then he slammed the car door shut and turned to face us fully.

"You must excuse my mother. She's a little bit out of it. I'm afraid the gathering she's referring to is for family only." And with that said, he pushed past us and got in on the driver's side.

Kit and I watched him back out. "He's just a bundle of charm, isn't he?" she said.

I looked around. In the time it had taken to have our brief exchange, all the other mourners had disappeared. The church parking lot was as empty as if a funeral had never taken place, as if poor Mavis had never existed at all.

Kit and I walked to her car, the only one left in the lot. "What should we do?" I asked. "Should we go?"

"Hmm . . . I don't think this is the time. But . . ." She held up her index finger. "We know where Mrs. Woodstock lives, so how about we pay her a visit another time, say tomorrow, when Herman Munster isn't lurking around?"

"That's a brilliant idea. Let's do it."

***

Back at Kit's house, Larry fixed us margaritas while we filled him in on the funeral.

I took a sip of the frothy green liquid. "It's funny; my mom said the Woodstocks were well-heeled, but they look anything but. Did you notice Lionel's coat? And Mother Woodstock's was straight from Goodwill."

"Yeah," Kit said. "And Lionel's car was about a hundred years old. Maybe the Woodstocks fell on hard times?"

Larry joined us at the kitchen counter and took a sip of his own drink. "Don't you believe it. I told you they have money. Have you heard of Lonstock Savings and Loan?" He waited.

"Of course," Kit said. "Who hasn't?"

"I deal with them all the time," I said. "They've done tons of mortgages for us. Tom does a lot of business with them."

"The Woodstocks own it. Get it? Lon, short for Lionel, and stock—"

"Yeah, we got it, Einstein." Kit held out her drink for a refill, and Larry rose from his stool. "Don't you hate how smug he is?"

"Sorry, girls," he called from across the kitchen. "But I'm surprised you didn't know that particular little tidbit already."

"Okay, so what else you got?"

"Let's see." Larry placed his wife's refreshed glass in front of her and kissed the top of her head. "The company was started by Lionel's grandfather and passed to his son, Mavis's father, both also named Lionel, by the way. The current Lionel is the CEO."

"I'm wondering why Tom never mentioned this," I said.

"Why would he?" Kit asked. "I doubt if Lionel's actually drawing up mortgages himself. Although, with his winning personality, he'd be wasted tucked away in a corner office."

"No kidding. But with all the talk about Mavis recently, Tom should have mentioned Lionel's connection."

"What about the other Woodstock boys?" Kit asked.

"Marcus also works at Lonstock, number two bean counter. But Will . . . now, he's a little odd."

"They are all a little odd." Kit wrapped air quotation marks around the word *odd*.

"Oh, he's odd, all right, but in a good way. Apparently, he's somewhat of a genius. After graduating from DePaul, he went on to MIT and ended up with a full professorship there. He's also got a doctorate in nuclear physics or something really brainy like that from UCLA. Yet now he works at some flunky job for bro Lionel. He was out of Illinois for a long time but came back a few years ago at Lionel's request."

"Gee, Lar, where'd you get this stuff?"

"We CPAs hear things."

"You mean you picked all this up at your sports bar?"

"Something like that."

I finished my drink and then spoke up. "The question is, with all that money, and obviously all those family smarts, what did *Mavis* do?"

"Sorry, girls, can't help you there."

"Okay." Kit sighed. "Here's the plan. First we see Ma Woodstock. Hopefully, we can get her alone without Lurch."

"Don't forget, Lionel and his mother live together in the family mansion," Larry said. "He never married. Big surprise."

Kit leaned forward on the counter. "So as I was saying, here's the plan: we go over to the house and have a little chat with the mother and try to find out just what her baby girl has been up to."

"Good." I nodded, glad that Kit seemed to be heading our investigation.

"Next—"

"There's a next?"

"You better believe it. Next, we go back to Mavis's house and do a thorough search."

I held up my hands in protest. "But do you really think—"

"Obviously, we missed something, and we gotta go back there before your boyfriend Flip—"

"Fletch. And he's not my boyfriend."

"Flip, Flop, Fuckhead. Whatever. He's looking for something, and we have got to get it before he does."

"It's not as if the house is still unlocked." Not to mention, I didn't add, that we didn't even know what it was we were looking for and that Tom would put a hit on me if I went back there.

"My bet is that the family will really want to sell it now, and that's where Tom comes in. And you too, Larry."

Larry held his hands up in protest. "Noooo, I'm not going to be a part of this. And by the way, forgive me for raising an obvious question, but just why are you two pursuing this?"

Kit turned to face her husband, her eyes open wide. "Because, dummy, we don't believe Mavis killed herself." It was good to hear Kit vocalize my own thoughts.

"Whoa." Larry rose from his stool and burst out laughing. "Have you lost your mind? What are you saying, that she was murdered?"

"If she didn't kill herself, it was either an accident or yes, murder."

"Forget it. I want nothing to do with this. You're going down a dangerous road here."

It was all Kit needed. Danger was a red flag to her bullheadedness.

"Larry," she said patiently, as if talking to a naughty child, "it's just a little investigation. If it was suicide, then no harm done, but if it was murder, then someone needs to look out for Mavis."

"Katherine," Larry said, equally patient, as if addressing the same naughty child, "you might not have heard, but in this country we have a little group known as the police force. It's *their* job to determine what's murder or suicide. It's not the job of a couple of bored housewives out for a lark."

"Now wait just a minute there, mister," I said. "First of all, I am not a housewife—"

"But I am," Kit said, "and just what has that got to do with the price of Cocoa Puffs in China?"

"Okay, okay. Sorry; that was wrong. I just wish you two would stay out of this. And much more important, leave me out of it."

"Larry, we need you," Kit said, and I was eager to learn just what part Larry would play in the latest can't-fail plan of hers.

"You don't need me."

"Ah, but we do, my darling. You have the most important job of all, ya know."

"I'm afraid to ask, and I want no part of any harebrained idea you've cooked up, but go ahead, lay it on me."

"Getaway driver. See, we'll go to Mavis's house at night, when it's dark, and you can be our lookout."

Larry and I turned to face each other and then burst into laughter. Kit was enjoying her plan way too much, but it did sound exciting.

"Sorry," Larry said. "I'm not driving or looking or doing any other crazy thing. You girls are on your own."

He kissed his wife on the top of her head again and then gave me a kiss on the cheek. He left the kitchen, laughing and shaking his head. At the doorway to the den, he stopped and turned. "Er . . . I don't suppose it would make a difference if I *forbid* you to do this?"

This time Kit and I looked at each other and burst out laughing.

"Yep, that's what I thought." He turned and waved a hand of dismissal over his shoulder.

CHAPTER NINE

I didn't even turn on the radio or play a CD on the drive home from Kit and Larry's. I was too preoccupied with my own thoughts. I kept thinking how all that Woodstock money hadn't kept the only daughter—and sister—alive.

My melancholy lifted when I entered my apartment and discovered phone messages from the women in my own life. The first message was from Emily, who left an excited voice mail begging me to call her immediately on her cell.

"Mom, Mom," she said as soon as she heard my voice. "Guess what?"

"Tell me."

"I got a job! A real job."

"Honey, that's great. Tell me about it."

Since Emily's employment goals are in acting, I assumed the job didn't have the longevity of, say, vice president of a bank or chief of medicine at Cedars-Sinai, and I was right.

"It's a commercial. There were more than a hundred of us up for the part, and I had a million callbacks. But I got it, Mom. They chose *me*."

I closed my eyes and remembered a fourteen-year-old Emily bursting into our living room, shrieking that she'd gotten the lead role in her school's rendition of *Romeo and Juliet*. For the next three months, her father and I were reduced to communicating with our daughter only in Elizabethan English.

Emily: *Mother, pray pass the Wheaties to thine daughter.*

Me: *It gives me most pleasure, and will mine Lady be having milk with thine cereal?*

It turned out that the starring role Emily had landed now was the coveted part of Young Mother with Baby extolling the joys of Coddles Diapers. She explained that she didn't actually have a speaking part; and when the camera moved in close to show Young Mother putting the diaper on the baby, a stand-in would be used. But that was even better, Emily assured me. "I have a *stand-in*."

I could feel her joy spread all the way from the West Coast, and I hung up feeling certain there was an Emmy in *my* Emmy's future.

My second return call was to my mother. I passed on her granddaughter's good news, and she immediately wanted to know who would play the part of the baby and if Emily had seen any stars out there in Hollywood. "That Humphrey Bogart was a good actor," she said. "Not conventionally handsome, but he had a presence about him."

I didn't remind her that Humphrey was dead. Surely she knew that. But we had a pleasant chat, which ended with her reminding me to lock all my doors and keep the phone line open. It felt comforting. At least I knew *she* would come to my funeral—if she outlived me. And unlike Mavis's mother, she would wear matching accessories. I immediately chided myself for having such a shallow thought.

Instead of turning on the TV or opening my latest book in the alphabet murder-mystery series (I was up to *V is for*

Vengeance), I decided to ponder the facts Kit and I had gathered so far about Mavis. (I might have read one too many murder mysteries, but I still believed we might be in the middle of a real-life one of our own. Call it *S is for Suspicious*, at the very least.)

I grabbed pen and paper to take to bed with me, all the better to ponder with. But my first thought didn't need to be written down. How the *hell* were Kit and I going to investigate Mavis's house again? Well, maybe we could finagle our way in through Mavis's mother.

We were planning to go see her tomorrow morning, anyway. Somehow, we would have to get her to let us into Mavis's house. That was in addition to getting her to answer our questions, which I also needed to formulate.

Once ensconced among my pillows, I began to write what we knew. It didn't take long.

We knew Mavis had seemed desperate to sell her house right before she died. We knew she and Lionel were not on speaking terms. We knew Fletch knew her and wanted to speak with her. Perhaps her mother would know why, I thought, moving from my *Facts* column to my *Questions* column.

And surely her mother would know why her oldest son and only daughter were on the outs. And why Mavis wanted to sell her house so quickly. And why anyone would think her daughter might want to kill herself. Or who might want it to *seem* that way. And finally, when did Mavis actually die?

Suddenly I recalled the woman in the photograph at Mavis's house. *Was* that Mavis? Kit and I still had no idea what Mavis looked like by the time she died. Unlike most funerals nowadays, the memorial service for Mavis had showcased no photos of the dearly departed, not even snapshots, let alone an elaborate DVD presentation picturing an entire lifetime. And the casket had remained as closed as the minds of most radio talk-show hosts.

Well, no doubt Mrs. Woodstock would have some recent photos.

I put down my pen and paper and turned off the light. My eyes had grown suddenly tired, and I knew I had to take advantage of that before becoming just as suddenly, inexplicably, wired—a not uncommon occurrence anymore. I drifted off with the thought that Mavis's mother was apt to be the only forthcoming Woodstock. I just hoped what came forth would be reliable.

***

Located on a wide street lined with stately oak trees, the Woodstock mansion sat among other three-story residences. But while the neighbors maintained their homes with the look of luxury only money can create, the Woodstock house sat on its foundation crying out with neglect and disrepair. It was young Oliver Twist begging for *more*. Please, sir, more paint, more roof shingles, more landscaping.

My Realtor eyes sized up at least thirteen thousand square feet and noted the vast front yard that undoubtedly bore similar marks of neglect under the layer of snow that covered it.

We hadn't called first, but we waited until after ten to arrive, figuring Lionel would be out of the house by then. Mrs. Woodstock opened the front door after Kit pounded several times. The doorbell didn't seem to work.

I was struck by how tired Mavis's mother looked. She wore a tattered gray cardigan and red stretch pants that did not flatter her chubby figure. Upon seeing us, she began trying to arrange her hair into some sort of style. I noticed a colossal diamond ring on her wedding finger, the only sign of any real wealth so far from the Woodstock camp.

Kit spoke first. "Mrs. Woodstock, do you remember us—"

"Oh, girls, come in, come in." A broad smile appeared on the elderly lady's face, and she waved us in. "It's so good to see you. I looked for you yesterday. But none of Mavis's friends . . ."

The look of despair on her face wrenched my heart. What parent doesn't want her daughter to have friends? "Oh, Mrs. Woodstock, we are so sorry we didn't come. We were just so . . . so . . . ."

"Distraught," Kit said. "Is this a bad time?"

"No, no, this is perfect. Lionel—he's my eldest son; you met him yesterday—left hours ago for work, and I'm just sitting here thinking. Come into the living room; I'll get us some coffee."

She led us through a wide, square hallway with a dark oak floor. To our right, a massive staircase led to the upper floors. It called to mind Scarlett O'Hara running down the stairs to a waiting Rhett. But this hallway had none of Tara's glamour. Instead, it was dark and musty, and the floor needed refinishing. How I would have loved to redo it all. And then sell it, of course.

Mrs. Woodstock continued through an enormous archway into an equally dark, musty, and tired-looking living room and motioned for us to sit on an old but ornate sofa covered in gold-and-olive brocade. I perched on the edge of the sofa and tried to picture Mavis growing up in such a mausoleum. It was the polar opposite of her own comfy house on Maple Lane.

"How nice of you to pay your respects to Mavis." I could hear Mrs. Woodstock's relief that her daughter did indeed have a friend, *two* friends. She insisted on serving us coffee and shuffled out of the room.

I glanced around, noting there were no family photographs, no knickknacks on the heavy wooden tables, no personal touches of any kind, with the exception of a large oil painting over the marble fireplace. It showed a severe man who was probably in his sixties glowering down at us. He was cursed with the long Woodstock face and frizzy hair. Mavis's father, I assumed. I shuddered and turned my gaze away.

Kit read my thoughts. "How'd you like to wake up to that face every day?"

"Shush. Be nice."

We sat in silence, our knees together, our hands in our laps, like two bad kids in school waiting for the principal to reprimand us. I almost expected the man in oil to point at us and dole out our punishment.

At last Mrs. Woodstock appeared in the doorway with a silver tray and coffee service that needed polishing. She placed it on a low table in front of us and proceeded to pour coffee into delicate china cups, which she handed to us. The liquid was too burned-tasting to even be sipped, in spite of a hefty dose of cream. Luckily, the applesauce cake a neighbor had delivered to her the day before was so moist it didn't require a drink to wash it down. I had two pieces.

After Mrs. Woodstock sat down in a wingback chair across from us, Kit spoke. "How are you holding up, Mrs. Woodstock? I am just so sorry about Mavis."

"Thank you, dear. That's very kind of you. You know, it's a terrible thing to outlive a child."

"Yes," I said. "It must be very hard."

For the first time, the thought of losing Emily washed over me, and I was filled with pain for this bereaved mother.

"Especially in *that* way." Mrs. Woodstock leaned forward in her seat and shook her head as she spoke. "They say she kill . . . took her own life. I don't understand it. It's so unlike her to do something like that." She sat back against the cushion and let out a loud sigh.

I leaned in toward her. "Mrs. Woodstock, what exactly happened?"

"They say she committed suicide." The harsh word brought tears to her bright blue eyes, and I was reminded of my own mother for a moment.

Mrs. Woodstock ran an aging hand across her cheek, sitting up as tall as she could. "They found her in her car. It had run out of gas. They say she'd turned it on and just waited—can you imagine?"

She stopped, as if she were doing just that: imagining her daughter waiting to die.

Her voice broke when she spoke again. "The garage door was closed and also the door leading to the kitchen. They found a towel in the tailpipe of her vehicle. Can you believe that? An ordinary kitchen towel had been stuffed into the pipe." Her expression indicated the towel was the culprit, not the carbon monoxide. And maybe she was right, in a way.

The room was silent for a moment, and Kit and I stayed as still as statues.

"The police took it, the towel, I mean. They say it proved she killed herself, that it wasn't an accident."

"I'm assuming they did an autopsy?" Kit asked. I was shocked at how clinical she sounded. She might have been questioning her car mechanic to be sure he'd rotated the tires.

"I expect so. You'd have to ask one of the boys. They did say she had a sleeping pill inside her. Ambien, I do believe."

I had a horrific vision of a single white pill rushing through Mavis's bloodstream. "Was that unusual? I mean, did Mavis often take sleeping pills?"

"Who doesn't?" Kit asked.

"Exactly," Mrs. Woodstock said.

"Well, I don't," I said. I felt as if I had been excluded from a private club.

"Oh, you will, honey," Kit said. "Give your ovaries a little time to realize it's much more fun to stay awake all night."

I didn't respond to Kit's prediction because I was wondering why a person who was planning to kill herself in the car would bother taking a sleeping pill first.

"It's just so terrible," Mrs. Woodstock said. "I can't stop thinking about it."

"It's going to take time," Kit said. "A lot of time. It's perfectly normal for you to be upset, ya know."

Mrs. Woodstock nodded in agreement. "Yes, and Lionel is so very upset too. All her brothers are, of course.

But Lionel, you see, he in particular has spent so many years angry with his sister."

"Of course," I said. I realized I had yet another reason to pursue answers about who did what to Mavis. Perhaps it would bring this dear old woman some comfort.

But Mavis's mother seemed unaware there might even be any questions. She was already off the subject of Mavis's demise. "I hope you won't think me rude, but I don't really remember you two girls. Were you in the same class as Mavis at school? Were you in contact with her recently?"

My shoulders sagged with my guilty burden. I was an impostor pretending to know this woman's daughter, when I really didn't.

"She loved movies," Kit said.

I stole a glance at her. Where did *that* come from?

"Oh yes, she did." Mrs. Woodstock seemed unaware that we hadn't answered her questions. "But her father didn't approve. And her brothers . . . they didn't have time for that sort of thing. But you are right; Mavis did love the movies. Sometimes she would tell us she was going to the library to study, but I always knew she was sneaking out to see a show."

That depressed me, imagining Mavis sitting alone in the movie theater.

"Did you ever go with her?" Mrs. Woodstock asked.

"Yes," Kit said, "we often met her there."

Mrs. Woodstock nodded. A smile formed on her face, and I silently blessed Kit for telling such a welcome untruth.

"The thing is," Kit said, "we lost contact with her . . ."

Mrs. Woodstock's smile disappeared. "I'm afraid we all did for many years. Even her family. As I said, she never really did get along with her two older brothers. But she and Will were always close. He's her twin, you know, four minutes older."

"Sometimes siblings just don't get along, and there's nothing you can do about it, ya know." Kit probably picked that up from Dr. Phil.

"Did she have any special, er, grudge against Lionel?" I gleaned the last crumbs of cake from my fork tines.

"Oh no. Mavis was a sweet girl; you know that. I suppose you could say Lionel held a grudge against *her*, though."

"Every family has at least one grudge being held, Mrs. Woodstock," Kit said. "What was Lionel's?"

"Please, call me Beatrice. I insist."

"All right, Beatrice." Kit smiled. "But about Lionel? What grudge could he possibly hold against Mavis?"

"It wasn't even Mavis's fault, really. It was her daddy's." She turned slightly to look up at the oil painting. "And it wasn't even his *fault*. It's just what he called checks and . . . checks and . . . what is that term? You know, it's in the Constitution, I think."

Kit and I looked at her open-mouthed. What *was* she talking about? And then, in the tricky way minds work, especially as they age, mine came up with the answer. "Balances? Checks and balances?"

"Yes, that's it. Her daddy made Mavis the majority stockholder of the company, just by a teensy bit. He didn't figure she'd have anything to do with actually *running* the company, being a woman and all."

I felt momentarily surprised she didn't elaborate with an apology on behalf of her husband, but then I remembered her age and my own mother.

"So he figured that was the way to keep the boys in line," Beatrice Woodstock said. "They couldn't run away with the company, alone or together. And there was plenty for everyone. All of us had more than we needed."

"But that stuck in Lionel's craw, huh?" Kit asked. "That Mavis controlled the company?"

"Oh, but she didn't. She could have, but she didn't. She didn't even know. She'd already disappeared before her daddy died and any of us knew what he'd done in his will. So she was never a threat to her brothers. All those years she was gone, she never once contacted her brothers about the company. About anything, in fact. But still, it riled Lionel, yes."

Then, just as I decided we had found our murderer, Beatrice said, "Marcus was equally unhappy about it."

I took a moment to be disappointed that Lionel wasn't necessarily as evil as I'd like to prove him to be. And then I asked, "What about Will? I suppose as her twin, he didn't resent anything about her?"

"Will never cared about the business, either."

"Mrs. Woodstock, uh, Beatrice," I said, "do you know the man named Ryan Fletcher who . . . found her? He goes by Fletch."

She stared at me, looking almost stunned. "Of course."

It was my turn to be stunned, even though I shouldn't have been. Fletch *had* said he knew Mavis. So why wouldn't he know her mother? And I had been hoping Mrs. Woodstock could shed light on Fletch and Mavis's connection. "How did he know your daughter?"

"Why, I'm surprised you don't know, Valerie, being a friend of Mavis's." Was she eyeing me suspiciously? *Was* she daft? Hadn't we already told her we'd lost touch with Mavis?

"Mavis and I had a gap in our communication. Didn't we, Kit?"

Kit nodded, and Beatrice Woodstock continued to scrutinize—suspect?—me.

"A rather large gap, actually," I said.

That seemed to satisfy her, and so she answered my question.

And then I knew the real meaning of stunned.

"Fletch is Mavis's husband," she said. "Rather, ex-husband."

CHAPTER TEN

Mother! Who are these people?"

We all looked toward the entrance to the room, where a short blond woman stood. I remembered her from the funeral. She was wearing a wool suit that was at least two sizes too small; and I noticed she, like Beatrice, had a huge diamond ring on her left hand. Did the Woodstocks own a diamond mine?

"Hilary, how nice," Mrs. Woodstock said. "Girls, this is Hilary, my daughter-in-law. Marcus's wife. These are two of Mavis's old friends, dear, from school. Valerie and Kit. Come join us; I'll get more coffee."

"Don't bother; we're late. Get your coat, and we'll go."

"But I—"

"I told you I'd pick you up at ten thirty," Hilary said, and at that precise moment a clock, somewhere in the house, let out a chime, confirming that Hilary was nothing if not punctual.

"Oh my, I completely forgot. Yes, yes, I have a doctor's appointment, and Hilary is driving me there. I'm afraid you'll have to excuse us."

"No problem." Kit stood up. "Perhaps we can come again. How about we do lunch one day soon, Beatrice?"

That sent Hilary marching across the room to her mother-in-law. "Mrs. Woodstock has a very strict eating regimen. She doesn't *do* lunch." She took Beatrice by the arm to guide her toward the doorway.

"No, but *you* obviously do," Kit said in a whisper.

"*Kit.*" I didn't think Hilary had heard, but I felt as eager to leave as Hilary was to usher us out. We were bid a hasty *good-bye, thank you for coming*, with an implied *don't come back*.

***

"I guess we'll just have to talk to Will," Kit said. We were sitting in her BMW, parked across the street from the Lonstock Building. Unlike the Woodstock family home, the office structure looked as though it had been built ten minutes ago. It was a four-story contemporary glass-and-steel building with the company logo splashed across the top floor. On one side of the building stood a parking garage. The other side housed a row of upscale shops, including a Starbucks, a ladies' boutique, and an antique shop.

"Hmm. How are we going to do that? Without Lionel seeing us? I mean, we can't just go into the building and ask for Will."

"Right, that wouldn't work." Kit had her elbows on the steering wheel and her head turned toward the building. "What can we do, what can we do . . ." She tapped on the wheel with her fingertips as she repeated her mantra.

I glanced at my watch; it was almost eleven o'clock. "How about we go and get some coffee?" I indicated the Starbucks. After the cake Beatrice had served, I wasn't hungry; but a cup of coffee sounded good.

"Great idea."

We left the car and crossed the street to the row of shops. With lattes in front of us and an oversize brownie for me (so much for not being hungry), we put our heads together to try to come up with a plan to meet Will the Twin.

"If we could find out where he lives, that would be good," Kit said. "Don't you have that sort of information at your office?" She took a sip of her coffee.

"Kit, I work at a real estate office, not the Department of Motor Vehicles." Sometimes I wonder if she has any real idea what I do all day.

"There must be some way we can find out where Will hangs his hat." She took another sip, and then her brown eyes opened wide as she gazed over my head. She spilled a little of her drink as she put the cup on the table with an unsteady hand.

I turned in the direction she was looking, expecting at the very least to see a masked man with a gun grabbing the pretty, young Starbucks employee by the throat. But it was even more exciting than that. A tall, thin man with frizzy, dark-blond hair entered the store, carrying a laptop.

I forced myself to whisper. "Will. It's Will. And he's alone."

We watched in awe as he ordered coffee and a sandwich and then proceeded to the table right next to us, placing his purchases down and opening his computer.

I suppressed a giggle. "Talk about good luck."

"Or being in the right place at the right time. Let's speak to him."

"What'll we say?" I asked, still whispering.

"Leave it to me. Where there's a Will, there's a way."

Kit ignored my groan and leaned over to tap the edge of Will's table with her fingers. She cleared her throat. "Excuse me, but aren't you Will Woodstock?"

He pushed his glasses a little farther up on his nose and peered at Kit, then at me. "Yes. And you two were at my sister's funeral yesterday."

"We were." Kit scooted her chair closer to his table. "I'm so sorry about Mavis. She was such a good person."

"Me too," I said, also edging my chair in his direction. "I'm sorry too."

He looked at me closely. "Valerie." I remembered then that he was somewhat of a genius, and obviously blessed with a good memory. "And Katherine. I believe you went by Kit. I remember you from school."

"Wow," we said in unison. But if he hadn't changed that much in appearance, we probably hadn't, either. Nevertheless, I said, "Good memory."

"Not really. I saw you at the funeral and looked you up in the yearbook. It was nice of you to come yesterday. But I'm surprised to see you here."

Did I hear suspicion in his voice?

"I'm antique shopping." Kit pointed through the wall of Starbucks toward the antique store. "What about you?"

"My office building is next door. I often have my lunch here. It's expensive, but it's a hot spot, so I can use my laptop." He tapped his computer. "I like to get away from the office sometimes."

"Ya know, it's funny because we were just visiting with your mother this morning. We stopped by to pay our respects."

"She was hoping to see you at the house yesterday. She told me she invited you back after the funeral." He had a pathetic air about him, and I pictured him and his mother waiting for Kit and me to show our faces at the house.

This was our first real conversation with him ever, and it was the day after his sister's funeral, but Will couldn't shut up. And Kit and I hung on every word he spoke.

It was true that after graduation from high school, Mavis had not gone to college. Apparently, her father, even though he could have afforded tuition anyway, had decreed college a waste of money for girls. He had, instead, found her a position in his bank, a sort of girl Friday role, Will called it. But she was never happy there and felt ostracized by the other employees. Since she was not one to exploit being the boss's daughter, it was a hindrance rather than a help.

One day she just took off. Will was still at DePaul at the time and heard the news from Lionel, who presented it in a good-riddance sort of way. But Daddy Woodstock was upset. And Beatrice, of course, was crushed.

No one knew where Mavis had gone for about ten years, and then only because a private investigator had been hired. The detective reported that Mavis was living in Florida and working at a club. Upon hearing this little tidbit, Kit kicked my leg under the table.

I could only imagine Mavis was some kind of coat checker or cashier; but no, apparently the club wasn't the kind where gentlemen checked their coats. They were too busy having their laps danced on (or whatever it is women actually do when they perform a lap dance). Either way, it seemed incredible that our frumpy Mavis would be hired for such recreation.

Will must have sensed our disbelief. He fished through his wallet and pulled out a photograph that showed a tall, beautiful woman who bore only the slightest resemblance to Mavis.

"That's her?" Kit put her reading glasses on and looked more closely. "That's Mavis?"

"Sure is." Will beamed. "Amazing what a little plastic surgery can do, huh?"

We both nodded in agreement, but I was filled with sadness that Mavis's change of appearance had led only to pole dancing, or whatever it was she did at the club. The photo was about twenty years old, and I tried to decide if the picture on Mavis's dresser was of the same person.

"What about Fletch? Ryan Fletcher? When did they marry?"

Will stretched a skinny arm out and looked at his watch. Then he stood. "I've got to get back to work." He shut the lid of his laptop and told us how glad he was we had come to the funeral; that would have meant so much to Mavis. Blah, blah, blah.

But I still had many unanswered questions. When had Mavis returned to Downers Grove to buy her little house? Who was the child in the photograph? And most important, who was her plastic surgeon? We needed that guy's name.

"Will, thank you for talking to us," I said. "And it was good that your father called an investigator. At least you found her again."

"Yes." He stuffed his used napkin into his empty coffee cup. "But by the way, it wasn't my father who engaged the investigator. It was me."

***

"Who's this Celestial DuBois?" Perry asked me, as soon as I arrived at the office. He'd obviously been to a tanning salon, judging from the artificial glow of his face that made his teeth look as if they would light up in the dark.

"*Celeste* DuBois," I said.

"Who is she? She's called for Uncle Tom three times this morning."

"I really don't know, Perry. Why don't you ask him?"

"Oh, *right.*" Perry swiveled around in his chair. "Like he'd tell me who this Celine—"

"*Celeste.*"

"Okay. Celeste. Whatever. Like I could ask Uncle Tom. I don't know if you've noticed, Val, but Uncle Tom hardly ever shares anything with me."

"And why do you think that is, Perry? *Why?*"

"That's what I'm asking you."

"Well, one reason could be that you still call him *Uncle* Tom." I took off my jacket and draped it over the back of my chair before walking over to him. On the corner of his desk, I could see three slips of pink paper, each showing a variation of Celeste DuBois's name in Perry's spidery handwriting.

"He *is* my uncle."

"And you *are* nearly thirty."

"What's that got to do with it? My mother said I should always address him as Uncle. It's a sign of respect."

"For Don Corleone's nephew, maybe." The messages were laid out in a fan, like a blackjack hand. I checked out the times of the Celeste calls, noting they were twenty minutes apart, like contractions in labor.

"We are also a very close family," Perry said.

"Also? Are you comparing yourselves to the Corleones now?"

"Val," he said, as he bent over to pull up his socks (thus giving me the perfect opportunity to swipe the messages and stuff them in my pocket), "what's pissing you off?"

I sat down at my own desk and stared hard at him. Perry's suntanned face looked concerned. It was a fair question. I had been in a good mood when I arrived only moments ago.

"Okay, Perry," I said. I leaned back in my seat, stalling for time to justify my suddenly vile mood. "Here's the thing. Nepotism."

"Have you seen a doctor?" he asked.

***

The great man himself arrived five minutes later. He glanced at Perry. "What the hell happened to you?"

I rose and followed Tom into his office. On the way, I gave Perry a severe look meant to suggest that next time he should *think* before he went to a tanning salon.

I leaned forward with my palms on the edge of Tom's desk. "Your girlfriend called."

He had reached the other side, and we stood facing each other, like two gladiators at the Roman Coliseum, ready to fight to the death.

"Three times," I said.

"Okay. Got it. Three times. Tell Billie to bring me coffee."

"We need to go over the new listings," I said.

"Okay. What you got?"

I didn't actually have anything, but I took a seat across from him anyway. "I do have one question for you."

"Okay, shoot."

"Tom, why didn't you tell me you have had business dealings with Lionel Woodstock? And why didn't you tell me that Fletch was married to his sister?"

"That's two questions."

"Well, answer me, dammit. When I was all over the Mavis thing, why didn't you tell me what you knew?"

"First, you didn't ask me then. And second, what is it exactly that you think I knew?"

I took a deep breath, deciding that Tom was, by far, the most frustrating man I'd ever met. "Okay, let's start with Fletch. You knew he was married to Mavis." It was a statement, not a question.

"As a matter of fact, I didn't. I had no idea until you just told me, Kiddo. I haven't been in touch with the guy for years. He just suddenly showed up here, and apparently you fell deeply in love with him."

"Not even close. And really? You didn't know?"

"No. Why would I know? You think he sent me an announcement? And by the way, what the *hell* was he doing married to Mavis Woodstock of all the—"

"Why? Why do you think it so unlikely they should be married?" If Tom even came close to saying he didn't think Mavis pretty enough for his precious Fletch, I would reach across the desk and strangle him.

"Because I seem to recall that Mavis was a nice girl, and as I've told you several times, Fletch is an asshole." Damn him. He was impossible to trap.

"Okay," I said. "They were married, but I think it was brief, and they were divorced a long time ago. I just think it's strange that he never mentioned it to me on our date."

"Probably too busy trying to get in your pants." Tom started to sort through a pile of golf magazines on his desk.

I ignored his remark. "Okay, so you didn't know about Fletch. What about Lionel Woodstock? You know him?"

"Hell yes, I know him. So do you. What about it?"

"You deal with him?"

"Deal with him? I use his bank to finance mortgages. Again, so do you. Will you get to the damn point?" He picked up one of the pink slips with Celeste's number on it and studied it.

He had me there. I wasn't sure what the point was. As usual, he had taken my words and switched them all around, confusing me. "Okay, I'll leave you alone so you can phone your girlfriend." I waited, but Tom didn't deny the fact, which only made me madder. I stood up.

"One last thing." He pulled a set of keys out of his pocket. "About Lionel. He wants his sister's house put on the market pronto. All her furniture and belongings are still there, but the family will remove them in the next couple of days. Meanwhile, get over there as soon as you can, take some pictures, and get the house on the market. And the good news for you is that this time you won't have to break the law in order to get in."

He flung the set of keys toward me, and I caught them with my right hand.

"And by the way, don't even *think* about taking that dizzy dame Kit with you. This is business, not a game of Clue."

I couldn't believe it. It was as lucky as having Will walk into Starbucks. I couldn't wait to call Kit.

"And tell George Hamilton out there to get his ass in here," Tom said.

I returned to my desk and reached into my purse for the leather notebook I'd started using to make notes of what we knew so far about Mavis. Through Tom's closed door, I could hear him yelling at Perry. I smiled to myself as I turned to a clean page and titled it *Fletch*.

Then I wrote *Married to Mavis. When? How long? What happened?* I was tapping my bottom lip with the tip of the pen when a soft hand on my shoulder forced me out of my detective mode.

"Billie," I said. Where had she come from? Well, I knew she had simply taken the five steps that separated her desk from mine. But the silence with which she had taken that journey seemed ominous. That's what I was actually thinking: *ominous.* I shuddered, willing away my melodrama. I had to get a grip.

Billie glanced down at my notebook. "You had a call, Val. From Mavis Woodstock's mother." She handed me a piece of pink paper on which she had written *B. Woodstock,* followed by a telephone number.

"Really?" I closed my notebook and tried to hide my excitement. "Thanks."

"Too bad about Mavis," Billie said.

"Yes, isn't it? She was an old school friend of mine." Billie probably saw through my promotion of the dead woman to friend status. On her worst day, Billie would be a far more perceptive detective than I could ever be, even if I'd walked in and found the perpetrator stuffing a towel into the tailpipe of Mavis's car.

"Well," I added, "I knew her in school. We weren't exactly friends. But I certainly knew her." As I babbled, I could hear the voice of my third-grade teacher admonishing *guilty conscience needs no accuser.* I hadn't been sure what she meant, but suddenly I could relate all too well.

"I see." Billie nodded toward my closed notebook. "Is that your little Murder Book, Val?"

"What?"

"You don't really believe she killed herself, do you?"

"Why wouldn't I? The police seem satisfied, and so does her family."

"Seems strange that she would want to sell her house one day and then kill herself a couple of days later."

"Actually, she e-mailed me, canceling her plans to sell."

"Oh, right. I forgot about that." But we both knew she never forgot anything.

I didn't ask her how on earth she knew Mavis had e-mailed me because I figured I probably didn't want to know. Not yet, anyway. I made a mental note to question her at a later date. Then I stifled a giggle. I could ask her *not to plan on leaving town anytime soon.* Or whatever the police say when they have a person of interest they might want to interrogate again.

When Billie was back in her corner of the office, I picked up my phone. But just before dialing, I changed my mind and took my cell phone out to my car.

Sitting in the front seat and shivering, from the chilly day as well as from nervous anticipation, I punched in Beatrice Woodstock's number. Her call to me was probably just about selling the house, but I didn't want to be overheard in case I *was* able to turn the conversation to Mavis.

CHAPTER ELEVEN

Hello, Beatrice? This is Valerie Pankowski. How are you?" I sat with a hand on the steering wheel, as if I really were planning to drive someplace.

"Valerie? How kind of you to call me back."

"I just got the keys to Mavis's house, so I'll be going over there soon to get the details for the listing nailed down." I cringed at my choice of words, suddenly filled with an image of the undertaker nailing down Mavis's coffin.

"Oh really? I suppose Lionel has arranged that. He didn't say anything to me. That's not why I was calling you, dear."

"What can I do for you? Is it about lunch? Could Kit and I take you some—"

She lowered her voice, and I knew I wasn't the only one who didn't want to be overheard. "It's difficult for me to get away; I'll have to let you know about that. But I'm calling because we never really finished our conversation this morning. Hilary rushed me out the door so quickly. She takes good care of me, but I didn't get to tell you . . ."

She stopped talking, and I waited for her to catch her breath.

"Are you still there, dear?"

"Yes, Beatrice, I'm still here."

"Okay, good, because I wanted to tell *someone*."

"I'm listening."

"It's just that I don't believe for a moment that Mavis took her own life."

"Beatrice, what do the police say?"

"Oh, them. They say she did it. And Lionel and the other boys do too. But I know better. She wouldn't do that. She had too much to live for."

"When did you last see Mavis?"

"That's just the thing. I hadn't seen her for about a week, but she and I met up fairly often since she returned to Downers Grove."

"When was that? When did she return to Downers Grove?"

"Oh, earlier this year sometime; let's see, it was after the holidays, but—anyway, she wasn't speaking to her brothers, at least not Lionel. So she never came to the house, but she called me often, and sometimes we'd meet for lunch. Hilary knew about our little secret; she often drove me to meet Mavis and then picked me up later. But she won't say anything, and you mustn't either. It would get me in trouble with the boys."

"I promise I won't tell the boys."

"Mavis lived in Florida for many years, but she came home to the Midwest for good. She was a dance instructor in Florida, but you probably knew that. Those Florida people love the tango and the mer . . . what's that dance that sounds like lemon meringue pie?"

"I think you mean the merengue." She reminded me of my own mother, who always refers to the "medicine" they put in her hair whenever she has a perm.

"Yes, that's what I mean. She had her own dance studio, you know."

I didn't correct Beatrice. Dance studio was more than enough for any mother to know about her daughter's "dancing" career.

"She loved Florida, Valerie. It never snows there; did you know that? You can go to the beach on Christmas Day if you want to. Can you imagine?"

We were both silent for a moment, as I pictured Beatrice Woodstock strolling along the Atlantic coastline in her mismatched outfits and accessories.

"So," I said, "you've been in touch with her a lot since she came back here?"

"Of course, and she was very happy. That's why it's ridiculous to think she would . . . do anything harmful. She took me shopping just last week to that mall. Oak something. They were having a good sale in one of the big department stores there. We liked to rummage around on the sale racks—"

"Beatrice?" I hated to cut short her pleasant memories, but I was getting colder and would have to start my car if we didn't finish soon.

"Yes, I'm sorry; it's just that . . ." She sniffed, and I thought she might be crying. "It's hard. I miss her so. But that's neither here nor there, and you don't have time to listen to all this. I just wanted to tell one of her friends that I know she didn't kill herself. And I can prove it."

I took a deep breath. "How's that, Beatrice?"

"Because she was taking me back to Florida so I could see it. 'Mommy,' Mavis told me, 'the sea is as blue as a sapphire. And the birds on the beach will eat right out of your hand.' Of course I never told the boys, but Hilary knew. Mavis promised me, Valerie. Did she ever mention it to you?"

"No. No, but it sounds lovely. I'm so sorry, Beatrice."

"Yes, but I guess I can live without seeing the West Coast. It's never seeing Mavis again that I can't bear."

I didn't stop for a geography lesson. Instead, I asked, "When were you planning this trip?"

"In two weeks. Mavis had the tickets all set up. She arranged everything on that Wide World Net thingy. We were going first class, too, on United, to Miami Beach. Can you believe that? I'll tell you a little secret, Valerie."

I held my breath.

"I've never flown on an aeroplane. Can you believe that? An old woman like me who's never flown on an aeroplane?"

"Oh, Beatrice, there are a lot of people who have never flown on an aeroplane," I said. The pronunciation conjured up images of glamorous Pan Am hostesses in cute pillbox hats, all looking like movie stars.

"I have to go. Someone is coming."

"Wait, Beatrice. There's something else I need to know. What about Ryan Fletcher? You said he was Mavis's ex-husband."

"Oh, him. Yes, she married him many years ago, and they weren't together for long. It was during all those years she was cut off from our family. I think he's a scoundrel, Valerie. But please don't tell anyone I said so. And now I really have to go. I just wanted to tell you that I don't care what anyone says. Mavis was taking her mommy on a trip, and she would never, under any circumstances, kill herself. She loved me, you know."

"I believe that very much, Beatrice," I said. But we'd already been disconnected.

Before returning to my office from the parking lot, I called Kit to relay the whole conversation to her. And I also wanted to give her the good news about Tom's handing me the keys.

Kit was on her stationary bike in her bedroom, watching TV, when I called, but in deference to the importance of the call, she muted the television and stopped pedaling. "So. It's confirmed," she said.

"You mean murder, not suicide."

"Duh. Yes. All we gotta do is prove who did it."

"Okay. But can we be sure that Beatrice is telling the truth and not just fantasizing?"

"Why would you say that?"

"Well, for one thing, she thinks Florida is on the *West* Coast."

"Easy mistake," Kit said. "She's about a hundred years old. She's allowed to get her coasts mixed up."

Again, I was reminded of my own mother. After a cruise to Hawaii several years ago, she brought back pictures of the Big Island that she was convinced was Puerto Rico. "Still, it doesn't mean the trip was ever really gonna happen," I said.

"Easy enough to find out. Larry's sister Carol. She's a travel agent, remember? She's got contacts. I'll have her check United flights to Miami. Even if Mavis wasn't legally Woodstock anymore, Beatrice sure as hell is."

"Good thinking. Okay, you get right on that and let me know. And by the way, don't make plans for this evening. I'm picking you up at five o'clock."

"Picking me up? What are you talking about? At five o'clock I'll be peeling potatoes to make Larry a shepherd's pie."

"Kitty Kat, I have the key to Mavis's house." My voice trembled at saying the words out loud, not to mention at the certainty I felt that we would uncover *something*.

"Ohmygosh, Valley Girl, how did you manage that?"

"I'll explain when I get there. Just be ready."

"Don't worry; I'll be ready. I *am* ready. Larry can order a pizza, and we're gonna *hang* that son of a bitch."

***

Tom telling me not to take Kit to Mavis's house was as effective as my mother telling me not to leave home after dark. But how would he ever know?

Well, *I* should have known not to underestimate him.

Then there was Larry.

From the moment I told Kit and Larry that Fletch had been lurking around Mavis's garage the day after her body was found and that he'd been the one to *find* her body, Kit had zeroed in on him as the killer. But even finding out that he was an ex-husband didn't convince Larry of his guilt. He was so frustrated at the leaps he thought his wife's imagination was making that we decided to drop him out of the loop. I wondered how Kit would explain her absence that evening.

For my part, my money was on Lionel. Or was it just too unbearable for me to think that I had been attracted to, and actually *kissed*, a murderer? I was counting on this visit to Mavis's house to point us in the right direction—point us to the right man.

Kit climbed into my car almost before I had come to a stop in her driveway. "I repeat: we're gonna *hang* that son of a bitch." Her auburn hair was pulled into a neat knot at the back of her neck, and her porcelain skin offset the red lipstick she'd no doubt reapplied right before leaving the house. She looked as good as she had when we'd gone to see Mrs. Woodstock that morning.

I knew I, on the other hand, looked as disheveled as I felt. But right now I had more important things to worry about. "I still don't see why you're so *sure* it's Fletch and not, say, Lionel," I said.

"Whoever it is, we're gonna *hang* him." She settled her Dooney & Bourke purse onto her lap like a baby she wanted to keep safe.

It occurred to me that for two women off to investigate a possible murder, we were in high spirits. We might have been going to the homecoming game at our school. That thought brought back another memory of poor Mavis—or rather *no* memory of Mavis. Whereas Kit and I had spent hours and hours primping and dressing for school events, I didn't recall ever seeing Mavis at anything outside of the classroom.

As we made our way up Mavis's sidewalk to her front door, my stomach felt almost queasy with . . . what? Anticipation? Fear? At least this time we were legit. I might have been rendered incapable of putting one foot in front of the other if we'd been sneaking. Nevertheless, however entitled we were to be there (at least me), I didn't like that it was so dark already.

I also didn't like entering the house and seeing that the family had already struck. And by family, I meant Lionel, but I reminded myself to keep an open mind. It might have been Hilary or Marcus or even Will who had removed the home's contents.

I suddenly wondered who really did legally own the house now, something I'd find out soon in my role as Realtor. Had Mavis left a will that had been shared with the beneficiaries already?

But rightful owner or not, any member of that family might have entered and removed evidence. Kit and I looked at each other, speechless in our defeat.

"We have to search anyway," she said. "Especially if it's Fletch we're after, he might have missed something."

And so we began in the kitchen. Kit opened all the cupboards, while I attacked the drawers. All were empty.

Next we moved into the living room. All the furniture was gone, so unless we were going to rip up floorboards, there was nothing to check.

The bedrooms proved as empty as the other two rooms. For some reason, I had imagined that the photograph we saw on our first visit would still be there, but it had disappeared along with the dresser it had been sitting on.

We had more luck in the bathroom. In a linen closet, a large cardboard box sat on the floor. It was full to the brim with the things people keep in their bathrooms. Maybe someone had emptied the medicine cabinet and cupboard under the sink and thrown everything in the box and then forgotten to remove it.

Kit dragged it out into the living room, and we both sat on the floor, ready to go through the contents. The room was chilly, and Kit rose to locate and adjust the thermostat. It didn't take long before warm air began circulating around us and we could remove our coats. I pulled the top item out of the box, an unopened roll of cheap toilet tissue. Single-ply. Next, Kit removed a tube of toothpaste rolled halfway up from the bottom.

"Hey, this proves something." She waved it at me, her glasses on the end of her nose, like a prosecutor wowing a jury with a vital piece of evidence.

"What?" I expected, at the very least, fingerprints of Mavis's killer.

"It proves Lionel didn't clear this place out. Or any Woodstock, come to think of it. This tube still has a lot of use left. The Woodstocks could make this baby last until next summer."

"Er, did you happen to get a look at Lionel's teeth? He could make that baby last until a *year* from next summer."

And so it went on. We took each item from the box as if it were a precious antique, but they all proved to be nothing more than used or unopened bathroom items. With most of the goodies spread out around us on the hardwood floor of the living room, we reached the bottom of the box. Only one item remained, a brown paper lunch sack, flattened by age and all the items that had lain on top of it.

"This is gonna be something," Kit said.

"Yeah, right. Probably some minipads."

I watched her peer inside and then look up at me with her devilish smile. "Eureka!" She reached into the sack and pulled out what looked like a stack of papers.

As if she were a gypsy laying out tarot cards for a reading, she placed each item from the stack on the floor between us. There were several photographs, all looking like the boy we had seen in the picture on Mavis's dresser. These pictures captured a boy ranging in age from baby to teenager. A blond woman was in some of them—Mavis, though not the frumpy kid I remembered. No, this woman was the blond bombshell Will had shown us in his picture. I held up one photo.

They were in a park; the boy looked about five years old. Mavis sat on a bench behind him and watched as he held out his hand. He might have been holding food for some unseen birds. Mavis had one hand shielding her eyes, like a visor, although she was wearing sunglasses. And as I picked up the other photos with Mavis in them, I was struck by the feeling that she didn't want her picture taken. I handed one to Kit.

"Hey, look at the fuck-me pumps," she said. "How'd she dance in these?"

I snatched the picture away, but Kit was already studying another item.

"Oh shit. Look at this." She held out what appeared to be a birthday card, handmade by a child. On the front was a picture of a stick dog drawn in brown crayon. Inside, the same crayon had been used to write HAPY BIRTHDEY TO MY MOOTHER. Underneath was another stick dog, this time drawn in red crayon. And then LOVE FORM YOUR SON SEAN XXXX.

It was just the sort of thing a mother, any mother, would keep stored away. I was filled with sadness at the sweetness of it. And then I became even sadder that it was the only card in the bag. I practically needed a U-Haul to store all the similar mementos I kept from Emily through the years. Just one card made it seem as if Mavis had been robbed of so many memories of her son.

"Ah geez," Kit said. "Look at this."

It was another picture of the boy, this time a little older, sitting on a couch with a chocolate Labrador at his feet. The boy beamed, his hand out as if ready to pat the dog's head.

"It's the dog he tried to draw on the card," I said. "Kit, do you think any of the family knows about this kid? Do you think Beatrice knows she has a grandson? And who's the father?"

"Mavis was married to your boyfriend. *He* could be the daddy, ya know."

I took my glasses out of my pocket and held the picture closer to my face, but all I could see was a boy who looked like a young Mavis. I shuddered and put the photo down on top of the others. "What else you got?"

"We got two credit cards, both in the name of Mavis Woodstock and both current," she said. "And then we have this." She held up an envelope yellow with age. It had been ripped open, the edges jagged. "You look inside." Kit held it toward me.

"Kit, I don't feel right about this." It was obviously a personal letter.

"What? Don't be an idiot. We've come this far; we have to read what's in there."

"Don't you feel just a tiny bit—"

"Give it here." She yanked it out of my hand. She pushed her glasses up and studied the postmark. "This says 1985, or is it a six?" She pulled a piece of paper out of the envelope. "Okay, ready?" She unfolded the letter.

I nodded, and she began reading:

Dearest M,

Please, please let me see you. I miss you so much and this separation is killing me. I promise I won't even touch you. I just want to see you and talk. That's all. Just talk. I followed you to work on Friday. That place is disgusting. It makes me sick to think of you working there. I saw some men come out, and I wanted to kill them. Then I saw you take Sean to the park on Saturday. I wanted so much to talk to you. But I don't want to make you angry again, so I just stayed hidden.

I promise it won't be like the last time. I know you have your life (although I hate it), but after all these years, and what we have been through, surely you can see that we have to talk sooner or later.

Please, please think about this. And know that I love you so much, I can't bear not being near you.

Kit stopped reading and looked up.

"Go on," I said. "Who signed it?"

"No one."

I snatched the letter from her. It had to have a signature. But it didn't. Who would write such a letter and not sign his name, unless of course he didn't want to be identified?

"See how it was written? Almost printed, like a child. You think it's Fletch?"

It was true the writing wasn't cursive, but it certainly wasn't a letter from a child. "Oh, this is getting just too creepy. What the hell kind of life did poor Mavis lead?"

"Yeah." Kit nodded. "Growing up with the Addams Family, then running away and working as a stripper or maybe worse, a son no one seems to know about, and then some maniac stalking her."

"Well, it appears her family doesn't know about her son. But that's not even the worst part."

"Right. You mean being murdered."

"That's what I mean."

We put all the items back in the sack and stood up. The empty house suddenly felt eerie. We placed what we'd removed, except the sack, in the box and returned it to the linen closet.

I hadn't done what I was supposed to do for Haskins Realty: take measurements of the rooms, take some photos, make notes so I could write a brief description. But that could wait for later, along with disposing of the box of bathroom junk. I would come back in the morning and take care of business. My heart just wasn't in my job right now. Safeguarding Mavis's sack of mementos seemed more important, like something I should do for her.

We turned the heat back down and locked the door behind us before walking to my car. "Here," Kit said. "You keep the sack."

"Really? I feel like it's evidence or something. Should we go to the police?"

She stopped in the middle of the pathway. "Okay, what is it, really? A letter written decades ago. It might have nothing to do with her murder. The writer doesn't threaten her. It could be from anyone. Maybe one of the guys in that club where she worked had the hots for her."

"Then shouldn't we take it to the police?"

"Let's sleep on it. The letter is so old, another night isn't going to make or break, ya know."

We drove in silence, the sack tucked safely in my briefcase.

When I pulled up in front of Kit's house, I said, "Well, we should probably tell the police we were there before Mavis's body was discovered."

"We don't even know if she was *in* her car when we looked in the garage that first time."

"True."

CHAPTER TWELVE

When I got home after dropping Kit off, I called Emily. Luke told me she was at work, and I noted the pride in her husband's voice, as if Emily were being directed in a Martin Scorsese movie.

"You should see her, Val," he said. "We went over her scene when she came home last night. They say the commercial won't air for three months at least, but can you imagine when we see our girl on TV?"

I am so glad Emily married Luke. He is a good guy, just what she deserves. "Well, tell her to call me. I want to hear all about it." I wished I could hold her in my arms and tell her how much I love her, how very proud I am to be her mother.

"Yes, I'll have her call you."

"No matter how late."

***

In the bright light of day, Mavis's house was not as creepy as it had been the evening before. And without Kit beside me, I was able to concentrate on my realty tasks.

But after accomplishing those, the only things that seemed able to penetrate my thoughts of Mavis's murder were my excitement for Emily and my curiosity about Tom and Celeste. Emily I could understand, but why did I care so much about TomCel? Probably because Tom shrouded their relationship with mystery, and I loved mysteries. Obviously. Or maybe I just wasn't used to him *having* a relationship, and I wasn't sure what was up with him and his French-chick wannabe.

Back at the office, I found Tom's door shut. He was on his phone speaking in a normal voice, which meant I couldn't decipher his words. I suddenly yearned for his bellowing that makes it clear what he has on his mind.

I was keying in Mavis's listing on the computer when the faux Frenchwoman herself walked in the door. Her expressionless face looked beautiful. I quickly discarded the notion that you have to smile to appear attractive, no matter what my mother taught me. Maybe it's okay to chew gum in public and slouch too.

Perry and Billie were both at lunch—although not together—and I was glad I was the only one in the outer office. Maybe I could learn more from Celeste than I had from Tom about the nature of their relationship. "Celeste, is it?" I said.

She nodded and then peeled off her calfskin gloves to reveal an impeccable manicure. "Is Tom in?"

"Yes, I'll let him know he has a visitor." I started to rise. So much for our little chat.

"No need. I'll just surprise him."

I sat back down and watched her approach his door. I felt like I was witnessing someone about to slip on a banana peel. Entering Tom's private office without a prior summons when the door is closed is something we office peons just never do. We always knock on the Great One's

117

door and wait for his directive before entering. Clearly, she was not in the office loop. But when she tapped on his door and then opened it, she somehow sidestepped the banana peel.

"Hey!" I heard him say, and then Celeste closed the door behind her, shutting me out. He even sounded happy to see her.

Just then the phone on my desk rang.

"Val, can you do lunch?" It was Kit.

"Can't talk now."

"Why are you whispering?"

"Celeste is here. Remember that woman Tom is seeing? Well, she just came to the office, and they are behind closed doors—"

"I can't hear a word you are saying. Can you have lunch or not?"

"No. I'll call you later."

I hit the *off* button and started scribbling gibberish on a steno pad, just in case they came out of Tom's office. I didn't want it to look like I was waiting for them. It didn't even occur to me that Kit might have something important to tell me about Mavis. *That's* how curious I was about Tom and Celeste.

About twenty minutes later, after I had written down the names of everyone I could remember from my high school graduating class, with my ear straining toward the closed door, Tom and Celeste burst out of his office. I kept my head down and made check marks by the names on my list as if it were going to somehow change the world.

I noticed Tom had one arm around Celeste's slim waist, and she was waving his car keys in her perfect hand. "Are you sure this won't be a problem?" She gazed into his face and actually batted her eyelashes.

"No, not at all. Val can give me a ride home. I'll see you later."

She smiled and kissed his cheek. "Okay, I'll see you at home."

And then she left. I hadn't noticed her arriving by taxi, but I doubted she'd walked to our establishment in what looked like two-hundred-dollar Kenneth Cole boots. Far more puzzling, however, was that she drove off in Tom's Mercedes, which was like the Vatican's lending the popemobile to an underage driver.

Tom and I watched her drive off. "So," I said. "You lent Celeste your car?"

"You're very astute today, Sherlock Holmes. What tipped you off?"

He returned to his desk, but I was on his heels like a Labrador itching to have him throw the ball.

"I'm just surprised, that's all. When I asked to borrow your car when mine was in the shop, you said, and I quote, 'I'd sooner give my keys to Helen Keller than to you.'"

"Let's face it, Kiddo, you are a crappy driver. Celeste knows her way around German engineering."

"Really?" I tried to perch on the corner of his desk. It might have been a classy move if I were in a black-and-white movie—*and* if I were Katherine Hepburn to his Spencer Tracy. But the reality was, my rear end slid off twice, so I gave up and sat in his visitor's chair instead. "Nice talk from someone who will apparently need a ride home," I said.

He chuckled. "How about I buy you a drink on the way?"

"Oh, right, that's just what every crappy driver needs. Alcohol."

This time he actually laughed. "You are a piece of work, Val, you know that?"

It was a loving pat on the head for the Labrador retriever.

***

"You know, I might have had plans tonight," I said, after Tom ordered our drinks at Brandon's, a swanky bar on the way downtown.

"Did you?"

"No, obviously not. But I might have."

"You didn't, so stop going on about it." He took a swig from his martini glass and visibly relaxed. "Here's to you, Kiddo." There's no doubt Tom does his best work in dark bars.

"So, Tom." I squirmed on the bar stool. "When we got the listing from Lionel, well, you said they'd be clearing out the house in the next couple of *days*, didn't you? But when we—when I went there just a few *hours* later, it was already cleared out. Doesn't that seem weird to you? Typically, it—"

Tom put his hand on my knee. "Valerie, don't *tell* me you are going to read something into that. Since when is it a crime to be a cooperative client?"

"Well, I'm just saying it seems unusually fast."

He sipped from his martini glass before answering, but his eyes never left mine. "And you don't think the Woodstocks are unusual?"

"Of course I do. But—"

"Look, no crime has been committed. And the sooner you get that through your head, the better for all of us. And by the way, Val, I'm not stupid, so don't *you* be, either."

"What are you talking about?"

"I'm reminding you not to take your girlfriend to Mavis Woodstock's house. *Ever.*"

"I—"

"I don't want to discuss it. Just do *not* involve Haskins Realty in *any* way with this Mavis's death."

I looked at him without saying a word. Had he caught my slip when I'd started to say "when *we* went"?

"And while I'm dishing out warnings, let me add that you're a fool if you keep dating Fletch. You can't be that desperate—"

"*That desperate?* I'm not desperate at all." I could barely get the words past my sudden anger. I wasn't sure if I was having a hot flash or a temper tantrum, but Tom's choice of words was making me break out in a sweat.

"Whatever. Just drink your drink. I gotta get home."

His authoritative tone was just too much. I gritted my teeth. "Yes, you do," I said. "And good luck with that."

I pulled my coat off the back of my chair and grabbed my purse off the bar, not sure if it was really Tom I was furious with. But I was furious. As I stomped toward the door, I stiffened my neck and resisted the temptation to look back.

I had no doubt he could get himself home. He was a big boy.

***

On the drive home I thought a lot about Tom. He can be frustrating and irritating and yes, often insensitive. But I've known him so long—our lives have woven around each other since we were teenagers—that I couldn't list his unappealing character traits without some of the good ones popping up, urging me to reconsider.

In high school, where our paths first crossed, he was neither the jock nor the brain, although he could easily have been both. He was never considered handsome, but he had a coolness about him. He was a friend of my older brother, Buddy, who now lives in Washington, DC, and unfortunately had no memory of any Woodstock when I called him. (In fact, he acted just like all the other men— Tom, Larry, and even my ex-husband—although his advice to stay out of it was at least tinged with brotherly love.)

I recalled how Buddy brought Tom to our house when we were all in high school. Tom teased me, the way guys tease their pals' little sisters. And I remembered the Friday night when I typed a paper for him while he was out on a date.

After high school Buddy left to attend the Naval Academy in Annapolis and then to become an officer in the Navy. Tom went off to the University of Texas in Austin, which seemed unlikely for a Midwestern boy; but it also added to his mystique. The summer before my senior year, I got a job waitressing at Barney's, a local hamburger joint. Tom came in every Friday night, sometimes with a girl, sometimes with a group of guys, and sometimes alone. He always sat at one of my tables, and always asked about Buddy before ordering. I was impressed by the large tips that college guy left me. When he was alone and the restaurant was not busy, I would sit with him and talk. He had big plans to make a lot of money.

And a few years later, after I finished school and was planning my wedding, we met up again. It was one of those chance meetings at the mall. Tom was already married by then to his first wife, and I was engaged to David. I was shopping for bridesmaids' dresses, and he was on his way to negotiate a lease for space to open a travel agency. We had coffee and talked about high school, and he gave me his business card.

From there our lives crisscrossed as if by some divine intervention. I booked our honeymoon with his agency (a disastrous trip to Hawaii, where everything went wrong), and David and I had dinner a few times with Tom and wife number one. Later, when it was time to move out of our apartment and get serious about buying a house, Tom, who by then had sold the travel agency and opened a real estate office, handled our first house purchase. Then our second. Then Tom got a divorce. I stayed married, but we had lunch occasionally. He was my guy friend, my brother's old pal, the man my husband didn't object to. Of course by then, my husband had a lot of playmates of his own.

Tom came to Emily's christening and played golf occasionally with David. I cooked him dinner a couple of times when he was between girlfriends and wives. It's a good platonic relationship, even if I still feel like his friend's little sister. And even if he sometimes seems to be the most insensitive lout on the planet, he certainly was there for me when I needed a job and when David was out of town and I needed to call someone in the middle of the night because I heard a strange noise in my garage. Even though I never expected Tom to rush over and beat up any would-be intruder, he did actually show up and drink David's twenty-year-old scotch, assuring me I'd make it through the night. And when I got my divorce, of course, Tom was there for me once more.

I remembered the silver cross he gave Emily when she graduated from high school, and of course the bracelet he'd just given me, and I began to grope through my purse for my phone.

Tom answered after one ring. "Yeah? Whaddya want, Val?"

"I'm just checking to see if you're okay."

"No, I'm not okay. I'm still sitting in the damn bar. You coming back to get me or what?"

"No, I am not coming back. Call Celeste. I just wanted to say—"

"Okay, okay, I'm sorry. I shouldn't have said anything about Fletch. But . . ."

"But what?"

"I just want to make sure you two . . . I was just hoping you two were done."

"Why? What is it to you?"

"Val, that guy is just not good for you."

"So you've said. But why do you care?"

"I don't."

"Then shut up about him. Now call the Celestial Body and go home. I'll see you tomorrow."

"Yeah, okay. And Val—"

"What now?"

"I don't like you driving and talking on the phone. You're a crappy driver, remember?"

"Yeah, I remember. And thanks, Pa, for the advice."

I ended the call, only to have my phone ring before I could put it back in my purse. I saw Kit's name light up. "Kitty Kat," I said.

"Where are you?"

"Driving home; just had a drink with Tom. Why?"

"Stop by here. We need to talk."

I saw there were no other cars around, and so like a NASCAR driver, I did a three-point turn in the street and headed toward Kit's house.

***

"Okay," Kit said. She ushered me into her kitchen. "I've been busy. Now listen to this."

I removed my coat and set it on a stool beside her granite countertop. Then I sat down on the neighboring stool. I could see the remains of some ravioli on the counter, which reminded me I hadn't eaten. Suddenly I was starving.

Kit caught my glance and reached into the cabinet for a plate. She spooned some of the food onto it. "So I checked with Carol this morning. Turns out Mavis did have a reservation for her and Beatrice to Miami. Paid for with American Express, which was *not*, incidentally, one of the cards we found in the sack, ya know. By the way, you do still have the sack, don't you?"

I took the plate and fork she handed me and speared some ravioli. "Oh, sorry. I accidentally dropped the sack in the river this morning when I was taking my run."

"Funny."

"Don't worry. It's in my briefcase, safe and sound. And this is delicious."

"Never mind that. So we know Beatrice isn't senile. Mavis really was planning to take her mom to Florida."

"Yeah, that's good," I said. "Well, not so good for Beatrice, since she won't be going, but at least it proves Mavis wasn't planning to kill herself. Doesn't it?"

"Probably. I doubt she'd off herself with a trip two weeks away. But that's not the main thing. There's something else."

"What?" I wiped my mouth with the cloth napkin she handed me.

"I called the Downers Grove police station."

I stopped wiping. I wasn't sure if I was angry she'd done that without my knowledge or glad she hadn't asked *me* to do it.

She got up and took a small dish of crème brûlée from the fridge and placed it beside my ravioli. "I spoke to a Detective Sergeant Billings. I told him we had been at the house on Friday and the car was in the garage, but no Mavis. Of course we never looked in the car. But we know you got an e-mail—by the way, exactly when did she send that e-mail?"

I had finished my ravioli and was plunging into the dessert. "Well, I got it Saturday . . ." It flashed through my mind that I didn't see a computer at Mavis's house on our first visit there, even though she'd referred to a "computer room" when she called me. So why no computer? And how had Mavis e-mailed me? She didn't have a workplace in Downers Grove. She could have gone to a library or some other public place, but that didn't ring true. If she *didn't* have a computer handy, she'd just pick up the phone to cancel her plans with me.

Where was her computer?

Kit interrupted my thoughts by waving a hand in front of my eyes. "Hey, are you pissed off? I figured you'd be glad I called the cops. Yesterday you were all about going to the police."

"No, no, forget that. I'm wondering *how* Mavis e-mailed me, not when."

"What are you talking about?"

After I told her, she said, "I suppose she might have had a laptop, and it might have been in a closet or something, but I have a hunch you're onto something, Val."

"Maybe you should run it by your police friends," I said. So I *was* irritated that she'd gone to them without me.

"Val, I'm telling you, it was a spur-of-the-moment thing. And I'm sorry. I guess I should have called you first. But the idea just hit me, and so I did it."

Well, that was believable. Kit does stuff first, then thinks about it afterward. I've probably lectured her on that little habit a million times during the forty years we've been friends.

Kit buys a convertible on a whim and then realizes it's hell on her hair and returns it the next day. Kit thinks they should take a cruise and buys the tickets before remembering how Larry suffers from seasickness. I decided a little phone call to the police was small potatoes in her great scheme of things.

"Okay," I said. "So you spoke to some detective inspector."

"Detective sergeant. And I can tell you he had no time for me *or* the letter, or anything else to do with Mavis. Death ruled a suicide. Case closed."

"Did you mention how improbable it is that a person takes a sleeping pill, then decides to kill herself?"

"Er, honey, according to Detective Sergeant Dickhead Billings, that's like your common, everyday suicide. By the way, turns out he's a pal of Lionel's, so that tells you what an asshole he is."

"What are you saying? It was a cover-up?"

"All I'm saying is that Billings sounded all misty-eyed when I mentioned Lionel's name. I thought he was going to break into song. He made it very clear to me that *Mister* Woodstock was mourning the suicide of his only sister and that I should keep my nose out of it. *If* I knew what was good for me."

"Did he really say that?"

"Not in so many words; but it was obvious he's a big Lionel fan, and he wasn't about to go stirring the pot."

"He didn't say *that*, either, did he?"

"Val, must you be so literal? I'm giving you my impressions—"

"Will you two quit, already?"

We both turned to see Larry coming through the archway from the den. "Katherine, did I hear you say you called the police? The Downers Grove police? Have you gone completely insane?"

"Oh, you." Kit rose and took another small dish of crème brûlée out of the fridge and handed it to him. Did she have an endless supply of the French dessert on hand to distract us? "Will you calm down? It was a perfectly logical thing for a taxpayer to do."

"And what letter are you talking about? Just what the hell have you two been up to? It's one thing to talk between yourselves about this cockamamie idea—"

She turned him around and ushered him back the way he had come. "Larry, darling, do us all a favor and go eat in the den. You already said you didn't want any part of this, so that's what you get."

Surprisingly, he let himself be pushed out of the kitchen, but he was shaking his head in disapproval.

Kit rejoined me at the counter. "So the hell with the police; we'll find out what happened on our own. Then we'll see what Detective Sergeant Fucking Billings has to say for himself."

CHAPTER THIRTEEN

L arry looked settled in his leather recliner in the den, a crème brûlée–laden fork to his lips, when Kit and I barged in and told him he'd probably want to leave. We wanted to use the computer, and he wasn't going to like what we were computing. Or, more accurately, googling.

"Can't you use your laptop?" His eyes never left his high-definition screen.

"No, it's upstairs. This is quicker." Kit had already typed the name *Sean Woodstock*.

Larry groaned and then lowered the footrest and heaved himself out of his chair. He seemed to decide that however awkward it might be to eat and watch TV in their bed (long before he was ready to go to sleep for the night), it would beat the hell out of being in earshot of whatever we were cooking up. Crème brûlée it wasn't, he knew that much.

"Damn," Kit said. "Nothing here. But wait a minute." I sensed she wasn't talking to me, but rather to the computer.

Then I watched as she typed in *Sean Fletcher* (as in son of Ryan Fletcher). "Kit!" I said. But she'd already hit Enter, and results appeared before our eyes.

She paged down past Sean Fletcher the athlete and a few other Sean Fletchers and stopped when she got to a Sean Fletcher the author, a memoirist to be exact. "Wow. What if this is him? Wouldn't that be too good to be true? What if our Sean Fletcher has written a *memoir?*"

"Well, then he'd be like most of the general population," I said. Still, it would be nice if we *could* just order a book on Amazon.com that would answer some of our questions.

As she transitioned from Google to Amazon, I ran back to the kitchen to grab my reading glasses from my purse. By the time I returned to the den, Kit was already scrolling down the page to read a summary of *Mother's Day* by Sean Fletcher. It was described as *a young man's turbulent childhood spent with his single mother and her life of high-class prostitution.*

"Good grief," I said. "Can that be Sean, the little boy from the photographs? And Mavis; can the mother really be Mavis?"

"Wow." Kit leaned back in her chair. "A high-class hooker? Way to go, Mavis."

"What do you think?" I plopped into the chair Larry had vacated.

"I think we gotta order the book." Kit stood and left the room. She returned with her wallet.

"But it seems so—"

"So what?" Kit took a credit card out of her wallet.

"So . . . I dunno, so invasive of her privacy. I mean, if she was a prostitute, that was her business. It feels wrong somehow for us to delve into—"

"Are you insane? Her *son* invaded her privacy by writing the damn book. It's out there, babe, on the Internet, for everyone to see. And it might just help us find out what happened to her. Besides, you know you want to read it; admit it."

"I suppose you're right."

Kit was already typing in her Amex card number. "I'll get express delivery."

"Are you girls done with your bullshit?" Larry stood in the doorway. "I need my computer. Now."

"Don't get your shorts in a twist, Larry; I'm almost done." Kit peered at him over her glasses. "Aren't you a little bit curious about what we've uncovered?"

"Let me guess. There was a shooter hiding on a grassy knoll with ties to the Mafia."

"Hilarious, Larry." Kit rolled her eyes at her husband and then held her credit card up to her face to double-check the numbers. "Okay, done. Now we just have to wait for the evidence."

"I mean it, Kit. I need my computer."

"Okay, okay, it's all yours."

I followed Kit back to the kitchen as Larry sat down at his computer and began to type. "He gets so paranoid about that computer," she said, "as if I'm gonna go through his files and blackmail his clients or something."

"His clients?" I knotted my scarf around my neck and then gathered my coat and purse. "He uses the home computer for his clients? Why not his office computer?"

"Exactly. But he's convinced that some of his high-profile clients' information should not be available to his office staff, ya know." She held up her fingers to form air quotation marks around "high-profile clients."

"I didn't realize Larry had high-profile clients."

"He doesn't really." She kissed me on the cheek. "He only thinks they have high profiles. Let's face it: he's a good CPA, but he's not filing 1040s for Brangelina."

We both laughed, and I slipped back to the den to say good-bye to Larry. He was still hunched over the computer, his back to me, and he gave a start when I leaned over his shoulder to give him a peck on the cheek. He said something, but I didn't catch it because what I saw on his computer screen stole my attention.

Two words jumped out from his list of folders. *Mavis Woodstock.* My lips stayed longer on Larry's cheek than I'd planned, as my eyes remained transfixed on the file name. Until Larry hit the key to close the screen.

"See ya, Val." He stood, freeing himself from me and covering the computer with his body. "Drive safely."

"Thanks." I put my arms through the sleeves of my coat, but I felt suddenly chilly.

On my drive home I debated whether or not to call Kit and tell her what I had seen. There must be a good explanation. Maybe Kit herself had made the file to log in all of our investigation info. But surely she'd use her own laptop for that. My gut told me not to mention it. Not yet, anyway. So instead, I followed Larry's instructions and drove home safely.

***

One benefit of showing houses for a living is the chance to see a lot of interior design. Some of it good, some of it scary. Khaki-colored walls and sage-green leather furniture are good. Big Bird–yellow kitchen cabinets and pink-flamingo wallpaper borders are scary. When I lived in the Big House, I prided myself on its décor, all of which I had designed myself. With the HGTV cable channel so full of ideas, I didn't need to pay a decorator to tell me my kitchen was screaming to be turned into a Tuscan village.

The morning after Kit's and my discovery of our Sean Fletcher (we hoped), while I sipped coffee and watched *Design on a Dime*, my present abode spoke to me, yelled at me, that its nine hundred square feet of white walls needed some fixing. Some color or something. *Anything.* Even if you choose to live in a box, it doesn't have to be one of those white Chinese-food containers.

It was Thursday, that day I often treat like non-Realtors treat Saturday. And Kit and I seemed to silently agree our next step was reading the memoir when it arrived. *Mother's Day* by Sean Fletcher would no doubt help us decide what to do—where to look—next. So after a quick stop at Starbucks for a venti mocha (way too expensive, way too fattening, but oh-so-delicious), I found myself in Home Depot's paint department.

After narrowing their paint-color choices down to a manageable five million or so, I settled at last on chocolate brown for my living room, buttery yellow for my kitchen, and medium blue for my bedroom and bathroom. I added some brushes and rollers to my cart and threw in some drop cloths, paint trays, and a few gadgets I'd never heard of that promised easy and flawless edging. Yeah, *right*. I'd loaded it all into the car when I realized I'd left the ladder with David, so I went back to drop another fifty bucks in the home-improvement store's coffers.

I was high atop that ladder, trying to get my brush into a corner without touching the ceiling, when the phone rang. Damn. Well, I'd just have to ignore it. There was no way I could get to it in time without breaking a leg or, worse, spilling paint.

"Val, it's Kit," I heard my friend's voice come over my answering machine at last, after four rings that pierced my every nerve. I don't know how people can blithely ignore a ringing phone. It's like letting a baby cry with no attempt to soothe it. It just isn't something I can do.

I also don't know why anyone would choose to have voice mail. I'd no sooner figured out my new system than I'd reverted to a good old-fashioned answering machine, which allowed me to hear Kit's voice now. That's something else I can't ignore.

And something was up. She meant business as she said, "Call me. Right away."

By the time I could set my brush on the edge of the tray of chocolate-brown paint and descend the ladder, taking care not to sprain an ankle or my back, she had hung up. I wiped two globs of paint off my hands with a paper towel and then picked up my phone to dial her number.

"Val, were you screening calls?"

"No, no, I was up on the ladder."

"What the hell are you doing on a ladder? Doesn't your place have a super?"

"I'm painting."

"Why on earth would you paint a rental?"

"Because I like to paint, and I don't like white walls that are already no longer white. They show every little thing, Kit, and they are so depressing to look at."

"Yeah, but why are you—"

"I said, I like to paint."

"Anyway, the book arrived. I'll be there in a few."

I wrapped my paintbrush in a couple of Walmart sacks and put it in the refrigerator. My paint job would have to wait a while.

***

The memoir was one hundred forty-five pages long. Not exactly *War and Peace*. And Kit had already highlighted many of the paragraphs with a yellow marker. As she read them aloud to me, I felt a churning in my stomach.

The most obvious fact that emerged was that Sean Fletcher did not like his mother. He described in excruciating detail his embarrassment at her profession and the men she brought home to their apartment. The times she was away for weekends, and he was left with an unkind babysitter. The bruises his mother sometimes appeared with and hid with makeup. But what saddened me most was the loneliness that engulfed mother and son, separating them from each other and the world around them.

"Well," I said, "that's just about the saddest thing I've ever heard."

"No shit." Kit removed her glasses.

"And do you notice he never mentions his father?"

"Actually, on page one hundred twenty-one he says he never knew who his father was. In fact, he never knew who his mother's family were, either, while he was growing up."

"He must know now. It wouldn't be that hard to trace," I said.

"Do you think Fletch the father knows about this book?"

"Good question. If Fletch is in fact his father."

"Sure he is," Kit said.

"We don't know. Seems strange Sean wouldn't have contacted him. Or maybe he did. Maybe it's linked to why Fletch came back here looking for Mavis."

The enormity of the whole situation was making me weary, and I poured us each a cup of coffee, even though I still hadn't eaten anything all day. At first I'd been too excited about my painting project; now I felt too sick because of Sean and his childhood.

"I don't know; I just don't know." Kit took the cup I offered her.

"By the way, have you written down everything we know so far?"

"Me? I thought you were doing that," Kit said.

"Well, I have my little notebook, but so much has happened, it's hard to keep up with it. I thought maybe you might have . . . you know . . . put it on the computer. To keep a record of what we know . . . so that it would all be in a file—"

"What do you mean?"

During our long friendship, I've never been able to conceal anything from Kit. This time wasn't going to be any different.

I sat down at the opposite end of the couch. "Okay. At your house last night, when Larry was on his computer, well, when I went to kiss him good-bye, I saw a file named *Mavis Woodstock*. I thought maybe you had—"

"*What?* You saw *what?*"

"A file titled *Mavis Woodstock*."

"And you wait until now to tell me?"

"I thought maybe you'd made the file—"

"Larry. That son of a bitch."

"Okay, maybe it's nothing," I said. "Maybe Larry is keeping a file. Maybe he decided to help us, after all, to surprise us."

But Kit was already heading toward the door. "I'm going home to find out just what he's up to."

"Okay." I followed her to the door. "But don't get into an argument, and don't tell him I told you, and be careful, in case . . ." I felt like that thirteen-year-old Val again, begging Kit not to get us into trouble by rushing headfirst into some teenage jeopardy.

But she was already gone.

CHAPTER FOURTEEN

I didn't feel like returning to my painting. The sadness of *Mother's Day* was too disturbing, and I needed something that would occupy my mind more than painting could. So I took a quick shower and headed to the office. Even though it was late in the day, and I didn't have any appointments scheduled, I had enough paperwork to distract me. Plus, I wanted to talk to Tom before he left for the day.

He was holed up in his office when I arrived. I rapped on the door and then—recalling Celeste's bravado—barged in.

He was sitting behind his desk, picking at the cellophane wrapping on a CD: *Mozart's Greatest Hits*. He looked up at me. "How the hell is a person supposed to get these things open?"

"Give it to me." I grabbed the CD from his hand and dug a fingernail into the sticky strip across the top. "So, Tom, about your old pal Fletch."

"Not him again." He leaned back in his leather wingback chair and put his hands behind his head. He looked dapper, with his starched blue shirt and maroon suspenders.

"Did you know he and Mavis had a son?"

"Valerie." He leaned forward, his elbows on the desk, the tips of his fingers forming a steeple. "The last time we discussed Fletch, you asked me if I knew he was married to Mavis. I told you no." He gave a condescending smile. "So if I didn't know he was married, how the hell would I know he had a son?"

"Okay, okay, calm down." I dug some more at the CD casing, which wasn't budging. My French manicure was closer to becoming unstuck than the CD was.

"What I'm wondering," he said, "is why you are so interested in Fletch. What the hell are you and that dizzy-dame friend of yours up to?"

I put one corner of the CD up to my mouth to tear the cellophane off with my teeth, thus protecting my nails. I managed to bite loose enough cellophane to make a gnat a new pair of pants. "This has nothing to do with Kit, who by the way is not a dizzy dame, as you so charmingly call her. I'm just curious, that's all. Since you seem to know Lionel so well, I thought maybe he had mentioned a nephew."

He rose and came around the desk, pulling the CD away from my mouth. "You'll break this friggin' thing; give it to me."

I plunked down in the visitor's chair, like a destructive child who'd had her favorite toy taken away from her.

He waved the CD at me. "This was a gift from Celeste, so I'd appreciate not having your teeth marks all over it." He went back to his side of the desk and took a pair of scissors from the top drawer. "Lionel Woodstock has never so much as mentioned the weather to me, much less if he has a damn nephew. And unlike you, I don't insist that an associate provide me with a family tree." I watched him insert the scissors into the edge of the cellophane and attempt cutting.

"Okay, okay, so the answer is no."

"I've forgotten the damn question."

"If you knew Fletch and Mavis had a—"

"No!" He remained focused on removing the cellophane and freeing the encased CD.

"Okay, got it. No need to shout."

"Just tell me this. Why do they make these things so difficult to open?"

"To drive us insane, maybe. Besides, you are not seriously going to play that, are you?"

"Of course. Play it and enjoy it. It was a gift."

"Well, talk about pretentious."

"Pretentious? What's so friggin' pretentious about it?" he asked.

"Because, you can have Barry Manilow's greatest hits and The Eagles' greatest hits, but not *Mozart*. It just doesn't work that way." Now I knew *I* sounded pretentious. After all, why shouldn't Wolfgang have a greatest-hits CD? He's certainly had the staying power.

"What's it to you?" He resumed edging the point of the scissors into Wolfie's plastic case.

"Nothing. Enjoy."

"Oh, I will. Celeste thinks it will help me relax. Like I need to relax. Like I'm not about to have a heart attack just trying to open the piece of shit."

"She's right. You do need to relax."

"By the way, what are you doing here? I thought you weren't coming in."

"Well, I was at home painting my apartment, but I got distracted and decided to come in and catch up on paperwork. The painting can wait."

"Wait? How the hell long could it take? Isn't your place like two hundred square feet or something?"

"Nine hundred, thank you very much."

"Oh, nine hundred. Excuse me. I didn't realize you had stables on the property. Why didn't you buy a house, like I told you to?"

"I love my apartment, I'll have you know, and if you'd ever bother to come see it, you'd know why."

He waved a dismissive hand in the air. "I've seen plenty of rabbit hutches; I don't need to see yours. And anyway, you never invited me."

"Come on; you don't need an invitation. You know that." I looked at my watch. I really did have paperwork to do, and clearly Tom knew nothing about Sean. "Okay then, I'll leave you and Wolfgang alone." I stood up.

"Val, wait. There's something I need to talk to you about. I'm glad you came in today, Kiddo." He threw the CD on the desk and flashed the boyish grin that always makes me think he's just stuck a tack on someone's chair. "I want to buy Celeste something. Something nice. I thought you could help me."

"Oh, is it her birthday?"

"No, I don't think so. But good idea; I should find out when that is."

"Well, Christmas is more than a month away. You've got a little time." I was pleased to hear that Tom didn't know when Celeste's birthday was.

"I just want to get her something, for no reason."

"For no reason?"

"Yeah, she's always doing sweet things for me, like the CD. I gotta reciprocate, don't I?"

"Well, if you want to. I mean, a CD's no big deal. It hardly warrants your undying gratitude."

"I'm not talking undying gratitude. I'm just trying to be nice. I don't know why you're against that."

"I'm not against being nice, Tom. Actually, I'm *for* nice. That's why I'm against Celeste."

"You're what?" His mouth fell open, and his eyes locked with mine. When I didn't respond, he took a cigar out of his desk and prepared to light it, even though the rules clearly forbade smoking in the building. "Why in the hell would you be against Celeste? You don't even know her."

I wondered how to answer that. It was true; I didn't know her. But her ridiculous gift to Tom had given me some psychological insight. Tom couldn't tell Mozart from Madonna. If she was his so-called girlfriend, why didn't she know that?

Finally, I said, "I know her type."

"Oh, this is really getting interesting now. And what type might that be, may I ask?"

Well, now I'd done it. I didn't have a single answer for that.

"Valerie, she doesn't need to be *your* type, you know. You're not dating her. I am."

"But you're my friend, Tom, and I hate to see you being used."

"Being used? What makes you think I'm being used? Oh, I get it." He laid his cigar in a glass ashtray on his desk, giving me his full attention. "Celeste couldn't possibly be in love—or even infatuated—with a lug like me."

"Tom, I'm not at all sure what you mean by lug, but I can assure you I do not think you are one. Nor, I'm sure, does Celeste. She is lucky to have a guy like you—to have *you*. I just don't think she's worthy of you. She seems shallow to me."

Before he could respond, I had a hunch and hurried on. "Tell me, Tom. Does she know the businesses you were in before Haskins Realty? Does she know you have parents alive and well in Naperville? Has she met them? Does she know how long you and I have been friends? Has she ever asked you stuff like this?"

"Why the hell would she care about my parents—or you?"

"Because, Tom, when you like someone, when you really care about them, you want to know everything about them."

"Then you must be madly in love with me, Val. You've never let anything about me go unresearched, un*scrutinized*. Why didn't you just say so? Why didn't you just tell me you were in love with me?" He laughed heartily at his own joke. Funny lug that he is.

Barely able to worm my way out of the hole I'd dug for myself in Tom's office, I scurried back to my desk, loaded some files into my briefcase, and left for home.

***

When I got back to my apartment and was faced with my half-finished paint job, I quickly put on my painting clothes and was just about to get up on the ladder again when the phone rang.

I was pretty sure it was Kit calling to tell me she had used the Chinese water torture on Larry and he had come clean, but it was Fletch. I was shocked to hear from him, but glad he had called so I could ask him a few questions.

"Valerie, I'm sorry I haven't been in touch. But things are pretty hairy right now—"

"Fletch, why didn't you tell me you'd been married to Mavis Woodstock?"

He was silent for a long time, and I thought he might have hung up. Eventually, he spoke. "I'm sorry I didn't say anything. It had nothing to do with you and me. It was a long, long time ago, and I hadn't seen her for many years."

"Fletch, did you know that Sean has—"

"Sean?"

"Yes, Sean. Your son. Did you know he has written a book that—"

"Wait a minute, Val. I don't even know who Sean is. Trust me, Mavis and I never had any children." He sounded sincere, believable.

But then who *had* written that letter to Mavis about seeing her at the park with Sean? And why did Sean go by Sean *Fletcher*?

***

For the second time that day, I put my paintbrush in the refrigerator. Fletch was on his way over. He wanted to meet for a drink, but I told him to come to my place. Not that I really wanted to see him, but I did want him to come clean about Mavis, and he seemed willing to talk, to set things straight.

I ran a brush through my hair and exchanged my paint-streaked sweats for jeans and a long-sleeved T-shirt just in time to press the buzzer to let him in.

He hadn't shaved, and I couldn't tell if that was deliberate or if he just hadn't had time. His hair needed trimming, and he was wearing holey jeans that looked like they'd seen better days but were more likely the latest fashion. Either way, the man could have easily made the pages—if not the cover—of *GQ*. He gave me a peck on the cheek, and I retreated to the kitchen for refreshments—and some breathing room.

I poured myself a Diet Coke and grabbed the last beer from the fridge. Then I joined him on the couch, where he'd moved aside some old sheets I was using to protect the furniture.

He took the beer I handed him. "Okay," he said. "This Sean? Who is he?"

"I thought *you* could tell *me*." I described the book, wishing Kit hadn't taken it home with her.

"He doesn't say who his father is, in this book?"

"No; in fact, that seems to be one of his many problems. He doesn't know."

"And we're sure he's talking about Mavis Woodstock as his mother?"

"No question."

"Interesting." He took a sip of his beer.

"Fletch, why don't you tell me everything you know about Mavis."

"Not much to tell."

"You were her husband, right? You must know something."

"Yes, I was her husband. For two years and two months. And that included the time it took for her to get a divorce. It wasn't very nice."

"Who divorced whom?"

"It wasn't what *I* wanted. I loved her; I really did. Still do, if I'm honest. If you can love a dead person."

Did his voice really crack? And was it sincere? His fingers caressed the beer can delicately, as if it were a crystal wineglass.

I decided to give him the benefit of my doubt. "I'm sorry, Fletch." Still, I had to press for more. "But what happened?"

He sighed and then took a long swig. "I met Mavis when she was twenty. She was sweet, smart, and pretty." He stopped then and looked at me as if waiting for a rebuttal.

"Go on."

"I saw pictures she kept of herself, growing up and in high school, and let's be honest, she wasn't Miss America back then. But when I met her, she was gorgeous, drop-dead gorgeous. She'd had some work done. You would not have recognized the girl you went to school with."

I nodded. "Did she have all that surgery to become . . . well, whatever it was she became?"

"Oh, not so she could be a stripper—"

"Then why did she do it?"

"Perhaps for the best reason of all. She didn't want to be recognized. She wanted to be a completely different person."

"That's understandable."

"When I first met her, she was working as a receptionist in a doctor's office. The doctor was a golf buddy of mine. I think I fell in love with Mandy—oh, did you know? She went by the name Mandy Woods. I think I fell in love with her on our first date."

"She changed her name to Mandy Woods?"

"Yes. Which is why it took me so long to trace her. I was looking for the wrong girl, Mandy Woods instead of

Mavis Woodstock. When we were together, I always teased her about being paranoid." He laughed, but not in a good way. "She was always looking over her shoulder. Sometimes I thought she was on the run or something. Which in a way, I guess, she was."

He crushed the empty beer can in his hand. When I apologized for not having more, he simply continued his story.

"So after a whirlwind romance, I convinced her to marry me. I say convinced because I don't think she ever really loved me as much as I did her. I was several years older and just starting out as a lawyer after my stint in the army. But we had a quick marriage ceremony in Minneapolis, and—"

"Wait a minute. Minneapolis? I thought you lived in Florida."

"No. We lived in Minneapolis. I found out that when Mavis left me, she moved to Florida. At least that's where I at last tracked her down. I even moved there myself. But we met in Minnesota."

"Did her family know?"

"Her family? Hell, I didn't even know she had a family. She told me she had been in foster care all her life and had no known relatives. I believed her; no reason not to."

"So you were married, and then what?"

"Things weren't right from the start. I suspected her of having an affair. I saw all the typical signs: putting the phone down when I came into the room, unexplained absences. She was an extremely private person. One day she just took off. Left me a note saying she wasn't happy, she was sorry for any pain she had caused me. I never saw her again. Not alive, anyway."

The facts were swimming around in my head. This was a whole new woman, this exotic Mandy who'd replaced the frumpy Mavis.

"What did she tell you about her family? What reason did she give you for being in foster care?" I asked.

"Not much. She was pretty vague. Her parents had been killed in a car crash. She was an only child. No other relatives. That sort of thing. All lies, as it turned out." He dug his hands into the pockets of his jeans and leaned back on the couch like a sullen teenager. "Anyway, through a detective friend of mine, I recently discovered a Mavis Woodstock who fit the description of Mandy Woods. And so I came here. I assume her family knows nothing about me."

"Actually, that's not true," I said. "Her mother described you as her ex-husband." I decided not to let him in on the fact that his ex-mother-in-law also called him a scoundrel. That seemed a little too much.

"I've been wondering whether to go see her."

"Hmm, not sure that would be good right now. You know, Beatrice Woodstock thinks her daughter was murdered."

He showed no surprise, as if Mavis being murdered was as likely as her making a trip to the grocery store. "And what about you?"

"I think it's a strong possibility," I said.

He seemed to mull the idea over for a few seconds, and then he abruptly sat up straight. "She surely doesn't think *I* did it."

"I don't know who she thinks did it, but you might not want to open that can of worms right now."

He stood up and dug his hands into the pockets of his jeans again. "Maybe. But one thing I will do is find my son."

"Wait a minute." I stood up. "How do you know Sean Fletcher is *your* son? You said on the phone that you and Mavis never had any children—"

"That I know of. But think about it: why wouldn't this kid be mine?"

"Er, there could be a million reasons for that. You said yourself she might have been having an affair. Besides, assuming you were the baby's father, why would she leave her husband if she was having his baby?"

"Unless she didn't know."

Or didn't want you *to know.* I didn't say it out loud because, for whatever reason, Fletch hadn't been Husband of the Year in Mavis's eyes. I didn't dare trust him.

"If I'm not the father, then who is?"

"Who, indeed?" Even to my own ears, I sounded like a bad character from an even worse British mystery novel.

I took the empty beer can from the coffee table and walked the couple of steps to my front door. Fletch was right behind me, ready to leave, and I had no desire to have him stay. "One more thing, Fletch," I said, one hand on the doorknob. "Why were you so intent on finding Mavis? It's been so many years since she left you, why not just cut your losses and move on?"

He hesitated, running his hands through his hair, a habit I had grown used to in the brief time we'd been acquainted. "Good question. Not one I can answer, though."

I waited. There had to be a reason.

"Like I told you, I was—still am—in love with her. For that short time we were together, I was happy. And I believed I made her happy. I just had to find out what happened."

"She was the one who got away?" I opened the door and stood aside so he could leave.

"That's right," he said. "And considering what happened to her, I'd say she got well and truly away."

CHAPTER FIFTEEN

I waited until I heard Fletch leave my building and then called Kit with my new information. I spilled it all out in a rush, trying not to forget a single thing. Only once did she break her silence while I talked, with a "*hot damn*" when I gave her Mavis's alias. She then told me she was waiting for Larry to get home from a business dinner so she could grill him about the computer file I had seen. After I hung up, my head was spinning, and I almost felt sorry for Larry.

I got ready for bed and turned on a rerun of *Law & Order*. Just as the NYPD Special Victims Unit was bringing in the murder suspect, the phone rang. I hoped it wasn't Kit calling to say Larry hadn't come clean and so she had buried the computer mouse in his forehead.

It was Tom. With one of Mozart's greatest hits playing softly in the background. "Hey, you okay?"

"Tom, what in the world? Are *you* okay? It's almost eleven o'clock."

"Yeah, I'm okay. Some people stay up past ten in Chicago. We're crazy night owls; sometimes we even spike our cocoa."

"You're hilarious. Why are you calling?"

"Just wanted to check on you. You seemed a little razzled when you left here today."

"Razzled?"

"Yeah, razzled. It's a word."

"I'm fine, Tom. Not in the least razzled. Are you fine with Celeste?"

"Yeah; she's in the bathroom getting ready."

"Whoa! Way too much information."

"Getting ready to take a *bath*. Geez."

I snuggled down under my duvet, thoughts of the Mavis/Mandy murder mystery fleeing my head. This was flat-out sweet. I pictured Tom creeping into the kitchen, or whatever room he was in, to make a call to check on me, while his girlfriend was preparing her bubble bath, completely oblivious.

"Thanks for calling, Tom. That's nice of you, but I'm okay."

"Yeah, yeah, hold your horses," I heard him call to Celeste. His voice returned to me in a whisper. "Get some sleep. And cheer up."

"G'night, Tom. And don't do anything I wouldn't do."

"Kiddo, that would just about make me the pope. And I ain't even a Catholic." I heard him chuckle as he hung up.

His comment about cocoa made me suddenly want chocolate, so I padded to the kitchen and found a package of Reese's Peanut Butter Cups in the back of the fridge. They were already old when I'd moved them from the Big House for just such an emergency, and the chocolate had turned white. While I stood at the counter, stuffing the candy into my mouth, a huge wave of something hit me as I pictured Tom in his palatial penthouse doing whatever the hell it was he and Celeste did. It wasn't jealousy I was feeling, or if it was, I certainly didn't know why.

Instead of turning the TV back on to help me sleep, I switched on the radio by my bed. I moved the dial until I came to a classical station, and to the strains of one of Mozart's greatest hits, I fell asleep. Celeste was right. It was relaxing.

***

I was on my third cup of coffee the next morning when my apartment buzzer rang. I'd been up since five thirty, thoughts of Mavis and Fletch keeping me from sleeping. Not that I don't wake up every morning by five thirty. Don't all fiftysomething women?

I pressed the intercom button to see who in the world was coming to my apartment. "Yes?"

"Uh, a delivery for a Ms. Valerie Pankowski," came the unrecognized voice that sounded like it could belong to a serial killer.

"I'm not expecting a delivery." I cursed myself for not putting in a dead bolt yet and started to retreat to my kitchen, where I had weapons in the form of my Chicago Cutlery. But the buzzer brought me back. "What?" I tried to sound as if I were very busy cleaning my .357 Magnum.

"Ms. Pankowski? I have some flowers for you. I mean, I'm from DG Florists, and someone is sending you some really beautiful flowers." He spoke so rapidly I could hardly understand him.

"I'll be right down." They were probably from Fletch, but I hadn't ruled him out as Mavis's killer, and if he thought a bunch of flowers would do the trick, he was way off base. Nevertheless, I hurried down the two flights of stairs to the lobby.

A guy who couldn't have been a day over sixteen thrust a bouquet of purple tulips at me and bolted out the front door before I could thank him. *Teenagers!* I felt relief that Emily is past that unstable age and almost halfway through her unstable twenties. I plucked a small white card from where it was nestled among the purple petals. Then I realized I'd have to look at it upstairs when I had my reading glasses on. I shoved it into the pocket of my skirt.

Back in my kitchen, and before arranging the flowers in my favorite Waterford vase, I found my glasses and pulled the card out of my pocket. I felt . . . what? Shocked? Delighted? Horrified? A mixture of all three? Neatly typed out was the message *I really do hope you are doing okay. I care about you. Love, Tom.*

It was with the same mixture of the same three emotions that I opened my door to a light knocking a few minutes later. I'd just finished applying my makeup and was about to leave for the office.

"Tom! What are you doing here? How did you get in?"

"You aren't as safe as you think you are. You know these rabbit hutches. Any ol' dog can get in. I just walked in when one of your neighbors happened to be walking out. And you know what he said to me?"

"What?"

"He didn't ask what the hell I thought I was doing, just letting myself in. No, he said *good morning.*"

"So I have friendly neighbors. But Tom, what *are* you doing here? And the tulips! They're so lovely. I'm . . . well, they're lovely."

"Yeah, I just figured you were never going to invite me here, so I decided to come see the joint for myself. Pretty nice, Kiddo." His eyes roamed the small space. "But this paint job you got going here . . . what are you using, a nailbrush? And why'd you pick black?"

"It's not black. It's chocolate—"

"Yeah, whatever. You should have asked me to help."

"You? Paint?"

"Yeah, I'm a good painter. Whaddya think? I'm all thumbs, just 'cuz my name is Tom?" He gave a belly laugh, and it was contagious, lame joke or not.

I laughed along with him, long and hard, realizing just how much I needed that, just how tense I'd become over

Mavis and her murder. Soon I was laughing so hard I was crying. And then I was just crying.

"*Geez*. Don't go getting all mushy. What the hell is wrong with you?" I was now wrapped in Tom's warm bear hug, and he didn't let go.

I pulled myself away and took the white linen handkerchief from the top pocket of his jacket. I blew my nose hard into the crisp fabric.

"*Geez*." He stepped back, as if my nose had produced a nuclear blast.

"Stop saying that." I blew hard again. "Here." I handed him back the soiled and scrunched-up handkerchief.

"I don't want that back *now*."

"I'll send it out and have it laundered."

"See that you do." He took off his cashmere coat and tossed it onto the couch. Either he was planning to stay a while, or he was afraid I'd make the next blow on his sleeve. "Okay, let's have a real look at this place."

"The next tour is starting in fifteen minutes. Want a cup of coffee while you wait?" I figured I didn't need to worry about looking like a slacker, rolling into the office midmorning. After all, I was with the boss.

"You got any good coffee?"

"I have Folgers. Is that good enough?"

"Just make sure it's strong."

It was already made, of course, but in spite of having been sitting for hours, it was probably still not strong enough for him. I stepped into my tiny kitchen and poured him some, anyway. I handed him a red mug.

"Don't Mess With Texas," he read the words wrapped around it. "What the hell is this?"

"Remember that convention you sent me to in Houston? Couple of years ago? This is your gift. I never got around to giving it to you."

"Geez, Val, you don't spare any expense. And I thought you didn't care."

"Well, now you know. I think that says it all."

"Damn Texans."

My tears had dried up, and I took a seat on the end of the couch after removing the pile of sheets that Fletch had rearranged the night before. Tom sat down at the other end. My apartment seemed smaller than ever with him in it. Even when he was still, he seemed to take up all the space.

"Okay, so tell me. What are you really doing here?" Not that I cared. I felt happy just to have him in my home.

He took a sip of the coffee and then scrunched up his nose. "Did you hear me say strong? This is dishwater."

"Give it to me." I held out my hand. "I'll make you some more. You are such a pain."

But he kept his hand on the mug and then put it down on the coffee table in front of us. "I wanted to talk to you," he said.

"Okay." I had a sudden sinking feeling. Was it something about the job? Had the bottom fallen completely out of the real estate world while I was busy chasing down murderers? Tom showing up out of the blue, following his purple tulips, was so un-Tom-like that I steeled myself for bad news. Maybe *he* was Mavis's murderer, and he'd come to confess.

"It's about yesterday, about Celeste; you never finished your thought. You said you knew her type."

"I just meant she wasn't *my* type. And as you so wisely pointed out, she doesn't need to be *my* type."

"What the hell type is she? What were you trying to say?"

"I was trying to—well, I don't know what I was trying to say. Other than she isn't good enough for you. Yes, that's it precisely. She isn't good enough for you."

"Really? You aren't just saying that 'cuz I said the very same thing to you about Fletch?"

"No, but now that you mention it . . . look, forget what I said. If Celeste makes you happy, then I guess that's all I need to know. She does make you happy, right? Forget everything I said; I was babbling—"

"You're babbling now."

"Probably. Let me fix you some stronger coffee."

I started to rise, but he put his hand on my knee. "Wait. There's more."

"Okay." I sat back down, and he removed his hand. Again, the sinking feeling flooded my stomach.

"I asked Celeste to marry me."

I could hear the clock on the kitchen wall ticking; I could hear a dog barking somewhere; I could even hear the traffic whizzing by on Hunter Drive, almost two miles away.

"So, whaddya think?" He picked up the Texas mug and rubbed his fingers over its arrogant message.

"I think that's wonderful."

"You sound like you just found another dead body."

"That's not funny, Tom." I rose and went to the kitchen to pour the remains of the coffeepot down the drain. "I think I've got some French roast somewhere. Let me look." I began opening cupboards and banging them shut.

When I turned around, Tom was standing there. He had put his coat back on. "Not such a good idea?" he asked.

"No, a terrific idea. You love her, right? Because I assume you wouldn't ask her to marry you if you didn't. And why wouldn't you love her? She's gorgeous. And sophisticated. She buys you *Mozart's Greatest Hits*, for heaven's sake. Who wouldn't love that? It's sophisticated and generous—"

"You're babbling again."

"Am I? I'm sorry. Really, I am. And I think it's good news. And you love her, right?"

"Love?"

"Yeah, love; remember love?"

"I remember it. I remember what a pain in the ass it was. Who needs love at our age?" He began leafing through a stack of unopened mail I had lying on the kitchen counter. "You just don't want to be alone. You want someone to read in bed with, someone who likes the same TV shows, preferably someone who doesn't have a kid in jail and another in some damn religious sect, someone you can go to Vegas with and not have to entertain too much. What the hell else is there?"

I stared hard at him. "You really think that's all you need?"

"Hell yes. Don't you? And how old are these bills, anyway? Do you ever open your mail?"

"I'll open them when I'm ready to pay them. And no, I don't think that at all. I think I need more than someone to read in bed with."

"Lots o' luck with that." He turned to go.

"Wait." I didn't want him to leave. I had handled it badly. I had to save it. "Look, I found some French roast. Well, actually it's Columbian roast, but it probably tastes the same, right? How badly can the Columbians screw up coffee? They seem to do a good job with coke." I smiled. "You know, coke? Like cocaine? Isn't Columbia one great big cartel or something?" I was pulling open drawers, rummaging around for the can opener, panicky that he might leave before I salvaged the situation. "And what is a cartel, anyway? Is it like a big club or something—"

"Val. Stop."

"No, really, I want to make you some coffee; I just need to find the blasted can opener."

"It's right there," he said, pointing.

"Oh, right; look at that. If it had been a snake, it would have bitten me." My idiot's smile was replaced by my idiot's laugh. I placed the opener on the can and squeezed the handle, punching through the lid.

"Forget it." He shook his head. "I'll get some coffee at the office. I like the way Billie makes it best. And you better get to work too. It's late."

"No, no, wait. There's something else I have to say." I finished circling the rim of the can and ripped off the aluminum top, and a dot of bright-red blood appeared on the tip of my finger. "Damn," I said. "Just dammit. Okay, go; you can leave."

"It might be best, Kiddo." A smirk appeared on his face. "I don't want to witness any more domestic injuries. You could lose a finger with that thing, and I don't want to be responsible."

"You're really funny." I sucked on my finger. I doubted Celeste ever cut her finger opening a can. She probably bought the kind with the aluminum-foil pull-off lid, the kind sensible people buy. "Go; just go." I made a shooing gesture, and a tiny droplet of blood flew in his direction.

He turned toward the front door, then stopped. "But what was it you wanted to say? You said there was something else."

"Oh yes; I just wanted to say congrats, Tom. Really."

"*Congrats?* You think you could muster up the whole word?"

"Okay, congratulations. I am very happy for you."

I guided him to the front door, my finger back in my mouth. I could taste my own blood. And then Tom did another un-Tom-like thing. He took my finger out of my mouth and put it up to his lips and kissed it. It was such an intimate thing that I thought I might start crying again.

"Try not to kill yourself in that kitchen. I'd recommend a bag of Starbucks from now on."

And then he was gone.

I held my bloody finger and went to his handkerchief that still lay on the counter. I wrapped my finger in the clean part. It was beginning to throb, and I sat on the edge of my coffee table to nurse my wound. What was he *thinking*?

More important, what was *I* thinking? I didn't want Tom for myself; that much I knew. But at the same time, I didn't want anyone else to have him, either. Or at least not Celeste. I liked things the way they were, Tom all crunchy on the outside and soft and marshmallowy on the inside. I liked his late-night calls to check on me, and I liked knowing he was there if I needed him to come over and kill a spider.

What it came down to was that I don't like change. I'd just been through a major one, but oh boy, leaving David was nothing compared to losing Tom. And I knew instinctively Celeste just wasn't the type to share.

***

I arrived at work about an hour later with a Band-Aid wrapped too tightly around my finger. Perry informed me Tom was in his office and not to be disturbed, under any circumstances.

"Fine. I don't need to speak to the old buzzard, anyway." On the drive to the office, I had gone from mad to sorry to desperate-to-talk-him-out-of-it to mad again.

"If you have anything you must see Uncle Tom about, you can run it past me."

"Perry, if I want to speak to Tom, I will. You won't stop me. So shut up and leave me alone."

"Oh boy," he said, more to Billie, who was dispensing the day's mail, than to me. "Looks like someone is grumpy."

"Your daughter called." Billie dropped a pile of letters on my desk and ignored Perry. "I told her you'd call her back."

I had opened one envelope and was beginning to peruse its contents, when I realized Billie was still standing over me. I looked up and raised my eyebrows. I watched her gaze follow Perry as he sashayed out of the office, no doubt for a check in the restroom mirror, an hourly ritual for him.

When he was safely out of earshot, she returned her attention to me. "So, Val, how's your investigation going?"

"Billie, there is no—"

"Whatever. Listen to me. Before Perry gets back."

I knew right then I should suggest having lunch together. I should tell her to save her information until then so I could question her further. But of course I couldn't wait, so I remained silent.

"What do you know about Kit's husband, Larry James?" she asked.

"Billie, what the hell kind of question is that?"

"I saw him in the Lonstock Building yesterday."

CHAPTER SIXTEEN

S o? So what if Larry James was in the Lonstock Building?" I asked Billie. "Big whoop." But my mind was swirling. It *was* a big whoop, a very big whoop. And not only that Larry was in the Lonstock Building, but that Billie was there too. "First of all, what were *you* doing there?"

"Delivering a revised lease to Whitworth's," she said. "They're in the same building."

I let out an inward sigh of relief. Billie was probably doing Perry's job, since she rarely leaves our office; but if we were carrying on business with other tenants in the Lonstock Building, so could Larry. Before I could pitch this to her, Perry returned to the office, just as Tom came out of his. I grabbed my briefcase and opened it, planning to at least put on a show of working.

"Don't you think it's time to spring for a new lunch sack, Val?" Tom's voice boomed from over my shoulder, and I realized he'd spotted the bag of clues taken from

Mavis's house, the bag I was still carrying around in my briefcase.

And why was I? Was I afraid someone would steal it if I left it at home? "What?" I asked, deciding to play dumb.

"Looks like that sack's been around for decades. What've you got in there, some stale pretzels?"

"Nothing you'd be interested in," I said, pretty sure *that* was a lie.

***

It was Kit's idea that we go back to see Beatrice Woodstock. If for no other reason, we should give her the contents of the brown bag. It didn't seem right that we should hold on to them, and if we turned them over to anyone, it should be someone who had loved Mavis. How we would explain having them in the first place was no problem for Kit.

"We'll worry about that when it comes up," she said. So we arranged for me to pick her up after work and go to the Woodstock residence, unannounced, armed with our brown sack of goodies.

When I pulled up in front of Kit's house, she hurried down the pathway and into my car. Then she slammed the door shut, her mouth set in a grim line. "I'm so mad I could just spit." She glanced at the time on her Movado watch, as if we were late for a very important date.

"What happened?"

"Larry, that's what happened. Val, are you sure you saw a Mavis Woodstock file on his computer?"

"Pretty sure." I eased the car back out into the street.

"Pretty sure? What does that mean? Did you, or didn't you? Because Larry insists there is no such file, and of course I can't check because he's changed his password."

"I did. I'm certain it was there, Kit." I hated the implication that Larry was lying, since I love Larry almost as much as I do Kit. But I didn't like the idea that she thought I

159

was lying, either. I recalled the file name I saw on the screen as I leaned over Larry's shoulder, and I was sure I was right. Pretty sure.

"I don't know what to think," Kit said. "Did you have your glasses on?"

"No, Kit, I did not have them on, but I assure you I know Mavis Woodstock's name when I see it."

"Whatever."

In all the years we've been friends, Kit and I have never had a real argument. I have, however, put that down to my giving in and letting her infrequent bad moods work themselves out. Fortunately, it's never long before her usual good nature returns.

We drove in silence to Beatrice Woodstock's, and when we reached the gloomy house, I didn't stop, but drove slowly past it.

"What are you doing *now*?" Kit asked.

"Checking it out. There's a car parked in the driveway."

"That's right; you've got that great eyesight."

"Yes, and without glasses too. Aren't you proud of me? I guess I'll return the white cane." I came to a stop at a palatial brick house two doors down from Beatrice's and shut off the engine. "Look." I turned to face her. "I don't want to go in there if you are in a mood. I'm certain I saw that file on Larry's computer, but if he says there was no such file, then I'll go with that. Larry's not a liar, so let's forget it." This was not the time to tell her Billie saw Larry in the Lonstock Building, even if it was probably innocent.

"Larry's not a liar, my ass. He can lie just like the rest of us; don't kid yourself. Why else would he change his password? Huh? Tell me that. He's had the same password for years, so why suddenly change it?"

"Well, let's not worry about that right now. Let's figure out what we're going to tell Beatrice."

"I'm more interested in what she's going to tell us." Kit put her hand on my arm. "Sorry, Valley Girl. I'm mad at him, not you. Let's do this."

Fortified by her change of mood, I restarted my car, and we headed back to the Woodstock mansion.

The car parked in the driveway was a small Mercedes. Even though it was old and needed a wax job, it had an air of luxury compared to the cracked driveway. The Woodstocks neglected everything, including the family's only daughter.

I put my car in park and then grabbed the brown sack from the back seat. I shoved it into my shoulder bag, and we headed to the front door.

Within a few seconds of our ringing the bell, Hilary Woodstock appeared. And she didn't look happy to see us. "Yes?" Her bulky frame blocked the doorway. I again noticed the giant diamond ring, but it did little to enhance her frumpy brown wool skirt and the brown ruffled blouse that had made way too many trips to the washing machine.

"We're here to see Beatrice." Hilary couldn't intimidate Kit.

"She's resting."

"Really?" Kit raised her eyebrows.

"Yes, *really*. I'll tell her you came by. Next time, try calling first."

"It's rather urgent that we speak to Beatrice now." Kit sounded as if she'd come directly from Scotland Yard on official police business.

"I just told you, she's resting."

I wasn't sure what our next move would be. Maybe Kit would punch Hilary in the face, knocking her to the ground and stepping over her body to gain entrance to the house. But before Kit made use of brute force, a tiny figure appeared behind Hilary. It was Beatrice herself, and she squeezed in between her daughter-in-law and the door frame, reminding me of a child who has come to see her mother's visitors.

"Girls, how wonderful. Come in."

"Mother," Hilary said, "you know I have to leave now. I have an appointment."

"Yes, and what a shame." The elderly lady's watery eyes twinkled. "You'll miss visiting with Mavis's two girlfriends. But that's okay." Beatrice steered us toward the living room, which looked every bit as drab as I remembered it.

"You run along, Hilary dear. I'll see you tomorrow," Beatrice said to her daughter-in-law, who still stood in the doorway, not sure which way to turn. But Beatrice suddenly had a purse in her hand that seemed to appear from nowhere, and she handed it to Hilary.

I was surprised Hilary could be so easily pushed out. Whatever her appointment was, it must have been more pressing than monitoring our visit.

Beatrice gestured for us to sit on the couch, and she joined us in a neighboring chair. She wore a heavy navy-blue cardigan that looked hand-knitted. It partially covered a red cotton blouse that looked as if it had been vacationing in the washing machine along with Hilary's.

"She's a dear girl, really," Beatrice said, although I wasn't sure if she was trying to convince herself or us. "I am so glad to see you. Tell me everything. What have you found out?"

We both set our handbags on the floor by our feet and removed our coats, at the same time assuring Beatrice we didn't want any tea.

Kit crossed her legs and picked at a nonexistent piece of fluff on her wool pants. "First of all, I've spoken to the police, and it seems they are not interested in any verdict other than suicide."

"Fools." Beatrice took a tissue from the pocket of her baggy slacks and held it to her nose.

"And we did run into Will, quite by chance," Kit added. "He's very upset."

"Oh yes. Will loved his sister very much. They are, were, twins. Did I mention that?"

"Valerie has spoken to Ryan Fletcher," Kit said. "And he gave us a little insight into Mavis's life after she left Downers Grove."

I held my breath, not sure where Kit would go with this. I should have insisted we plan what we were going to say.

"Oh my," Beatrice said. "Ryan Fletcher. That was such a long time ago. You surely don't think he has anything to do with this, do you?"

"Beatrice," I said, "what did Mavis tell you about him?"

"Not a lot. They were married; I told you that. But for a very short time."

"You said he was a scoundrel."

"Did I? I've never even met the man, and Mavis didn't have too much to say about him. I wonder where I could have come up with that."

Oh great. The last thing we needed was to discover that Beatrice was fabricating what little information she had given us. "Did any of your sons meet him?" I asked.

"Only Will. Yes, that's it. Now I remember. Will did say that he met Ryan Fletcher, and he was a scoundrel. He might not have used that word, exactly, probably something much worse, but that's what he meant, I'm sure. I can't imagine where they met, but they did; I'm sure of it."

Beatrice, who had been focusing on Kit and me, suddenly looked over our heads to the entrance of the room. Her expression changed, and I thought for a minute the dreaded Hilary had returned. But it was even worse, I realized, when I turned my neck to see who was holding Beatrice's attention.

Lionel and his out-of-date suit stood in the doorway.

His mother said, "Lionel, what in the world are you doing home?"

"Hilary called me and said she had to leave. She didn't want you to be alone." He stepped into the room, and when he reached the couch, he bowed slightly before each of us. On anyone else, it might have been an elegant, stately gesture, like a courtier greeting a queen; two queens, in our case. But coming from Lionel Woodstock, it just creeped me out.

"I'm not alone. These are two of Mavis's old girlfriends, dear."

Lionel straightened and turned toward his mother. "I know who they are, Mother." He turned back to look down his nose at us, appearing about twelve feet tall. "You must excuse my mother," he said. "It's way past her bedtime."

"It's six thirty," Kit said. I wondered how she knew, since she hadn't looked at her watch, and the grandiose clock on the fireplace mantel had probably stopped working back in the late 1800s.

"Precisely," Lionel said. "We must maintain a very strict schedule." Then he partially cupped his hand over his mouth, as if to prevent his mother from hearing. "We get very confused if we don't stick to the schedule."

Not to be outdone, Kit cupped her hand partly over her own mouth and whispered to me, "Does she get up at three in the morning?"

"So it's very nice of you to visit, but I must insist that you leave. Perhaps the next time you would like to visit, you could telephone first."

I rose; it seemed the only thing to do. Kit sighed and did the same. Beatrice remained seated, looking confused, but I gave her a kiss on the cheek, and Kit followed my lead.

"We'll call you, and perhaps we would be permitted to take you to lunch," she said. Beatrice nodded, but I wasn't sure she heard Kit.

I looked over at Lionel, who was already standing at the entrance of the room, his arm outstretched like a doorman in a fancy hotel ushering the riffraff out. We slipped into our coats and gathered our purses, and he led us to the front door. When he opened it, a rush of cool air blew into the house, and I dug into my pockets in search of my gloves.

"Good of you to call. Do give my regards to Tom Haskins," he said.

The mention of Tom's name gave me a sudden burst of bravado, as if he were standing behind me urging me to take my best shot. "One other thing. On the phone, when we first spoke, uh . . . you mentioned that Mavis was living in Florida."

"What about it?"

"Well, it's just that you seem to have lost touch with her. I just wondered how you knew she was living in Florida."

"I know a lot of things. And I know that the whereabouts of my family is *my* concern, not yours. Do I make myself clear?"

I nodded, as if he'd just satisfied any doubts I might have about his character and I thought he really should consider running for office. I stepped across the threshold before Kit did, but not before I heard her say, "Lionel, have you heard anything from Sean?"

I thought my heart had stopped beating, and when I turned, Kit and Lionel were staring each other down, like a Rottweiler and a poodle—Kit, of course, being the poodle.

After a brief silence Lionel smiled and said, "Sorry. I don't know any Sean."

Kit returned his smile, and I noticed how white her teeth were compared to Lionel's yellow chompers. "Mavis's son. Your nephew. I just wondered if you had heard from him lately."

"Once again, I'm sorry, but you are mistaken. I do not have any nephews. And Mavis certainly never had a son."

"Oh yes—"

"And one other thing while I have your attention. I understand one of you ladies made a visit to the police. Now, while your interest in Mavis's death is certainly understandable, since you claim to have been such great friends, I do not appreciate your discussing my family's business with the authorities. In fact, I insist you leave my family alone. Please don't come back to see my mother, and please discontinue this . . . this . . . witch hunt you seem to have undertaken."

"But—"

"Good evening."

"Wait!"

But before Kit was cut off for a third time, I took her arm and pulled her to my side of the threshold. And then the door slammed shut.

"Wow," Kit said, when we were buckled in the front seat of my car. "Wow, fucking wow. Did you see his face? That was awesome." Once more I was struck by the greatest difference between Kit and me: I wanted to throw up; she thought it was awesome.

When my stomach returned to its proper location in my body, I spoke. "Why did you do that? Why on earth would you ask him that?"

"Why not? And he knows; couldn't you tell? He knows, all right."

"But Kit, why tell him like that? What if he didn't know?"

"Trust me, he knew already, and I just want to give him something to think about when he's tucked into his coffin for the night."

"But what did you gain by that? I don't understand."

She rolled her eyes. "Don't you get it? Now he knows that *we* know too."

I still didn't understand what ground we had gained, but Kit had a broad smile on her face. I assumed she was already hatching our next plan of attack. The brown sack, in the meantime, still lay in my purse. And that was just as well. It might not have been the best time to unload it on Beatrice.

Kit suggested we stop for a drink somewhere, and that sounded like a good idea.

We were no sooner seated at El Palenque, a Mexican restaurant close to her house, than she pulled a pen out of her purse and began writing on a napkin, even before the margaritas served in glasses the size of fish bowls were placed before us. I sipped my drink through a straw and watched as she scribbled down what we needed to do, as easily as if she were preparing a grocery list.

"By the way, Valley Girl," she said, not looking up from her notes, "that was a brilliant move you made back there."

I stopped sipping. "Me? What move did I make?"

"Asking Lionel how he knew Mavis was in Florida. I never even thought about that little gem."

"Ah." I took a long sip. "I don't know where that came from. But what did you think about his answer?"

She tapped the end of her pen on her chin. "It makes sense, ya know. Really, perfect sense. He *would* make it his business to find out where she was. He wouldn't want little sis making a surprise visit back to town, what with her controlling the company and all. I'm sure he loved having her safely tucked away in another state. And shaking her butt every night for the local perverts kept her out of trouble. At least the kind of trouble *Lionel* cared about."

"Yes. But when she *did* come back, his little empire was in great danger of crumbling before his beady eyes."

"Exactly. A threat like that might even make a person want to do something very bad. Although not a person as warm and fuzzy as Lionel, of course."

If it hadn't been so gruesome, or if we had been discussing a movie we'd both seen, we might have laughed. But instead, we both shuddered.

Then Kit returned to her list. "I still need to find out what the hell Larry is doing with a Mavis file. And what the hell's in it. And then we have to somehow contact Sean."

"Sean? How do we do that? And more important, what do we say? Er, Sean, you don't know us, but we were slight acquaintances of your mother about a hundred years ago, and by the way, we think she was murdered?"

"Exactly."

CHAPTER SEVENTEEN

I was getting ready for bed when my phone rang. I hoped it was Emily. I hadn't had a chance to return her phone call, and I was ready to have a long conversation that didn't involve the Woodstocks, illegitimate sons, or murder.

But it was Tom.

"So I heard you made a little house call this evening," he said.

I could hardly believe what I was hearing. Had Lionel Woodstock called him? How else would Tom know we had been there? But just in case he didn't, I remained silent.

When I didn't respond, he spoke again. "I just got off the phone with Lionel Woodstock."

I *had* to speak then, to tell him our side of the story (whatever that was). I felt like a teenager explaining to an angry parent how the car got dented. "Okay, okay," I said. "I stopped by—"

"*You* stopped by? I heard you had your nut-job friend with you."

"Okay, so Kit was with me. But it was very spur-of-the-moment. I had a few personal items of Mavis's from her house, and I only wanted to return them to her mother. It was no big deal, and really, Tom, I resent—"

"What? What do you resent?"

"I resent your implication that there was something wrong or sinister about returning Mavis's things to her mother. I, we, did nothing wrong. And for your information, your pal Lionel showed up before I could even properly speak to Mrs. Woodstock. And he asked us to—no, he *threw* us out of the house. Clearly, he didn't want either one of us to speak to her. He may be a business client of yours, ours, but I don't see that—"

"Way to go!"

"Really?"

"Yeah, really. I was proud of you girls, ruffling that son of a bitch's feathers."

"Oh. Well, it wasn't really me, more Kit."

"Yeah, that's what I figured."

I felt slighted to be considered the wimpier of the crime-fighting team, but I couldn't deny it. Then something occurred to me. "By the way," I said, "how well is Lionel connected in this city?"

"What do you mean?"

"Well, for instance, would he have any influence with, say, the police? I mean more so than a regular person?"

"Do you mean do the police look the other way when he parks that boat of his illegally?"

"Well, I was thinking something a bit deeper than that."

I heard Tom sigh before he responded. "Val, Val, Val . . . he's got money. People with money can influence anyone they want. They live in a different world than schmucks like you and me."

"Well, you have money—"

"Not that kind, I don't."

"They're really that rich?"

"Yeah, they're really that rich."

"Well, I'm glad you're not mad at us—at me."

"Nope. You're not the only one who likes to ruffle feathers, Kiddo."

We said good-bye, and I hung up. I was still smiling when the phone rang again.

I could hear Tom's bellow before I'd even had a chance to say hello.

"Why the hell were you asking about Lionel being connected? You haven't been to the police, have you? Val, tell me you—"

"Relax." Suddenly I was really glad Kit had dealt with the police alone, so I didn't have to lie to Tom. "No, I haven't been to the police. You know me better than that."

"Good; make sure you keep it that way."

***

"Mom, Mom, I got another job."

I glanced at the clock by my bed, just as the red numerals turned to six minutes after five. I had answered the phone immediately, not giving myself a chance to worry that something terrible had happened somewhere to someone I love.

"Em?"

"Were you sleeping? Guess what I'm doing. Go on, guess. Oh, you'll never guess; I'll tell you. It's a movie, a real movie, and guess who's in it? Go on, guess."

"I'm sure I can never guess." I eased myself up to a sitting position in the dark bedroom.

"*Matt Damon*. It's a mystery-type thing starring Matt Damon and I'm not sure who else. But probably someone else as good. Mom, I'm sorry if I woke you, but Luke and I just got home from a party. It was at an agent's house, with all sorts of people there. Hollywood types, real movie people. Agents, writers, actors, the whole works."

"Slow down, honey," I said, catching her excitement and not wanting to miss anything. "First, tell me about the commercial. Is that done?"

"Oh, that. Yes, it'll air in the next couple of months. I'll tell you when. But this movie—I mean, it's not a speaking part or anything; it's more of an extra role. I'll be in the background on the phone in a railway station, but the money is good for a day's work, and Matt Damon is in the scene."

"That's great, darling. Really, well done." Then I had a thought. "Say, Em, this party you were at? You say there were agents there?"

"Yeah, like I said, the whole works."

Sean's book had been published by a New York publisher I'd never heard of, but I recalled his acknowledgements on the first page. He had thanked an agent from Los Angeles, Sally Someone-or-Other from Truth Be Told, for all her encouragement and hard work. While Emily prattled on about the glamour of the movie industry, I debated mentioning the agent's name.

"He's such a good actor, not to mention hot. *Luke*." Her voice cut away as she argued with her husband about the hotness of Matt Damon. "He is hot; you know he is. Mom, Luke doesn't think he's so hot."

"He's the hottest," I said. But I was only half listening.

"Mom, are you falling back to sleep?"

"No, sorry, I was just thinking of something else."

"Something else?" I hadn't heard her sound so disappointed since she'd lost her bid for the sorority she wanted to join.

"Sorry, Em, but I was just wondering . . . were any literary agents at the party?"

"A bunch. Why?"

"Have you ever run across an agency called Truth Be Told?"

"Sounds weird, Mom. What are you up to?"

I pulled the duvet around my shoulders, debating what to say. This was where I had to lie to my daughter, but hey, where did she get her acting skills in the first place? "I'm on the verge of a big sale back here, but there's a lien against the house, apparently by this Sally person from Truth Be Told. I'd like to get in touch with her, but it's proving difficult. I do know she's out in LA somewhere."

I held my breath for Em's reply, but of course she didn't doubt her mother's truthfulness. "Do you know her last name?"

"It's at the office. Can I e-mail it to you?"

"Yes, do that. Luke can find her. He can find anyone on the Internet."

"Okay, honey, I'll do it when I get to work. And really, congratulations. Should I start shopping for a dress to wear to the Oscars?"

"I'll be getting mine at Tar-jay." She giggled. "Jewels by Monsieur Walton."

"Sounds divine, dahling. Give Matt a kiss for me. And Luke too."

***

I called Kit on my drive to work, first relaying the previous night's conversation with Tom. "I can't believe he was on our side," I said. "That man . . . he can be so tough, but then he can do the softest or most supportive thing. And he's actually *proud* of us. He—"

"Geez, you two should get a room."

"Who?"

"You and Lionel. Duh. I mean you and Tom, of course."

"I'm so sure." I changed the subject, telling her about my conversation with Emily.

"Good thinking, Valley Girl. Hold on; let me get the book right now." Kit had forgotten the agent's name mentioned in the front of Sean's book, too, an all-too-common fiftysomething foible. "Okay, here it is," she said at last. "Sally Stapleton."

"Okay." With no way to write it down while I was driving, I logged it into my brain. A combination of *All in the Family* stars Sally Struthers and Jean Stapleton. What fiftysomething couldn't remember that?

I told her about Emily's big role with Matt Damon, and she was impressed. Then my thoughts returned to Sally Stapleton. "Let's hope Luke is really the whiz Emily thinks he is," I said.

"He's so hot," Kit said.

"*Kit!* That's my son-in-law you're drooling over."

"Not Luke, dummy. Matt Damon. But Luke ain't so bad, either."

***

When I got to the office, I composed an e-mail to Emily and Luke. Then it occurred to me that if Luke was such a whiz and could locate Sally, he could probably locate Sean Fletcher too.

I added his name to the e-mail.

I felt I'd done almost a full day's work in the five minutes it took me to ensnare my child and her husband in the web of lies I was creating. Leaning back in my chair, I felt, rather than saw, Billie staring at me from her desk behind me. I whirled around to face her.

"Any luck with the Woodstock house?" she asked, before taking a sip of coffee.

"Not yet. I haven't even shown it."

"It's such a cute house; I can't imagine it will take long."

"Hmm." I closed my e-mail page.

"Great for a young couple or empty nesters," Billie said. "Good-size kitchen. Some of these older houses have such tiny kitchens, but that one is a nice size."

"Sure is." How did *Billie* know so much about the kitchen? She rarely, if ever, sees any properties. "Er, Bill, do you think there are enough cabinets?"

She smiled at me over her cup. "Dunno, Val, not having actually been there myself. I only go by the specs."

"Of course." I forced a smile in return.

"Been where?" We both looked toward the door as Tom filled the entrance to the office.

"I was just asking Val if she'd had any bites on the Woodstock house," Billie said. She headed toward the kitchenette to make the boss some fresh coffee.

"Yeah, about that. Val, in my office. Right now."

I hurried after Tom and took his suit coat that he foisted on me, presumably to hang up for him like a butler in his service.

"The house is off the market," he said. "Pull it from the listings."

"What? Why?"

"Doesn't matter why; just pull it."

"But I thought—"

"Never mind what you thought. Pull it."

"Tell me why." I plunked down in the chair across from his desk and crossed my arms around my chest, like a child who'd just been told she couldn't stay up late.

Tom gave an exaggerated sigh, like that child's parent about to explain the benefits of going to bed early. "Okay. Here's the thing. Apparently, Lionel, who wanted the house for sale in the first damn place, is not the owner. It doesn't belong to him. Seems a will has surfaced, and Mavis left it to someone other than her mother or brother."

"And let me guess who she left it to."

"Go on, genius. Tell me what you think you know."

I returned his smirk. "Well, I bet she left it to Sean Fletcher. Right?"

A smile spread over his face, causing a corresponding batch of goose bumps to spread over my arms. "Wrong," he said.

I remained speechless. Who would Mavis leave her house to, if not her son? "Okay," I said, with what little wind I had left in my sails escaping overhead. "Who is it?"

Tom opened his top drawer and pulled out a fat cigar. Extracting it from its metal tube, he twirled it in his fingers like a majorette warming up. Then he held it to his lips, and I wasn't sure what he was looking more forward to, lighting up or sharing with me who the lucky beneficiary was.

"If you don't tell me in the next two seconds, Tom Haskins, I'm going to yank that cigar out of your mouth and stuff it someplace else."

He burst out laughing. "Good one, Kiddo. Okay, the new owner of the house, after probate and all that shit, will be none other than . . . drum roll, please . . . Hilary Woodstock. How about that?"

***

I had to call Kit immediately. Like I'd found some giant missing piece of a puzzle and had to share it with my accomplice before she started pounding the wrong piece into an empty spot to make it fit.

"Wow. We gotta talk to Hilary," Kit said.

"Right away. But do we even know where she and Marcus live?"

"Don't need to; doesn't she spend every waking moment watching over Beatrice like a Doberman pinscher?"

"Good point. But Kit, let's please call first." I wasn't ready to confront Hilary's icy reception again so soon. I hung up after promising Kit I would call Hilary and set up a time. I dreaded the task but believed I would handle it better than Kit.

For the rest of the morning I made Tom proud by doing what he actually hires me to do. I placed a few phone calls on behalf of Haskins Realty and made a dent in the growing paperwork I had neglected during the past few days. Feeling like a productive member of the real estate community once again, I gave Billie ten bucks when she left at lunchtime to bring me back a tuna sandwich from Quiznos.

Since I was the only one in the office, after Tom and Perry left for their respective lunch dates, I was in charge of the phone. I was busy doodling and pondering the best way to approach the formidable Hilary when it rang. "Haskins Realty," I said.

"Valerie? This is Hilary Woodstock." It was one of those moments when you aren't sure if you should thank God or blame the devil.

I crumpled up the page of my doodles, as if Hilary could somehow see them through the phone line. "Hilary! How good to hear from you," I said. I sounded as grateful as if she were calling to sell me Girl Scout cookies just when my Caramel deLites habit needed a fix.

"I wonder if we could meet," she said, as if we were old pals. "Would that be possible? Perhaps you and your friend could spare me a little time?"

"Shuuuuur." I tried to push the image of our previous encounters with the Ice Queen way, way out of my mind. "That would be great. What's good for you?"

"Actually, I'm always tied up in the daytime looking after my mother-in-law, and Marcus and I have plans for tonight. But I could meet you gals tomorrow at, say, six o'clock, somewhere for a drink, perhaps?" Hilary's referring to Kit and me as *gals*, as if we were sorority sisters, was as ludicrous as the idea of meeting her in a bar for a few belts during Happy Hour. But I worked with what I had.

"Sounds like fun," I said.

"Great. There's a place called Dexter's on Olsen and Main; do you know it? It's next to Barnes & Noble. Wanna meet me there tomorrow, then? Let's say six thirty, to be on the safe side?"

I almost told her that would be heaven, but even with our newfound best-friend status, that would be going a little too far. So instead, I told her I'd call Kit and we'd see her at Dexter's the following night.

***

After a slow Sunday afternoon at the office—made slower by the fact that I couldn't concentrate on something as mundane as selling houses when I had a murder to solve—Kit and I arrived at Dexter's at six o'clock, mainly so I could have a strong drink before Hilary arrived.

The best that could be said about the place was that it was dark. There were a few customers sitting at the bar, the singles and unhappily marrieds who just didn't want to be home on a Sunday evening.

Kit and I seated ourselves at one of the empty tables for four at the back of the room, where we had a good view of the door.

"I wonder if we'll have to ask her about the will or if she'll just tell us," I said. I had, of course, filled Kit in on the will.

"Val, don't sweat it. She called us, ya know."

"I know, but she was so bitchy the last time we saw her. I don't trust her, although maybe her good fortune has softened her up."

"Just remember that she *was* a bitch, so don't go falling for any crap."

At exactly six thirty the Budweiser sign hanging on the back of the wooden entrance clattered as the door swung open, and Hilary appeared. She spotted us and waved, as though we three met on a regular basis for a girls' night out.

"Hello," Hilary said. She took off her leather coat, which looked as if it had been removed from its rightful owner back in the 1960s, and arranged it across the back of the vacant chair. Pulling down her tweed skirt, she took a seat as she eyed our cosmopolitans.

"What are you girls drinking?" she asked. "Do they still sell manhattans? I used to drink those all the time, but honestly, I haven't been to a bar for years." She waved her left hand in the air, signaling the waitress, and the glint from her huge diamond caught the light of the neon St. Pauli Girl sign over her head.

"Your ring is magnificent," I said.

"Oh, this?" She smiled, turning her hand to examine it. "It is lovely, isn't it? It belonged to my mother."

That was no surprise since it was hard to imagine a Woodstock man springing for a piece of jewelry that must surely have cost twenty thousand dollars. I wondered if Beatrice's ring had come from *her* mother.

The waitress appeared, and Hilary ordered her manhattan and refills for Kit and me. Once the drinks had been placed on the table, Hilary waited for the waitress to disappear before she continued. "So you are probably wondering why I wanted to meet."

"You bet," Kit said.

I glanced at my friend, taking in her Prada suit and Mikimoto pearls, realizing how they made Hilary's outfit look all the cheaper.

Then I noticed for the first time that even with her outdated clothes, there was a certain something about Hilary. In the dim light of Dexter's, in spite of her excess weight and frumpy hairstyle, she exuded a touch of class, the kind that comes naturally—you either have it or you don't, and no one can take it away from you, not even the Woodstocks.

"Okay," Hilary said. "Let me start right off by saying that I know I probably sounded like a—"

"Bitch?" Kit said, and I kicked her under the table.

Hilary gave a short laugh. "Okay, I'll give you that. And I do apologize. But I didn't really like you two, right from the get-go. In fact, I was rather suspicious. What were you doing? Why had you suddenly appeared, claiming to be old friends of Mavis's?" She punctuated each question with a dramatic hand gesture. "I don't recall Mavis ever mentioning you two. In fact, from what Mavis told me, she never had any friends in high school."

"Yeah, we get it. We weren't exactly doing each other's hair every Saturday night," Kit said. "But we did know Mavis, and we did like her."

Hilary didn't challenge that. Instead, she took a long sip of her drink and continued her story. "Mavis and I really *were* good friends . . ."

CHAPTER EIGHTEEN

When Hilary finished what she had to say, she peered at her watch and gasped. Certainly no Movado like Kit's—in fact, probably a cheap brand she'd purchased at Walmart—the watch looked absurd against the giant diamond on her finger. But it obviously worked, and like a teenager past her curfew, she expressed dismay at how late it was and bolted out of Dexter's.

Kit and I ordered another cosmopolitan and a coffee, respectively, and then remained speechless until we'd been served. "Well, what do you think?" I asked, before taking a sip from the cup that was so large it guaranteed my coffee would be cold long before I finished drinking it. Give me a 1980s-size cup any day over the large vessels currently in vogue.

Kit didn't answer me as she sipped her own beverage, undoubtedly still pondering Hilary's presentation.

"As I'm sure you can imagine," Hilary had said, "I wasn't exactly welcomed into the Woodstock family with open arms."

She'd met Marcus in college, she told us, at DePaul. It was the only period in his life, at least in the thirty-three years she'd known him, that he'd seemed *normal*.

"He didn't act like a Woodstock in college," Hilary said, sounding like someone who had been duped on a lemon of a car.

"What do you mean *like a Woodstock*?" I suppressed a giggle as the Woodstock bird from the Peanuts cartoon suddenly flashed into my mind. Under different circumstances, it would have been one of those moments where I kicked Kit's leg under the table to be sure she got the joke. But her face was set as grim as a prosecutor's at a murder trial.

"In twenty-five words or less, they are tight: tightly knit, tightly wound, and tightfisted." Without being asked to, Hilary elaborated. "They really don't trust anyone but another Woodstock, which makes it increasingly difficult for them to function in a world with fewer Woodstocks in it all the time. And they're pathologically frugal, a condition that's contagious no matter how much you despise it."

"You said you and Mavis were friends?" I asked. "How and when did that come about?"

"When Marcus took me home to meet the family," she said, her tone giving the age-old phrase a note of irony, if not bitterness. "Mavis and Beatrice were the only ones who were kind to me, especially when the men weren't around. Beatrice is a sweet lady; she really is. And Mavis is, was, a lovely person. I'm not talking about looks; I'm talking about what was inside." She tapped her left hand over her heart, and her huge diamond blinked in agreement.

For the first time, I noticed a sadness in Hilary, as if she really had lost a good friend.

She stirred the ice in her manhattan. "I'll miss Mavis so much. She was the only friend I had. How sad is that?"

I nodded in agreement and almost grabbed Kit's hand in recognition of *our* friendship. But from the look on Kit's face, I could tell she was thinking Mavis's death was a lot harder on *Mavis* than on Hilary.

"Okay," Kit said, "you and Mavis were buddies, but what about the men?"

"Not thrilled to welcome me into the family, to say the least."

"What about Will?" I remembered thinking Will had seemed decent.

She ignored my question and continued. "Marcus and I had already married. He was adamant we get married before his family knew anything about me or our plans. We got married in a chapel on campus with only my parents and a couple of my friends. So his family wasn't exactly jumping up and down with delight when we showed up."

"Lionel?" I asked pointedly, giving her a chance to confirm that he was indeed the bastard he seemed.

"He's bad, like their father. Their father was a cruel man. Even his making Mavis majority shareholder was a mean trick he played on his sons. In those days Lionel was merely his puppet, like all his children, really, and I hoped when the old man passed away, things might improve a bit in that household. But Lionel assumed his father's reign, and if anything, he's worse."

"Why did you stay in such a hostile environment?" I asked.

"Good question." Hilary took a sip of her drink. "For one thing, I loved—love—Marcus. He's a good man, despite everything his family has put him through. And to be honest, my own family wasn't exactly the Waltons, if you know what I mean. I think the happiest I ever made my parents was when I got married and moved away."

As pitiful as Hilary's story sounded, we wanted to know *Mavis's* story. So I was glad, if a bit uncomfortable, when Kit asked, "About Mavis, just how much, er, just what do you know about her life since she first left Downers Grove?"

"Everything. I know everything." Hilary looked Kit squarely in the eyes.

She told us, as Will had, that Mavis left Downers Grove when it became obvious her family wasn't going to support her in school *or* the family business. Even Marcus, in spite of his wife's pleas to help, had done nothing. Only Will, apparently, had stood up for her—to no avail.

Hilary also reported, not surprisingly, that Mavis refused to buck Lionel and her father. That was decades ago, Hilary pointed out. She paused a moment as if to search her memory. "A year after Mavis graduated from high school, that's when she left Downers Grove. Ironically, she ended up owning a majority of the business after their dad died, but by then she'd disappeared. By the time she found out, she didn't really need the money and didn't want to come back. Not that Lionel, at least, didn't expect her to pounce any minute."

I noticed Kit's eyes beginning to glaze over, and she even yawned. I didn't know whether it was from her cosmopolitan or if it was body language for *tell me something I don't know.*

"She got a job in a plastic surgeon's office. I think she got hired because the doctor figured he could get her cheap by throwing in some free work. Maybe he wanted a guinea pig."

I recoiled at the metaphor as Hilary continued. She said Mavis had sent her photos of her new self and wrote of her brief marriage to Fletch. Later, Mavis wrote of her overwhelming feeling of unworthiness that sabotaged the marriage. "I guess she was still the same Mavis with no self-esteem, after all," Hilary said. "But I didn't dream she'd go from marriage to dancing and . . . other stuff."

"Why do you think she told you about that . . . stuff?" I asked. "I mean, she was in Florida; she didn't have to let you know."

Hilary was silent for a moment, as if considering that question for the first time. "I suppose we all need someone to talk to, confess to, don't we? And I'd always been open with Mavis. Our friendship was not one-sided. I didn't just help her. She helped me too. Plus, I was the only link to her mother. She knew she could trust me to look after her. And I kept Mavis up to date on Beatrice."

"Did you know Mavis had a son?" Kit made it sound like a challenge, as if she felt she had some information that Hilary did not.

But yes, Hilary also knew Mavis was raising a son named Sean. She hastened to add that she didn't know who his father was. "It's absolutely irrelevant, anyway," she said. "Whoever he was, he was not in Mavis's life. Or Sean's."

I looked at Kit. Her raised eyebrows told me she and I were wondering the same thing. *Why do I feel she's trying to head us off at the pass?*

"I promised Mavis I would raise Sean if anything ever happened to her, though I never knew how I'd pull that off with Marcus. He refused to even have kids of our own, let alone raise . . . a sibling's son . . ."

"Hilary," Kit said, "when did Mavis come back to Downers Grove and buy a house? And why?"

"Oh, that was years ago, in the eighties. She had me buy the house for her, as a safety net for Sean, in case she ever died. Kind of an investment, or even a guaranteed roof over his head. I mean, she paid for it, but I did all the legwork and stuff so she wouldn't have to come back here."

"So she wasn't living in the house?"

"Not until this year. It was rented out for all those years before that, most of the time to an elderly couple who took good care of the place. I had a rental agency handle everything. Once in a while I'd drive by to check it out, just to see that everything was being kept up, to protect Mavis's investment."

"And she left it to you in her will," Kit said.

"Now look, if you think there was any funny stuff going on, you are dead wrong. When Mavis had her will drawn up, she told me her plan to leave the house to me. It was with the understanding that I would keep it for Sean—in case he ever needed it or wanted it. But . . ."

"But?" Kit said.

"Okay, it was kind of a safety net for me too. You have to understand, Lionel runs that family. If anything ever happens to Marcus, I'll be out on my ear. But to be honest, after all these years, and with Mavis living there now, I forgot about the house coming to me if anything . . . er, happened to Mavis. I was almost shocked when the will was read. Although not nearly as shocked as Lionel. He was fit to be tied. It was nice to have the upper hand for once."

"Did she say why she came back to live in the house?" Kit asked.

Hilary waved a hand in the air. "Oh, she wanted to be closer to her mother. Beatrice is getting older and not in the best of health. I think she wanted to spend whatever time she had left with her. Also . . ."

"Also?" Kit said.

"Let's be honest. The kind of lifestyle Mavis had chosen for herself was long since over. That couldn't go on forever, could it? I mean, if you are making your living being attractive to men, eventually you're going to run out of time. Mavis was still attractive, but she could hardly compete with those young kids, could she?"

I felt a sick churning in my stomach at the facts of Mavis's seedy lifestyle. "So are you saying she sort of retired?"

Hilary looked at me. "She'd stopped doing whatever it was she was doing, yes, if that's what you mean. Everything was aboveboard when she was back in Downers Grove. She had a little money; she was planning to spend a quiet life here, taking care of her mother."

"Hilary, are you shocked by her . . . what she did?" I asked.

"Of course not. I don't judge. You do what you have to do to get by."

For the first time, I felt a smidgen of respect for Hilary.

"And what about Sean?" Kit asked. "Do you know where he is?"

"No idea. Mavis lost contact with him when he was twenty or so. He just took off. She was heartbroken, of course, as any mother would be. But their relationship was, as far as I could tell, very rocky, to say the least. Of course I've tried to find him since all this happened, to let him know he does have a family in Illinois, but I've not had any luck."

I doubted her efforts to find her nephew. After all, if we had located his memoir so easily on Google, how hard could it be?

"Did any of the uncles know about Sean?" I asked, presenting one of the many pieces of the puzzle that still needed a home.

Hilary shook her head. "Absolutely not. I had to promise never to say anything. She didn't even tell her husband—ex-husband."

"And yet she told you."

Hilary nodded.

"One other thing," I said, the Realtor in me refusing to let the house go. "Mavis contacted me to put the house on the market. She sounded so anxious, but then she abruptly changed her mind. Why do you think she did that?"

Hilary looked down at her half-finished drink and swished the melting ice around in the glass. "She had the idea that maybe Beatrice could move in with her. The poor old lady is miserable living with Lionel. Who wouldn't be? Mavis thought she should find something a little bigger and farther away. She was always worried that Lionel would find out where she lived, so once she'd made her mind up to sell, she wanted to do it quickly. But as for why she changed her mind, I have no idea. She never discussed that with me."

"You think Beatrice would have been allowed to live with her daughter?"

"If you mean because of Lionel, he has no great love for his mother. He'd probably be thrilled to get rid of her."

I thought about Beatrice's telling me how her little trip to Florida had to be in secret, as if Lionel wouldn't want her to go. Was that just an old lady's fantasy, and *would* Lionel really have been glad to unload his mother?

"Hmm . . . I don't know if Beatrice has told you or not," Kit said, "but she—and we—suspect foul play in Mavis's death. Since you were her friend—her best friend— I'm sure you want to help us get to the bottom of it. And Hilary, what we think—correct me if I'm wrong, Valerie— what we think is that if we find out who Sean's father is, it might shed light on why she was murdered."

"Maybe," Hilary said, "but I really don't think it has any significance."

And then her cheap watch told her it was time to go.

"So, what do you think?" I asked Kit again now. "Hilary was very honest."

Kit stared intently into her drink. "You think so?"

"Well—"

"I wonder why she wanted this little meeting. Why make such an effort and then not give us anything really new?"

"You don't believe her?"

"What's not to believe? She never revealed anything of great importance, ya know. Seems it was more of a pity party for Hilary than for Mavis. Did you notice how she painted such a fine picture of herself?"

"Yeah, you're right. Do you think it has anything to do with the will and her little inheritance? I mean, the day after the house is pulled off the market and we discover she's the owner, she turns from superbitch into . . . well, almost normal. For a Woodstock."

"Good point."

"Well, maybe Luke will have something to tell us about Sean soon," I said.

And indeed he did.

***

I knew I wouldn't go right to sleep when I got home, so I didn't even try. Instead, I finally unpacked my computer and set it up on the counter that separated my kitchen and living room. Maybe I'd have an e-mail from Luke and some answers—answers that wouldn't just bring more questions, for a change.

Marveling at the wonders of modern technology—did the youth of today take them for granted? *I* never would—I watched while four new messages were delivered. And I felt as happy as a schoolgirl finding a note from a boyfriend in her locker when I saw the name Lucas appear in my in-box. I clicked on his message.

Is this what you want, Val? I found this phone number for a Sally Stapleton. And it's probably the right one because it's the same number I found for one Sean Fletcher.

I read the ten-digit number over and over, as if it held the solution to my murder mystery. And then I *cursed* modern technology and caller ID's ability to thwart my making an anonymous call. I thought there was a way around it, like dialing something else first that would keep my number from showing on Sean's—and Sally's—caller ID screen.

But I didn't know how to do it, so I put my pajamas on and crawled under my duvet for what I figured would be a mostly sleepless night.

***

The next morning, after a hurried cup of coffee and slice of toast at home, I called Kit from the car as I drove toward my office. I had to run an errand on my way and was excited to tell her about it. I expected her to sound sleepy since it wasn't yet seven thirty and she has the stay-at-home-wife luxury of getting up whenever she damn well pleases. But her response surprised me.

"Hey," I said. "Sorry to call so early, but I've got a million things to do today, and I wanted to tell you about this e-mail I got from—"

"Forget about that. Where are you? Never mind; just get over here and pick me up. We've got to get over to the Lonstock Building as early as possible."

"What's going on?"

"I've been thinking. We've got to talk to Marcus without any of the others around. And the only way I can think of is intercepting him at the office. We can assume he goes there every day, and hopefully we'll avoid The Phantom of the Opera."

"Phantom? What are you talking—"

"Lionel, dum-dum. We'll just wait in the lobby and pray that Marcus shows up alone."

"Oh, *right*. A good plan. Should we throw a blanket over his head and force him into the ladies' restroom?"

"Fun-ee. If we don't catch Marcus alone, we'll come up with something else. But I have a good feeling about this."

She hung up, and I changed course, heading toward her house. Never mind that I really did have a million things to do, all related to Haskins Realty except for my one quick but important errand. And never mind that if I didn't start pulling my weight a little more around the office, I'd be looking for another job instead of a murderer.

I just prayed that Kit's feeling foretold *quick* as well as good.

***

At eight fifteen we were seated on a small marble bench across from the elevator in the lobby of the Lonstock Building. Not surprisingly, a crowd of workers formed in groups near the two elevator doors, waiting to be dispatched to their respective floors and subsequently to their desks.

"Kit, this is crazy. I don't know if I'll recognize him, even if he does show up."

"We'll recognize him, all right; he'll be the one who looks like a homeless man."

"What if he's with Lionel?" The thought of confronting *him* so early in the morning terrified me, but I knew Kit probably hoped for such an encounter. I didn't have to worry about Lionel, however. In the next moment, the glass doors swung open, and there was our mark—or Marc*us*, to be more accurate.

Yes, Marcus Woodstock entered the building—alone. I was struck immediately by the family resemblance; and if you'd had a gun to my head and asked me to pick the best-looking Woodstock, it would have been Marcus.

He was no movie star, to be sure; and of all the people we had witnessed that morning coming into the building, apparently Marcus was the only one who had taken the wind-tunnel entrance. His frizzy hair was too long and blown in several directions, giving him a mad-scientist look. He wore a battered raincoat, à la Columbo, over an equally battered suit, the pants of which were much too short, bringing to mind the old expression about expecting a flood. His left hand gripped a bulging briefcase, its leather cracked and dry from years of wear.

Before I could ask Kit what our next plan of action would be, she jumped off the bench and ran to Marcus, just as he was pressing the elevator button. "Marcus? I don't know if you remember me, us, but we are old friends of Mavis's, and we wondered if we could have a quiet word with you."

He gazed at us through his John Denver glasses. He didn't look fierce, the way Lionel did. In fact, he had a lost look on his face, and I felt sorry for him (although I wasn't sure why).

"There's a coffee shop around the corner here." He indicated a corridor to the right of the elevators. "I could spare a few moments." He looked at his watch as he said it—a cheap-looking watch like his wife's, probably a matching Walmart special, perhaps a buy-one-get-one-free.

Then he motioned for us to lead, and we headed off, acting like we knew where we were going—and even more preposterous, what we were doing.

CHAPTER NINETEEN

One thing Marcus had over his brothers was nice manners—at least judging from his order of three cups of coffee in Styrofoam cups. He pulled out two chairs for us in the tiny coffee shop and then placed his tattered briefcase on the empty seat beside him.

"So, ladies, what can I do for you?"

It occurred to me he might think we had some business-related matter to discuss with him, as I watched a congenial smile spread across his face.

"We met with Hilary last night, ya know." Kit took a sip of the weak coffee and managed to swallow instead of spitting it out. I was sure it was no Starbucks, but maybe it was going to be all right.

"Yes, she told me. Why wouldn't she?" Defensive. The congenial smile sagged a little.

"No reason. It's just that we're looking into the matter of your sister's death, and—"

"Are you with the police?" He withdrew his smile, causing his bad teeth to disappear, as if they'd all been pulled.

"In a manner of speaking. A third party, shall we say an interested third party, has asked us to look into the matter," Kit said.

I spit out the coffee I'd just sipped, and not because it was weak—although it was, almost undrinkably so. I grabbed a napkin from the holder on the table as I hit Kit's out-of-sight knee with my own.

"Hilary tells us she was good friends with Mavis," I said, hoping to avoid any more references to Kit's third party. "But we were hoping you could fill us in a little on your childhood, before Hilary joined your family."

"It's true Hilary has no knowledge of Mavis as a young girl growing up. And I wouldn't exactly say Hilary and Mavis were good friends. Good enough, I suppose." He stopped and picked up the coffee cup. After holding it to his lips for a drink that he seemed to savor (I guess no one had ever bought him a Starbucks gift card), he proceeded. "But not good childhood friends like you two were with Mavis, for instance."

I noticed then for the first time a keen intelligence behind the John Denvers and realized he was playing with us. "Okay," I said. "We were not friendly with Mavis in school; we all know that. But we never disliked her. And since her death, we have taken an interest in what happened to her."

"Too bad." He put the cup down. "Mavis could have used a couple of good friends back then. Things might have turned out different for her."

"How so?" Kit asked.

Marcus sighed. "Ladies, I guess there's no point in covering up. We Woodstocks have done way too much of that all our lives. Let me tell you what you don't know about our childhood. Our father was a monster. He treated his wife and his children like his personal property. He was tyrannical, and extremely cruel when he was crossed. We were all victims of his . . . his insanity, but he was the hardest on Will. My younger brother is a damaged adult today because of it. Actually, we are all damaged, but Will came off the worst."

We all three sat in silence for a while, as Kit and I digested this revelation. Then she spoke softly. "At least he's still alive. I'd say Mavis came off the worst."

"Would you, now? Mavis took her own life, I'm sure. And her reasons could probably be laid directly at my father's door. But she suffers no more. Will lives with the scars of his childhood every day. And his only ally was my sister. When he was beaten so badly for some trivial offense that he couldn't even leave the house, or locked in the cellar of our home overnight with only mice for company, my sister was his sole comfort. His only reason for living, if you want to be dramatic about it, was his love of Mavis."

"What about you?" Kit asked.

"Me? You mean was I beaten too, or why didn't I comfort Will?"

"Either one. You pick."

He took off his glasses and rubbed them against his sleeve. I could see his eyes fill with moisture, and then I knew why I had felt sorry for him earlier. He carried a sadness around with him like a second briefcase.

"I'm not proud of my conduct. We all do what we have to just to survive. Growing up, my life's purpose was to keep my father happy and away from me, like a rodeo clown distracting an angry bull. Selfish? Yeah, but it was all I knew. By doing so, of course, I deflected his wrath toward Will. Bullies often pick the weakest to practice their craft on, have you noticed? Will was our weak link. He served as a scapegoat for the rest of us, often sparing us our father's punishment."

I felt sick. The horror of the Woodstock legacy was hard to take so early in the morning, and the bad coffee wasn't helping. I flashed back to our schooldays, realizing another reason Will was hard to remember: he probably had been absent from school a lot.

"Look," Marcus said, "I think you probably have your hearts in the right place. And I have no doubt Mavis would appreciate your interest. But I'm convinced she took her own life, and really, you should leave it at that." His smile returned as he put his glasses back on. "You'll have to excuse me; I really must get to my office."

He rose, picked up his briefcase, and stood before us, looking every inch a beaten man. Then he repeated his earlier reflection. "It's too bad your, er, third party's interest in Mavis came so late."

Kit and I sat in silence, watching Marcus disappear from the shop.

Finally, I spoke. "Creepy as that was—and I know, it's as creepy as it can get—I don't see how it gets us any closer to proving Mavis was even murdered, let alone who did it." I wanted to add *what have we gained, making that poor man relive his tortured childhood?*

I had the sudden feeling we were out of our league, perhaps even out of our minds. Mavis probably *had* committed suicide. The only wonder was why she hadn't done it earlier. About forty-five years earlier.

But Kit spoke before I could voice those thoughts in kinder, gentler terms. "Unless Marcus is the murderer, ya know."

"Wha—why would you—"

"Val, I'm just trying to think of every conceivable scenario." She took another sip of her coffee and still did not flinch. She was indeed a tough cookie. "Don't you wonder why Marcus was so eager to blab? And what about Hilary last night? All that blah blah blah. Why didn't either one of them tell us to go jump in the lake? I know I would have."

"Well, yes, *you* would have, but they are not like you. I think he was telling us the truth. Why would anyone make all that stuff up about his own family?"

"Actually, I agree. But was he telling the *whole* truth?"

We sat in silence for a moment, and then Kit spoke again. "I can't drink this crap anymore. Let's go to Starbucks."

Maybe she wasn't so tough.

When we were settled across the street in our cushy chairs, sipping lattes that had never tasted so good, I finally told her just why I'd been off to such an early start that morning. "I'm going to Walmart on my way to the office."

"Going to buy a watch?" She laughed. "Just gotta keep up with those dashing Woodstocks, eh?"

"No, I'm going to buy a phone, one of those throwaway cell phones. Then I can call the number for Sean without . . . whoever's there . . . Sean, Sally . . . without them knowing it's me."

"Very smart, Valley Girl."

"I saw it on TV."

***

It seemed like a badly written episode of *Monk,* but there he was, Will Woodstock, at the jewelry counter in Walmart, looking at *watches.* I saw him as I was leaving, heading from the electronics department to the store exit. My first instinct was to hide from him. The last thing I needed was Will having me arrested for stalking. But I was, after all, *innocently* in the same store as he, albeit to buy a throwaway phone to call his nephew—to try, ultimately, to solve his sister's murder. And if handed an opportunity to further investigate a person of interest—and surely Will was at least that—how could I possibly pass it up?

Knowing Kit would be proud of me, I approached Will and tapped his back, which was bent over as he examined the watches. But I had no idea what to do after my tap caused him to straighten up and look at me, like a small, frightened animal caught rummaging in a garbage can. So I just watched as recognition flooded his face.

"Kit," he said. "I mean, Valerie. You're Valerie, right?"

"Yes. But you can call me Val." Why didn't I just tell him to call me Valley Girl, while I was being so inane? We had far more serious things to discuss, no matter what he called me.

"I just spoke with your brother," I said. "Say, could we go over there?" I nodded in the direction of the McDonald's that was attached to the Walmart, for the ultimate in one-stop shopping. "Let me buy you a cup of coffee." I didn't want to scare him off by making him think *he* would have to pay. Then, more in Kit-fashion than my own, I turned and started to walk toward McDonald's, willing him to follow. Which he did.

I dropped my purse down on a table and fished out some dollar bills. When I looked up to ask him what he would like, I noted his color was more ashen than it had been when I first spotted him at the jewelry counter.

"Coffee. Black." His eyes scrutinized my face, as if for clues.

I returned with our coffees and placed them on the table. Then I sat down across from him.

"Lionel talked to me too," he said. "And he forbade me to talk to you or your friend. Didn't he tell you that? And why are you following me?" He didn't touch his coffee. It sat in the middle of the table, protective lid still on it, and his arms hung down by his side. I could imagine them touching the floor, making him seem even less evolved and more peculiar than he really was.

"First of all, I wasn't following you," I said. "And second of all, it wasn't Lionel I spoke with."

His voice quavered. "Marcus? You spoke with Marcus?"

I nodded. "Yes. And Hilary too."

He stared at me for a few seconds, as I picked up a blue packet of Equal and turned it end to end, as if it were a miniature ace of clubs. "Marcus and Hilary have always been jealous of me," he said.

"Jealous? Of you? Why?"

"They were jealous of my close relationship with Mavis. We were twins, you know, and she simply never felt as close to Marcus as she did to me; and contrary to what Hilary likes to think, Mavis certainly wasn't as close to her as she was to me. Blood is thicker than water. Mavis and I were like one person; we stuck together. She was my rock."

"And you hers? Were you her rock?" As if this discombobulated man could be anyone's rock. He was more like an annoying pebble in a shoe.

"Of course. I told you: we were like one. Why? What did Hilary and Marcus tell you? Why were you talking to them in the first place? Lionel . . . Lionel wouldn't like that. I'm sure if I'm not supposed to talk to you, they're not, either."

"Why doesn't Lionel want you to talk to us? And why does Lionel call the shots?"

"Because . . . our family's business is not any of yours. And Lionel is the head of our family. Now, if you'll excuse me . . ."

He rose, and my eyes followed him as he walked right past the jewelry counter and left the store. He probably didn't want to spend so much money on a watch, anyway.

***

I planned to wait until I got home from the office to use the phone I bought at Walmart, but it lay among the clutter of my purse, tempting me like a flask would tempt an alcoholic. So I headed to the ladies' room and dialed the phone number Luke had e-mailed me. I should have gone to my car, no matter how freezing it was, but I recalled how cold I got when I phoned Beatrice Woodstock from there, and I wimped out.

"H'lo." The woman sounded as if she had a bad cold. I didn't realize Californians could actually *get* a cold in all that sunshine.

"Uh, yes. I'm looking for Sean. Sean Fletcher. Is he in?"

Just then Billie entered the tiny washroom. I was in the only stall, with the door closed, but I could see her shoes walk over to the sink. The sound of running water made me worry I'd missed the woman's response. But I didn't dare speak again. Damn Billie and her inconvenient sense of hygiene.

And then I could hear the woman on the other end crying, softly at first, then more loudly. I wanted to comfort her and silently cursed Billie again for making that impossible. At last, the woman seemed to gain control of herself, just as I saw Billie's feet retreat from the sink and head toward the door.

After I heard it close, I spoke. "Are you still there, ma'am?"

"Yes; I was wondering if *you* were."

"Sorry; I got distracted. Are you all right?"

"Yes."

"*Is* Sean there?"

"Who *are* you? Did you read his book?"

"Uh, I'm an old friend of his?" Why had I made it a question? I should have had Kit do this.

"Then I guess you have a right to know," she said. "Sean is dead."

CHAPTER TWENTY

Hello?" the woman on the phone said, when she got no response from me. "Look, who is this?"

"I'm sorry." I came out of the bathroom stall, and my reflection in the mirror spooked me for a second, as if another woman were facing me with a cell phone to her ear. "I didn't know; I'm so sorry," I said. And I was. This was Mavis's baby, after all, and who was going to mourn him? "I really am so, so sorry. What happened?" I turned my back on the other Valerie.

"You say you are an old friend?"

"Yes. Well, no, not really. I never actually met Sean, but I knew his mother."

"His *mother*. You think that woman was any kind of a mother?"

"Yes, I do," I said, although I had no idea what kind of mother Mavis had been, never mind her occupation. I realized she might have stuffed Sean in a pillowcase and dropped him out of the Sears Tower, for all I knew, but somehow I doubted it. "What happened to him? How did Sean die?"

"He committed suicide, if you must know. Shot himself in the head." She was softly crying again.

"Oh no." I went back into the stall and closed the door.

"So you can tell his so-called mother just what her tawdry life did to Sean. She can do anything she wants to now, and she can't hurt him anymore, but if she thinks she's going to come to our apartment and go through—"

"She's dead too." I felt suddenly defensive of Mavis and wanted to protect her reputation with this stranger on the other side of the country. "She died over a week ago."

"Oh shit."

There was a silence on the line.

The Californian broke it first. "That might explain it, then."

"What do you mean? You think Sean knew?"

"I know his uncle called him the day before . . . the day before he did it. I came home and found him sitting in the dark, clutching that damn book of his. You know, I think he was sorry he wrote it, and he probably blamed me for getting it published. But it was good, not to mention the greatest therapy in the world. I just hoped after it was done that Sean would be able to move on, and we could finally start our lives together."

"You're Sean's agent?"

"Was. But we also lived together. Who knows? We might even have gotten married one day. But he was just so tormented about his childhood and who his father was."

"Did he know?" I held my breath as I waited for her to answer.

"No. That was the major part of his problem. He never knew, and she wouldn't tell him."

"And his uncle called him?"

"Yes. That day when I came home, he was very upset, said he'd spoken to his uncle. This uncle must have told him his mother had died. Next day when I came home from work, I found Sean dead."

"How terrible for you. I can't imagine what that was like."

"Damn him! Damn him for being so friggin' weak. Why couldn't he just move on and forget them?"

"Did he happen to say which uncle it was?"

"No; is there more than one? He just said his uncle was demanding, *threatening* is the actual word he used. Wanted to know all sorts of things about what Sean had been doing all this time. Apparently, he wasn't very pleased about the book, either. Poor Sean; he was so weak, really. He sounded a little afraid of this guy. Look, I have a million things to do."

"Of course; I'm so sorry. Please let me know if there's anything I can do for you."

"Like what?"

"Anything at all."

We hung up, and then I made one more call. Kit answered on the first ring.

"Okay," I said, "you better be sitting down. I have news." And I immediately launched into a reenactment of my meeting with Will, plus a near-perfect word-for-word recitation of my call to California.

"Well done, Valley Girl. Good work."

I'm sure I blushed at the praise. "Thank you. But isn't it sad?"

"Hmm, yes, sad. I suppose."

"You suppose? You don't think our Sean had enough shit to deal with, without Uncle Lionel calling to bully him and break the news his mother was dead? And I'm sure that was done gently, with all kinds of sympathy."

"If in fact it was Uncle Lionel who called."

"You think it was someone else?"

"Could be." I could almost hear Kit's brain ticking over the cheap phone.

"You surely don't think it was Will or Marcus. Neither one is what I would call threatening. Weird, yes, but hardly threatening." Even as I said it, though, I knew she could be right. "What do we do next?"

"I think you should call the LAPD and ask them to pull the LUDs on Sean's phone so we can clear up exactly which uncle called him. Then you need to get your ass down to Florida and find out just whose name is on Sean's birth certificate. And while you're at it, run a check on this chick in California, see if she's got any form."

I smiled. I knew she was poking gentle fun of my love for TV detective shows. So I played along. "Okay, boss. And while I'm gone, you try to wrap up that ol' Jimmy Hoffa thing."

"No problem. Just as soon as I diaper the Lindbergh baby."

We both laughed, and then Kit said, "Oh, I forgot to tell you my big news."

"Shoot."

"I cracked Larry's code. I got the password to his computer: Flemming. It wasn't difficult to guess."

"Flemming?"

"His mother's maiden name, for crying out loud. You know what a mama's boy he is. He changed it from Maybelline, her first name, to Flemming, her last name. Geez."

"Brilliant on your part."

"Not really. But the thing is, I found the Mavis file, and it was very interesting. Seems even hookers need accountants. The son of a bitch had a record of her earnings for the past five years. Turns out Mavis was loaded, and I don't mean from her family's dough. She had a couple of accounts overseas, one in Switzerland and one in the Cayman Islands."

"That doesn't sound like our Larry, being mixed up in—"

"Wait, Val. None of it is illegal. Larry wouldn't get involved with anything like that. But it does mean that the two of them obviously met, probably more than once. And he never said a word to me; can you believe that? Pretty impressive, eh?"

Actually, I could believe it. I'd trust Larry with my life; and for whatever reason Mavis needed to consult an accountant, she couldn't have picked a better one. The fact that they had gone to the same school and Mavis would have recognized his name made it even more believable. "Have you mentioned this to Larry?" I asked.

"Are you nuts? He'd kill me."

Before I could respond, the bathroom door flew open, and I'm sure the whole building heard Tom's shouting. "Valerie Pankowski! You better be giving birth in there because I don't pay you to sit in the john all day and yak to your girlfriends. You have clients waiting for you and houses to sell. You think they sell themselves? This is a place of business, not some friggin' Tri Delta sorority house."

"Gotta go," I whispered to Kit. I opened the door to the stall. Behind Tom's furious face, I noticed Billie standing there. *Rat.*

I followed Tom back to his office and closed the door, shutting us both in. Tom still looked furious, more than catching me in the bathroom on a personal call warranted.

"Okay, mister." I leaned against the edge of his desk. "Spill. What's eating you?"

He stared up at me blankly, and I quickly backed out of my Mickey Spillane detective mode. "Tom," I said. "Why are you so upset? Has something happened?"

"Nothing has happened." He shuffled papers around on his desk. "That's just the point. My top saleswoman is in the bathroom making personal calls, and we got a business to run here, Val. This ain't a joke."

"Okay." I moved away from his desk and took a chair. "First of all, cut the top salesperson crap. It's not like I have competition. And second, since when can't I make a personal phone call? And third, I work damn hard for you 24/7, so don't ever question my work ethic. And fourth—"

"There's a fourth?" Tom's face relaxed a little.

"Yes, there's a damn fourth. Since when do you barge into the ladies' room? I could probably report you to . . ."

"Do go on. This oughta be good." He smiled his I-got-ya smile.

I smiled back. "I dunno, the Bathroom Police, perhaps? By the way, did Billie tell you where I was?"

"What if she did?"

"I'm not sure. She's just acting a little strange lately, that's all."

"*She's* acting strange? What about you? Do ya think you could take a little time from your crime solving to sell a house or two? That's all I ask. Just sell me a house, Kiddo, and I'll be happy."

"No problem. I'm all over it, Boss." I rose and smoothed down my pants. "Ready for action. I'll rearrange Downers Grove. By the way, how's Celeste?"

Tom's face turned to stone. "Who?" He patted the breast pocket of his jacket and removed a cigar.

"Celeste. Don't tell me there's trouble in paradise."

He removed the cigar from its metal case. "Valerie, just do your job, and I'll be happy. And don't mention that broad to me."

I didn't respond. After all these years, if I've learned nothing else about Tom, it's when not to push his buttons. I did, however, take a tiny detour around his side of the desk and give him a sisterly peck on the cheek. For some reason, I felt happy.

"Get out of here and make me some money," he said. But his expression told me he was a little bit happy too.

I headed back to my desk to start earning my keep, but I had to deal with Billie first. At her desk, she had her head bent over a document that took all her attention. I put my hands on the edge of the desk and leaned forward.

"Ratting me out to the boss, Billie?" I whispered.

She looked up, but not in a surprised way. More like it was the shoot-out at high noon, and she was Gary Cooper to my bad guy.

"Got something to say, Val?" she whispered back. We both turned to watch Perry, who literally had his ear cocked in our direction.

"Very subtle, Perry," I said, before spinning back to face Billie. I leaned in closer. "Yes, I have something to say. Did you tell Tom I was in the bathroom?"

"Yes, but only because he demanded to know where you were, and I was worried about you. Who were you talking to?"

"Billie, I know you've read my e-mail." It was past time for me to confront her about knowing Mavis e-mailed me to cancel her plans to sell. "And now you're spying—"

"Come with me, Val." She stood and took my arm, steering me back to the bathroom, where she closed the door behind us. "Look, there's stuff you should know about Sean Fletcher."

"*Sean Fletcher?* How do you know about Sean Fletcher?"

"Oh, I know a lot about Sean Fletcher. I know he was Mavis Woodstock's son and that he had a miserable existence. So bad he even wrote a book about it."

"You know about the memoir?"

But of course. Billie knew everything. I should ask her what happened to Mavis.

"I met Sean," Billie said. She turned to the mirror and ran a finger across a perfectly groomed eyebrow. "It was at my book club. We had a series that focused on authors with local connections, and someone found out Sean had relatives here, so we invited him. He seemed like an okay guy, if a bit odd."

"Why didn't you tell me this before?"

"You never asked me, Val. You should have known I could help you and Kit with whatever it is you're doing."

I decided the most sinister thing Billie was guilty of was feeling left out.

"Okay, then how about helping now, Billie? I'm asking. Do you have any theories on what really happened to Mavis?"

"Buy me lunch, and I'll tell you what I know." The old Billie had returned, the good kid who had saved my butt a million times.

"You're on, and do you mind if I invite Kit?"

"Not at all. The more the merrier."

***

Billie insisted we stop at her apartment, where I waited in the car while she ran up to her place and returned with a large brown envelope sticking out of her purse.

I pulled my Lexus out of her parking lot. "By the way, what's up with Tom and Celeste? I thought they were engaged."

"Forget it." Billie waved a hand in the air. "That's over. He dumped her, or she dumped him; that part I'm not sure about."

"Oh, come on, Bill. You probably know more than Tom does. What happened?"

"Okay." She turned to face me. "From what I gather, she wants some kids. Tom wants some arm candy. They agreed that wasn't perhaps the basis of a good marriage, and then they agreed to disagree and go their separate ways. And why do you look like the cat that just slurped up the cream?"

I didn't realize I was looking any particular way, but when I glanced at my reflection in the rearview mirror, I could see she was right.

Billie leaned back in her seat. "Anyway, Tom's waiting for you, Val. You know that."

"What? Tom's not waiting for me. He and I would kill each other in five minutes. We practically do that now, and we're not even married."

"Yes, you're all Rhett and Scarlett. I enjoy watching you two. But take a little advice, Val. Tom won't be around forever. One of these days, a Celeste is gonna come along who will agree to Tom's terms, no matter how archaic they are, and you'll lose him. He's very eligible, for an old guy."

207

We both laughed, and I turned into the restaurant parking lot, glad to see Kit's BMW already there.

Once Billie had a cheeseburger, fries, and Diet Coke placed before her, she reached down into her purse on the floor by her feet and removed the brown envelope.

Kit and I watched in awe as Billie removed two large black-and-white photographs and placed them on the table before us, like a card shark laying out a winning hand. "Sean Fletcher," she said. Then she took a large bite of her cheeseburger.

Kit and I each picked up a photo. In the picture I held, Billie and Sean stood in front of a table covered with books, a sign that read The Downers Grove Bookworms behind them. Sean looked tall, with arms and legs that seemed to go on forever. I felt sorry for this young man. There was no question his stringy body as well as his long face and unruly hair were courtesy of the Woodstocks. *Didn't his father have any genetic input?* Not that it mattered any longer.

"He's a Woodstock," Kit said.

"No kidding." Finally, I pried my eyes off the picture I held and looked at the one in Kit's hands: a photo of Sean in the center of a handful of women, presumably The Downers Grove Bookworms. "Billie," I said, "I never knew you were such a literary buff."

She smiled. "There's a lot you don't know about me, Val. I'm actually the president of this here little organization." She tapped a mustard-smeared finger on the photograph I held.

"Way to go," I said.

"You do know he's dead, don't you?" Kit asked.

"Yes, a member of the San Pedro Bookworms called me. I was so bummed. What a tragedy; he was a cool writer. But frankly, I'm not surprised he blew his brains out."

"Why do you say that, Bill?" I scooped some of my tortilla soup onto my spoon.

She shrugged. "Just the way he was. I mean, on the surface, he was a nice guy, but right beneath that, he seemed edgy and scared, as if he was always looking over his shoulder."

"Did he meet up with the family when he was in Downers Grove?"

"No, that's just it; he didn't. He wanted nothing to do with them. I suggested it, but he wouldn't hear of it. And hey, it wasn't my place to go digging up family scandal." She looked at us both pointedly.

"Billie, all we want to do is find out what happened to Mavis," I said. "We just don't believe it was a suicide, that's all. And anyway, don't you think it's weird that he didn't even want to connect with his own mother when he was in her hometown?"

"Er, Val, have you even *read* the memoir?"

"Of course; we've both read it," Kit said.

"Then you know he hated his mother, and with good reason too."

"Billie," I said, "there are two sides to every story. And did you ever think that at least some of it might have been made up by Sean? You have only his word for it that it ever really happened that way."

Billie shook her head. "No, it happened, all right. I'm not saying Mavis didn't have her own set of demons to contend with, but I do know she wasn't exactly Mother of the Year."

"Okay, okay, let's just agree that we'll never know who was telling the truth," Kit said. "But what exactly does this tell us, about Sean, that we didn't already know? So he was a mixed-up kid with a crazy upbringing who didn't know who his father was. You could say the same, and worse, about thousands of kids."

Billie gazed over the top of our heads, lost in some deep thought of her own. "No," she said. "It was more than that. Sean was more than a crazy, mixed-up kid. There was something totally unbalanced about him. I said he was nice, but truthfully, he gave me the creeps. To begin with, I never really believed that he came back to Downers Grove just to meet the fabulous Bookworms. It doesn't make sense. A book club in a Midwest town?"

"Which, incidentally, just happens to be the same town his mother and family live in," Kit said. "But you said he wanted nothing to do with them?"

"Right. That's what he said. But you know he wrote that book to punish his mother, and a person who goes to that much trouble surely wants a reaction. You don't fly all the way here and just attend some stupid book club gathering when the object of your hatred grew up here."

"What are you saying?" I asked. Sean as the murderer wasn't something Kit or I had ever even considered.

"All I'm saying is Sean was full of hate. And it would have been easy for the guy to snoop around—especially since he wrote in his book that he'd found out her real name—and learn his mother had recently moved back here, and then come back and . . . get rid of her."

"But what about Sally? She said he received a call from one of his uncles."

"Big deal. Maybe he just told her that, or maybe one of his uncles was onto him. Or maybe the guilt just got to him. I told you, the guy was unbalanced."

Billie's words threw us into silence once more, and then it was broken by her phone ringing from inside her purse. She pulled it out and glanced at it. "Speaking of unbalanced, it's Perry. I gotta take this."

CHAPTER TWENTY-ONE

S o," Billie said, once we said good-bye to Kit and settled in my car, "what do you think we should do next?"

"That's simple. I'm going to take us back to the office, then I'm gonna finish the paperwork on my desk, and then I'm going home. I'm gonna run a bubble bath and soak for about six hours with a good book."

"*V is for Vengeance?*"

I smiled, turning the corner onto Highland Avenue. "How'd you know?"

"You're a big Sue Grafton fan. We discussed *U is for Undertow* about three weeks ago. You were about halfway done, and you're the type who could read alphabet mysteries only in sequence."

"Billie, you should be a detective."

***

A couple of hours later, the papers on my desk squared away, I shut down my computer and headed out. I needed time to think, to digest everything we had learned. On my way home, I pulled into Dominick's. In order to carry out my thinking session, I needed to purchase a few things. With my shopping basket half-full, I headed toward the checkout and placed my items on the conveyor belt: a bottle of pinot grigio, a can of deluxe mixed nuts, and a bar of Hershey's Special Dark Chocolate.

The woman at the cash register smiled. "This looks good." She scanned the chocolate.

"It can't hurt." I opened my purse and dug through to get my wallet. Only it wasn't there. "Damn."

"Problem?" The woman held the wine in her hand, not sure whether to continue scanning or not.

"My wallet. I can't find it."

"Oops." She put the bottle down. No way was she going to continue without the promise of payment.

I took out the entire contents of my purse and placed everything on the end of the counter reserved for sacking groceries. Not surprisingly, my large purse yielded far more items than the grocery basket. But no wallet, where I kept my credit cards and checkbook as well as my cash. "Oh crap." I shook the purse in case my wallet had found a rip in the lining and worked its way into hiding.

"Where'd you last use it?"

"Good question." Kit had paid for lunch, pulling her credit card out before I'd even thought to find mine. So when had I last bought something? I watched the sweet cashier transform into a guard from a women's prison as she returned my items to the grocery basket. Meanwhile, half the population of Downers Grove had formed a line behind me, every face pinched with annoyance at the inconvenience I was causing them.

I mumbled a halfhearted *sorry* as I shoved my sunglasses, camera, Franklin Planner, dental floss, makeup bag, phone, gum, and all the other necessities I keep in my purse back into their home. I still couldn't recall the last time I had seen my wallet.

When I was back in my car, with no pinot and no chocolate, I concluded it had to have been at McDonald's, where I had bought coffee for Will. And since I was closer to home than to the McDonald's at Walmart, I decided to head to my apartment and call the store.

***

I was craving Brazil nuts and Hershey's chocolate as I inserted the key into my apartment door. The instant I took a step inside, I knew something was wrong.

It was like every bad scary movie I'd ever seen.

As I reached for the light switch, I almost expected a clap of thunder to shake the building and the electricity to be simultaneously knocked out. Instead, my new Stiffel lamp flooded the room with a soft glow. Still, something felt wrong.

My first thought was that some unknown wallet thief had my driver's license and credit cards and decided to surprise me with his/my purchases before he murdered me. I stood in the open doorway, not quite sure whether to go in or back out, when the decision was made for me. From the galley kitchen, a figure emerged. It grabbed my arm and pulled me completely into the apartment, shutting the door behind me. Well, good. At least I didn't have to make *that* decision.

It was Will, but it was a different Will from the one I'd bumped into that morning at Walmart. His meek expression was gone. Instead, he wore a smile as charming as Jack Nicholson's when he stuck his head through a door and proclaimed, "Here's Johnny!"

He yanked me into the room and shoved me down onto the couch. I saw my wallet sitting on the coffee table, and for an insane moment, I felt relief that I wouldn't have to replace all those credit cards.

"Will, I'd offer you a glass of wine, but it seems someone stole my wallet and I had a bit of a problem at the grocery store."

"Shut up," he said loudly. But unfortunately, it wasn't loud enough for anyone outside my apartment to hear.

I made a mental note to get to know my neighbors, in case I survived and needed help with some other lunatic.

"Will, what are you doing here?" What I really wondered was, *What was the best way to calm a madman—possibly a murderer?*

He sat down across from me, on the edge of the coffee table.

"Will, I know you are upset—"

"You don't know shit."

I decided that he might be right. So I shut up and waited.

After a few moments of a staring contest that was making me extremely nervous—even though *he* seemed to be enjoying it—he slowly reached into his pocket and pulled out an object that he placed carefully next to the wallet beside him.

It was a gun.

Okay, so now he really had my attention. It occurred to me I had never actually seen a real live gun before. Not this type, anyway: small, compact, easily concealed. I tried to speak, not sure what I might say, but my throat had gone dry and no sound came out.

I watched with fascination as Will picked up the gun, then rose and went behind the couch. Once he was behind me, I felt something at the back of my head. Breathe, breathe, I told myself. This isn't happening. This is a scene from *Law & Order*. Only please God, don't let it be the first scene, where victims always meet their fate.

"You are pissing me off," I heard his voice. His normally wimpy, high-pitched squeak had been replaced by a deeper voice that meant business.

"I'm sorry." Now *I* sounded wimpy.

"I tried to warn you off today," he said. "But I could see it wasn't working. So I decided I had to take care of you once and for all."

"You mean you didn't meet me by accident at Walmart?"

"Oh, I've followed you more than once. You think it was a coincidence I ran into you at Starbucks? I'd never *been* to Starbucks before that. But I hadn't followed you to your home yet, and someone else lives at the address that the phone book has for you. So I took your wallet when you left your purse on the table, when you went to fetch our coffee at McDonald's, in hopes your new address would be in there. And it was. You made it so easy. Almost as easy as getting into your building with one of your nice neighbors and into your apartment with your own credit card. By the way, you really should invest in a dead bolt."

I remained silent.

"You just couldn't leave it alone, could you? You were warned off so many times by my family, but you just wouldn't quit."

I turned around. I couldn't have this conversation without seeing his face. I stood, not sure if it was fear or stupidity that motivated me, and moved around to where he stood.

He looked surprised, and I could see red blotches dot his white skin. I suddenly thought of Will the grocery sacker all those years ago.

"Will, I was only trying to find out what happened to Mavis."

"No! You didn't give a fuck about Mavis. No one did, not my brothers, not her fucking husband, not even my mother."

"Wait a minute; your mother cared very much."

He grabbed my arm and led me back to the front of the couch, where he threw me down again. At least this time I could see him and the gun still in his hand. "My *mother*. She knew what was going on. She knew everything our father did

215

to us. And she didn't stop him! She's as responsible for everything that happened to us as kids as he was."

"I'm sorry, Will; I really am."

"Why should you be sorry? Why should anyone care?" He lowered the gun and sat down on the coffee table again, staring at a place over my head. "I tried to make Mavis see that our mother was just like our father. All I wanted to do was be with her. I tried to tell her how much better it would be if we could just go away and be together. Our son . . ."

At these words, he placed his hand with the gun onto his lap and slowly began to cry. "Our son . . . we had a son. Was that so wrong? We loved each other. Why shouldn't we have a son? But he's dead too."

"You had a son—you mean Sean was *your* son? Yours and *Mavis's*? But . . . what happened to Mavis, Will? How did she die?"

He stopped crying and looked up at me. "She said she didn't love me. *Me*." He pounded his chest with his left hand.

"She'd been in bed when I got to her house," he said. "She told me to go, leave her alone. She had the nerve to just go back to bed, as if I were a . . . a . . . rodent that would make his way back out, afraid of her. I showed her I wasn't afraid. I got her ass back out of bed. Then I outsmarted her. I'm smart, smarter than her; all the Woodstock men are smart. She was just a stupid little slut, really, nothing more. Father was right not to waste money on an education for her. She was as dumb as our mother."

Then he stopped speaking, and his brow furrowed.

"How did you outsmart her?" I asked.

"I pretended she hadn't hurt me. I calmed down and asked her if I could have something to drink, if she would join me." He gave a laugh that should be used only at Halloween to scare little kids.

"Go on, Will."

"We went out to the living room, and I pretended to be calm. I brought us both a glass of wine from her kitchen.

But I'd seen her sleeping pills on the counter, and I knew what I had to do. I crushed some pills into her glass."

He paused as if to give me time to appreciate how clever he was. Then he continued. "I watched her take a sip. Then another. She rattled on and on about some dumb trip she was planning to take with our mother. I listened carefully, giving the pills time to do their job. I wanted so badly to tell her that she was going to hell, not to Florida. But she didn't get it. She was too fucking stupid to get it."

He took a deep breath, and then he stood up, the gun dangling from his right hand. "After a while, she started to get sleepy. I kissed her on the cheek and told her I was leaving. She was stretched out on the couch by then, and her eyes were closing. I went into the garage and got the car ready. I put a towel in the tailpipe. I got her car keys from her purse. Then I went back to the living room to retrieve my wineglass, which I washed and put away. Then I wiped my fingerprints from the bottle and put it in the sink along with her wineglass."

He actually touched the side of his forehead with his fingertips, indicating what a genius he was to think of everything. "And oh yes, I put her fingers around the bottle. You know, a wine bottle with no prints wouldn't be believable. Then I carried her out to the car. That's how I left her, sleeping on the front seat with the engine running. It was so easy."

He had a satisfied look on his face, as if he had just shared his secret for the best way to prepare a Thanksgiving turkey. "She died without ever waking up." He said it like a revelation, his eyes bright and focused, and a chill ran through my body.

Then he continued. "I took her laptop with me. She'd told me she was planning to meet you about selling her house, to get away, away from me. And because you so conveniently left your business card with your e-mail address on it in Mavis's door, I was able to send you that e-mail and cancel her plans to sell."

"So you went back to the house?" Surely he wouldn't have been that bold. Or stupid. But he must have. How else could he have seen my business card?

"Yeah, I went back the next day, to make sure I hadn't overlooked anything. I hadn't, of course." He sounded as if the only thing stupid he'd done was to doubt himself in the first place.

"Will." I sat forward and gripped the edge of the cushion, as if it might offer me some protection from this madman. "Why don't we call someone?"

He focused his watery blue eyes back on my face and his gun toward my chest. "And say what, that I had to kill my sister, that I loved her more than anything, but she wouldn't accept my love, that she spent all those years in Florida fucking every man who came along, but she didn't have any time for me? That when I called our son and told him I was his father, he took his own life? Who wants to hear *that*, Valerie?"

"So what are you planning to do now? Are you planning to kill me?" I couldn't believe I actually asked that. Giving a killer fresh ideas is perhaps not the best way to go, so to speak.

"You arrogant bitch. You're not even worth killing." Slowly, he dropped the gun from its aim at my chest, and then just as slowly brought it back up and pointed it at his own.

"Will, don't be crazy!"

"Oh, but I am crazy, Val, that's what Mavis said. She wanted me to turn myself over to a doctor. That night at her house, she looked just like you. Afraid. I could tolerate anything from her, except fear. I loved her, Val. I'd never seen her like that before—except for that one time."

I held my breath, wanting to listen to every word but trying to form some plan to get the gun out of his hand. "What time?"

"The time we made love. I'd followed her to Minnesota, where she was living with that man. Her husband, she called him. I should have been her husband, not him. She didn't call it love, of course. It repelled her. I had to hold her down, and I could see it was hurting, but I couldn't help it."

He was crying by now. "And then I stood across the street from her place in Florida and watched for so many years. All those men—she gave every one of them her love, Valerie. Why not me? We loved each other. Why couldn't she give me her love?"

Was he expecting an answer? I watched his grip become tighter on the gun still pointed at his chest. I watched the tears running down his cheeks. And then the phone rang. A piercing sound that flooded the room, causing Will to look around like an animal trapped by a dozen rednecks with shotguns.

I grabbed the gun away from him, and he almost seemed relieved as he put his hands up to his ears to cut off the sound.

"Let me get that." I ran to the kitchen and looked around the small space for a place to shove the gun out of sight. "Hello," I said, as I closed the kitchen drawer.

I heard my front door open at the same time I heard Kit's voice come through the phone. Before I could tell her to call the police, I was back in the living room and realized I didn't need help, after all. Will was gone. I peered out the open door into the hallway, and even though I couldn't see him, I could hear the wail of the doomed animal he had become.

***

"So," Tom Haskins said. He had the paper opened in front of him on his desk, and he was staring down at the headline, cigar stuck in the side of his mouth. "You hear what happened to Will Woodstock?"

"Yes." I took a seat in front of his desk. "Run over by a car."

"Up in your neighborhood too." He tapped the page. "Says here he was running down the street and darted in front of an oncoming car. Driver couldn't avoid him."

"I know; I read the paper too."

"Strange, huh?"

I looked up at him. "What do you mean, *strange*?"

"What do you think I mean? His sister kills herself, you spend a good part of the time I pay you for to dig into it, then the brother kills himself too. In your neighborhood."

"So what are you saying, Tom? That I'm somehow responsible?"

We stared at each other across the desk, me holding my breath, Tom chomping on his cigar.

"Are you?" he asked.

"No."

"Good. Then get out of here and do what I pay you for."

***

Later that night I took the gun from my kitchen drawer and put it in an Ann Taylor shoebox. I would take it to my bank the next morning and lock it in my safety-deposit box until I could decide how to permanently dispose of it.

Kit and I had agreed there was no reason to mention it to anyone. As far as the police were concerned, it was another suicide. They'd done little to investigate the murder of Mavis, so why bother with her brother? The driver of the vehicle that hit and killed Will had not been charged. There were too many witnesses to Will's erratic behavior and death. If his family was going to hold any kind of funeral, Kit and I did not plan to attend.

We also agreed there was nothing to be gained by passing on Will's confession to anyone. It wouldn't bring Mavis, or her son, back to life. It was also possible that Lionel already knew the sordid details of what had happened between his twin siblings. Besides, I was done with the

Woodstocks. I felt a little guilty about ditching Beatrice Woodstock; but maybe Will was right, and she *was* responsible in part for the tragic lives her children led.

I got ready for bed and turned on the TV. Instead of my usual *Law & Order*, I tuned into a rerun of *Friends*. It was silly and funny and helped me forget for a few moments the trauma I'd experienced. Just as I began to feel the welcome difficulty of keeping my eyes open, the phone rang. I smiled, knowing it must surely be Emily. I was right.

"How's my detective mother?"

I wanted to tell her I'd hung up my badge and was ready to concentrate on the real estate market and not a damn thing more, but all she knew was that I'd requested a phone number for Sean and Sally. I wasn't about to tell her what Kit and I had been through the past two weeks.

"Tell me what's going on with you," I said. "How's Hollywood?"

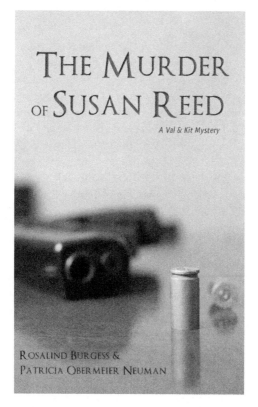

The Murder of Susan Reed

Susan Reed's body was discovered at nine thirty on Saturday night, April 5, by her mother. Marjorie Reed had used her own key to get into her daughter's apartment and found Susan lying dead on the kitchen floor. There were two bullets lodged in Susan's chest.

At least that's what the newspaper said. When I read the article the next day, I felt as if I had two bullets lodged in my own chest.

***

During the twenty-five years I was married to David Pankowski, I suspected he was unfaithful many times, but I was always reluctant to admit it. At least out loud. I didn't want to upset our applecart. The fabulous house, our outwardly perfect life, and most of all, our daughter, Emily. Looking back, I realize what an idiot I was. That applecart was more than upset: it was broken, squashed, ground into applesauce.

When my best friend, Kit, approached me with her own wobbly applecart, it was even harder for me to accept. Unlike my ex-husband, her Larry's a good guy. I would trust him with my life.

There is no way he would cheat.

"Wear these, Val." Kit handed me a pair of Versace sunglasses.

We decided a decade ago, when we entered our forties, that sunglasses improve our looks more than any makeup or beauty cream. Sunglasses shave years off our faces, we only half joke.

But they didn't seem appropriate right now. So I asked, "Why?"

"Disguise."

"Kit, it's raining, and it will be dark out. Don't you think the sunglasses are overkill? We might look suspicious." I fixated on the form our disguise would take, rather than why we needed a disguise in the first place.

"Not in the least. Bono wears sunglasses 24/7."

I shook my head like a dog that has just come in from the rain. "Wait a minute; what have you got planned? And what does an Irish pop singer out to save the world have to do with it?"

"Bono has nothing to do with it. These glasses are for you to wear when we spy on Larry. Oh, and let's find you a hat. A hat would be good."

"Ah," I said, as if the brilliance of her plan were starting to sink in. "But just one question. What will *you* be wearing? Groucho glasses and a false nose?"

"I'll be crouching down in the front seat, so no need for me to wear any disguise." She'd clearly thought it through and was pleased with herself.

"Front seat of what?"

"We're borrowing a car."

"Well, why don't we just steal one instead? Wouldn't that be better? Then we can switch out the plates and—"

Kit put a firm hand on my shoulder, her face close to mine. "This isn't a game, Val; this is serious."

I was about to disagree, laugh even, but her tone and the tiny little quiver of her lower lip stopped me. "Okay," I said. "It's not a game. But you haven't really told me what this is all about. If it's not a game, just what is it?"

"I still think Larry's having an affair," she said.

"You haven't convinced *me* of that yet. So tell me why I should wear this getup and spy on him."

"Susan Reed, from his office. She's been there almost a year. You met her at the office Christmas party. Dyed black hair. Bad teeth. No boobs."

"I remember." I sat on a stool facing her.

"What else can I say?" Kit waved a hand in the air, as if a bad dye job proved her husband's infidelity.

"Give me the details."

"Ah, the details. Oh, it's all so cliché. Late nights at the office. The answering machine kicks in after hours when he's supposed to be there, and apparently he's forgotten how to turn on his cell phone, so I can never reach him. Unexplained charges on his credit card. Lipstick on his collar."

"Wait." I held up a hand to stop her. "Lipstick on his collar?"

"Okay, no lipstick; I just added that. But something is going on, Val. He's different. Distant. We hardly ever talk anymore. The few hours he is home, he's locked away in his den doing who knows what."

"Kit, it's April."

"So what?"

"Well, isn't April for accountants like December for Santa Claus?"

"Oh, please. Larry's got ten thousand drudges down at that office of his. He should be no busier in April than any other time of the year."

"And you've asked him what's going on?"

"Yes. No answer. Just mumbling and bullshit."

"Okay, so let's assume Larry is consumed by another woman. Why do you think it's Susan? Because honestly, if I were going to have an affair with someone in his office, it would be that redheaded chick who wears the slit skirts. Or wait; what about Daphne? Talk about a blond bombshell. What about her? Why Susan?"

"That's the point entirely. Why would Big Red or Blondie be interested in Larry? Susan's got desperate written all over her."

"Well, that still doesn't explain why Larry would find *her* so fascinating."

Kit did a little jump off the stool. I thought I saw her lip quivering again. But she crossed to the Sub-Zero fridge and took two Diet Cokes from the door. "He said her name, Val. In his sleep. He said her frigging name. Soooooosan, Soooooosan." She sounded like the Ghost of Christmas Past calling to Ebenezer Scrooge. She stopped her moaning long enough to open and sip from one of the soda cans.

"Is that all you have to go on? He said her name in his sleep?"

"I have this." She rummaged in her purse that lay on the granite counter and retrieved a telephone bill. She handed it to me, and I was indeed struck dumb by the number highlighted at least twenty times. "This is Susan's number. Larry called her eleven times when he was in Las Vegas at that golf thing three weeks ago. He called me once. And that was only to remind me to record some stupid golf match."

"Okay. He called her eleven times. Could have been work-related calls."

"Work-related calls, my ass."

I could have kept trying to explain away the eleven phone calls, but by now my stomach was starting to churn a little. I had been through all this before. Only I had been so dumb that eleven phone calls wouldn't have sounded any alarms. In those days a dozen fire trucks racing through my kitchen wouldn't have alerted me to any danger. I suddenly felt determined to help my pal in her quest. And I was cashing in my membership to Larry's fan club.

"Okay," I said. "Tell me what you have in mind."

***

An hour later we were parked in the lot across from Larry's one-story building, with a perfect view of his office. Reluctantly, I had agreed to tuck my freshly bobbed and highlighted blond hair under a Yankees baseball cap. My blue eyes were hidden behind the Versace sunglasses.

Kit, who for some reason felt it was safe to sit up in the passenger seat when we weren't in motion, had a Chanel scarf wrapped around her head, the way Queen Elizabeth did when she walked her corgis. We had borrowed a 1994 Lincoln Continental from Kit's neighbor on the pretense that neither of our cars was working. Since the neighbor, an eighty-year-old widower, just handed over the keys, requiring no further explanation, I assumed he was either senile or in love with Kit.

After an hour of watching Larry's back as he sat at his desk, we finally saw him stand, put on his jacket, and turn off his computer. Then he glanced at his watch, took his trench coat from the rack, and left the room.

I glanced at my own watch, where I learned it was five minutes after six on April 5.

"Son of a bitch," Queen Liz said.

"What? What do you see?"

"That son of a bitch leaving the office at six. He hasn't been home this early for months. Now we'll catch him in the act."

We watched in silence as Larry came through the glass front doors of the building. His white Suburban was parked in his reserved spot. We watched him get in and make a phone call. A few minutes later he backed out of his parking spot.

As I put the Lincoln in gear, another figure emerged from the building and headed in our direction, toward the parking lot.

"It's her," Kit whispered, as if Susan could hear us.

"Are you sure? She looks taller."

"Wearing fancy five-inch heels, no doubt, for her little date with Larry."

We watched the figure enter the parking lot and then disappear. I swung our car out through the exit, trying not to lose sight of Larry's Suburban. Wearing dark glasses made it difficult (I assume Bono has his own driver), but by the end of the road, where Larry's brake lights came on at a stop sign, I was right behind him in the mammoth Lincoln. So far, so good. Except for my poor vision and Kit yanking at the leg of my pants from where she was crouched down on the floor.

"What's going on?" Kit asked. "What do you see?"

I flung the glasses onto the back seat. "That's better," I said.

"What? Do you see her? Where is her car? Is she in the car with Larry?"

"Kit, Larry is alone; you know that. Unless he had Susan stashed in the back seat all afternoon."

"Huh." Disgust. "That wouldn't surprise me."

"Well, if that were the case, who did we see leaving the building?"

My friend and partner in crime didn't answer. Seemed she had more questions than answers.

Five minutes later Larry's Suburban turned onto Ogden Avenue, and I lost him in the traffic. We drove up and down the busy road for another ten minutes. But at six twenty we decided to call it a day. Or night.

Next time we'd do better.

Patty and Roz
www.roz-patty.com

About the authors ...

Now a proud and patriotic US citizen and Texan, Rosalind Burgess grew up in London and currently calls Houston home. She has also lived in Germany, Iowa, and Minnesota. Roz retired from the airline industry to devote all her working hours to writing (although it seems more like fun than work).

Patricia Obermeier Neuman spent her childhood and early adulthood moving around the Midwest (Minnesota, South Dakota, Nebraska, Iowa, Wisconsin, Illinois, and Indiana), as a trailing child and then as a trailing spouse (inspiring her first book, *Moving: The What, When, Where & How of It*). A former reporter and editor, Patty lives with her husband in Door County, Wisconsin. They have three children and twelve grandchildren.

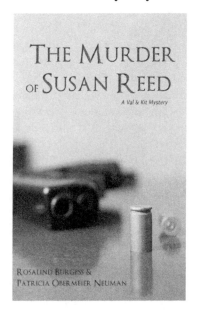

The Murder of Susan Reed

When Kit suspects Larry of having an affair with one of his employees, Susan Reed, she enlists Val's help in uncovering the truth. The morning after a little stalking expedition by the lifelong friends, Val reads in the newspaper that Susan Reed was found shot to death in her apartment the night before, right around the time Kit was so certain Larry and Susan were together. *Were* they having an affair? And did Larry murder her? The police, in the form of dishy Detective Dennis Culotta, conduct the investigation into Susan's murder, hampered at times by Val and Kit's insistent attempts to discover whether Larry is guilty of infidelity and/or murder. As the investigation heats up, so does Val's relationship with Detective Culotta.

FIVE STARS! "I couldn't wait to get this Val & Kit adventure after reading the authors' first book, and I was not disappointed. As a fan of this genre . . . I just have to write a few words praising the incredible talent of Roz and Patty. One thing I specifically want to point out is the character development. You can completely visualize the supporting actors (suspects?) so precisely that you do not waste time trying to recall details about the character. . . . Roz and Patty practically create an imprint in your mind of each character's looks/voice/mannerisms, etc."

FIVE STARS! "Even better than the first! Another page-turner! Take it to the beach or pool. You will love it!!! I did!!!"

FIVE STARS! "Great writing. Great plot."

FIVE STARS! "I enjoy reading about Larry and Tom as much as I enjoy reading about Kit and Val's relationship. The stories are always very exciting."

FIVE STARS! "Once again Val & Kit star in a page-turner mystery! It's always fun to see where a book series story picks up and where it will take you! Getting to know the characters is half the fun and . . . you can look forward to the next!"

FIVE STARS! "Val and Kit's interactions and Val's thoughts about life in general were probably the best part of the book. I was given enough info to 'suspect' just about every character mentioned."

No. 3 in
The Val & Kit Mystery Series

Death in Door County

Val embarks on a Mother's Day visit to her mom in Door County, Wisconsin, a peninsula filled with artists, lighthouses, and natural beauty. Her daughter, Emily, has arrived from LA to accompany her, and at the last minute her best friend, Kit, invites herself along. Val and Kit have barely unpacked their suitcases when trouble and tension greet them, in the form of death and a disturbing secret they unwittingly brought with them. As they get to know the locals, things take a sinister turn. And when they suspect someone close to them might be involved in blackmail—or worse—Val and Kit do what they do best: they take matters into their own hands in their obsessive, often zany, quest to uncover the truth.

FIVE STARS! "I love these stories and hope there will be more to come. I was reading in the car and laughing out loud. My husband looked over and just shook his head. Thanks again for another good one."

FIVE STARS! "Really enjoy the Val and Kit characters. They are a yin and yang of personalities that actually fit like a hand and glove. This is the third in the series and is just as much a fun read as the first two. The right amount of intrigue coupled with laughter. I am looking forward to the next in the series."

FIVE STARS! "The girls have done it again . . . and by girls, do I mean Val and Kit, or Roz and Patty? The amazingly talented authors, Roz and Patty, of course. Although Val and Kit have landed themselves right smack dab in the middle of yet another mystery. This is their third adventure, but don't feel as though you have to (albeit you SHOULD if you haven't done so already) read *The Disappearance of Mavis Woodstock* and *The Murder of Susan Reed* in order. This book and the other(s) are wonderful stand-alones, but read all . . . to enjoy all of the main and supporting characters' quirks?/habits?/mannerisms? I can't seem to express how much I love these books . . .

"Speaking of characters . . . This is what sets the Val & Kit series apart from the others in this genre. The authors always give us a big cast of suspects, and each is described so incredibly . . . It's like playing a game of Clue, but way more fun . . . the authors make the characters so memorable that you don't waste time trying to 'think back' to whom they are referring. In fact, it's hard to believe that there are only two authors writing such vivid casts for these books. So come on, ladies, confess . . . no, wait, don't. I don't want to know how you do it, just please keep it up."

Lethal Property

In this fourth book of The Val & Kit Mystery Series (a stand-alone, like the others), our ladies are back home in Downers Grove. Val is busy selling real estate, eager to take a potential buyer to visit the home of a widow living alone. He turns out not to be all that he claimed, and a string of grisly events follows, culminating in a perilous situation for Val. Her lifelong BFF Kit is ready to do whatever necessary to ensure Val's safety and clear her name of any wrongdoing. The dishy Detective Dennis Culotta also returns to help, and with the added assistance of Val's boss, Tom Haskins, and a *Downton Abbey*–loving Rottweiler named Roscoe, the ladies become embroiled in a murder investigation extraordinaire. As always, we are introduced to a new cast of shady characters as we welcome back the old circle of friends.

What readers are saying about . . .
Lethal Property

FIVE STARS! "My girls are back in action! It's a hilarious ride when Val is implicated in a series of murders. We get a lot of the hotness that is Dennis Culotta this time around . . . Also, we get a good dose of Tom too. But the best part of *Lethal Property*? Val and Kit. Besties with attitude and killer comedy. The banter and down-to-earth humor between these two is pure enjoyment on the page. Five bright and shiny stars for this writing duo!"

FIVE STARS! "Rosalind and Patricia have done it again and written a great sequel in The Val & Kit Mystery Series . . . full of intrigue and great wit and a different mystery each time. . . . *Lethal Property* is a great read, and I did not want to put the book down. I do hope that someone in the TV world reads these, as they'd make a great TV series. . . . I cannot wait for the next. Rosalind and Patricia, keep writing these great reads. Most worthy of FIVE STARS."

FIVE STARS! "OK . . . so I thought I knew whodunit early in the book, then after changing my mind at least 8-10 times, I was still wrong. (I want to say so much more, but I really don't want to give anything away.) Just one of the many, many things I love about the Val & Kit books. I love the characters/suspects, I love the believable dialogue between characters and also Valley Girl's inner dialogue (when thinking about Tina . . . hehe). I'd like to also add that (these books) are just good, clean fun. A series of books that you would/could/should recommend to anyone. (My boss is a nun, so that's a little something I worry about . . . lol) Thanks again, ladies. I agree with another reviewer . . . it IS like catching up with old friends, and I can't wait for the next one."

FIVE STARS! " . . . Val and Kit—forever friends. Smart, witty, determined, vulnerable, unintentional detectives. While this fourth installment can be read without having read the first three books (in the series), I'm certain you'll find that you want to read the first three. As has been the case with each book written by Rosalind Burgess and Patricia Obermeier Neuman, once I started reading, I really didn't want to stop. It was very much like catching up with old friends. Perhaps you know the feeling . . . Regardless of how long the separation, being together again just feels right."

FIVE STARS! "As with the other books in this series, this can be read as a stand-alone. However, I've read all of them to date in order and that's probably the best way to do it. I'm to the point where I don't even read the cover blurb for these books . . . because I know that I'll enjoy them. This book certainly didn't disappoint. Plenty of Val and Kit and their crazy antics, a cast of new colorful characters and a mystery that wasn't predictable. And yes, more of Tom. As much as I like him and am hoping for a Val and Tom hookup, Dennis grew on me this installment."

FIVE STARS! "Enjoyed reading *Lethal Property* as well as all by Roz and Patty. Written in a way that I felt connected with the characters. Looking forward to the next one."

FIVE STARS! "Reading *Lethal Property* was like catching up with old friends, and a few new characters, but another fun ride! I love these characters and I adore these writers. Would recommend to anyone who appreciates a good story and a sharp wit. Well done, ladies; you did it again!"

Palm Desert Killing

When one of them receives a mysterious letter, BFFS Val and Kit begin to unravel a sordid story that spans a continent and reaches back decades. It also takes them to Palm Desert, California, a paradise of palm trees, mountains, blue skies . . . and now murder. The men in their lives—Val's favorite detective, Dennis Culotta; her boss, Tom Haskins; and Kit's husband, Larry—play their (un)usual parts in this adventure that introduces a fresh batch of suspicious characters, including Kit's New York–attorney sister, Nora, and their mother. Val faces an additional challenge when her daughter, Emily, reveals her own startling news. Val and Kit bring to this story their (a)typical humor, banter, and unorthodox detective skills.

Foreign Relations

After sightseeing in London, Val and Kit move on to a rented cottage in the bucolic village of Little Dipping, where Val's actress daughter, Emily, and son-in-law are temporarily living and where Emily has become involved in community theater. Val and Kit revel in the English countryside, despite Val's ex-husband showing up and some troubling news from home. The harmony of the village is soon broken, however, by the vicious murder of one of their new friends. The shocking events that follow are only slightly more horrific than one from the past that continues to confound authorities. The crimes threaten to involve Emily, so Val and Kit return to their roles as amateur sleuths, employing their own inimitable ways.

What readers are saying about . . .
Foreign Relations

FIVE STARS! "Blimey! What fun! . . . These girls bring a sense of humor and a lot of fun to their search for who dunnit. I so enjoyed traveling with them across the pond for their latest adventure. They always keep me guessing until the end—not only about the who but the why. I especially liked the thoughtful way this book navigates the delicate challenges experienced by older children and their parents after divorce. Well done."

FIVE STARS! "Loved this fun book and a chance to catch up with my two favorite girl authors (and detectives). I particularly enjoyed that it was set in England as I am an Anglophile and some of the observations were so 'spot on' . . . a really great story that captured my attention from beginning to end. Just waiting to see what comes next and if Val will ever find a 'friend' and settle down? Please keep the books coming, Val and Kit!"

FIVE STARS! "Better than bangers and mash! These two ladies in England . . . what can possibly go wrong? A marvelous adventure punctuated with enough wit, humor and suspense to keep me a fan of Val & Kit for a long time."

FIVE STARS! "Fun series. . . . just finished reading all . . . and am already missing the stories. The characters were fun to follow as they solved the murders."

FIVE STARS! "This is my favorite series. I know I could be BFFs with Val and Kit. Characters are real. Writing is smart and funny . . . who could ask for more?? Well, I could . . . more books, please!!!"

And if you want to read about the mystery of marriage, here's a NON–Val & Kit book for you . . .

Dressing Myself

Meet Jessie Harleman in this contemporary women's novel about love, lust, friends, and family. Jessie and Kevin have been happily married for twenty-eight years. With their two grown kids now out of the house and living their own lives, Jessie and Kevin have reached the point they thought they longed for, yet slightly dreaded. But the house that used to burst at the seams now has too many empty rooms. Still, Jessie is a *glass-half-full* kind of woman, eager for this next period of her life to take hold. The problem is, nothing goes the way she planned. This novel explores growth and change and new beginnings.

FIVE STARS! "Love these writers!! So refreshing to have writers who really create such characters you truly understand and relate to. Looking forward to the next one. Definitely my favorites!"

FIVE STARS! "This book is about a woman's life torn apart . . . A lot of detail as to how she would feel . . . very well-written. I have to agree with the other readers, 5 stars."

FIVE STARS! "What a fun read *Dressing Myself* was! . . . I have to admit I didn't expect the ending . . . It was hard to put this book down."

FIVE STARS! "Great, easy, captivating read!! The characters seem so real! I don't read a lot, but I was really into this one! Read it for sure!"

FIVE STARS! "Loved it! Read this in one day. Enjoyed every page and had a real feeling for all of the characters. I was rooting for Jessie all the way. . . . Hope there's another story like this down the road."

FIVE STARS! "*Dressing Myself* deals with an all-too-common problem of today in a realistic manner that is sometimes sad, sometimes hopeful, as befits the subject. My expectation of the ending seesawed back and forth as the book progressed. I found it an interesting, engaging read with fully developed characters."

FIVE STARS! "Great book! It has been a long time since I have read a book cover to cover in one day . . . fantastic read . . . real page-turner that was hard to put down . . . Thanks, Ladies!"